MW00638442

CHRISTMAS CRIMES AT THE MYSTERIOUS BOOKSHOP

CHRISTMAS CRIMES AT THE MYSTERIOUS BOOKSHOP

EDITED BY
OTTO PENZLER

THE MYSTERIOUS PRESS
NEW YORK

First Mysterious Press edition

Interior design by Maria Fernandez

Library of Congress Control number: 2024942167

ISBN: 978-1-61316-572-0
Ebook ISBN: 978-1-61316-573-7

10 9 8 7 6 5 4 3 2 1

Printed in the United States of America
Distributed by W. W. Norton & Company

CONTENTS

INTRODUCTION

The Mysterious Bookshop opened its doors on Friday the 13th of April, 1979, at West 56th Street, more or less behind Carnegie Hall. It was in an old gray stone building that is now about a hundred and thirty years old. You had to go down two steps to enter a tight area filled with new paperbacks and a center table of new hardcover arrivals.

Just behind the table was the spiral staircase that led to the second floor, which was a more spacious space with twelve-foot-high ceilings and rolling ladders, where hardcover books filled the shelves, all in a single alphabet mingling new books with used and out-of-print volumes. We stayed at that location for about twenty-seven years before moving to our current location in TriBeCa, where we've been in much larger quarters for the past eighteen years. I still call it the new store.

We had struggled to stay in business during the early years, but things had improved dramatically after the first decade and I wanted to do something to thank our customers. I thought a free story from a favorite author might be nice, so starting more than thirty years ago, a holiday tradition was born as I commissioned an original story from some of the finest mystery writers in America each Christmas season.

These stories are then published in handsome booklets and given to my customers as a Christmas present. The only criteria for the authors to follow were that the stories should be set during the Christmas season, involve a mystery, and have at least some of the action take place at The Mysterious Bookshop.

The resultant stories have ranged from humorous to suspenseful to heartwarming. They have been so loved that customers from whom we rarely hear (alas) make a point of ordering books during the holiday season just to be sure they get a copy of the latest booklet. They have become highly collectable, too, single stories selling on eBay and ABE for more than the price of a new hardcover.

None of it would be possible without the warm friendship shown by the authors of these stories, of course. Trust me when I tell you they didn't do it for the money. An enterprising publisher discovered a few of the stories and asked if he could publish a collection of them, so Vanguard issued a hardcover of *Christmas at The Mysterious Bookshop* in 2010 (long out of print), followed by a paperback the following year with an extra story that is still in print and is one of the bestselling books in the store, year-round.

We've had so many good stories since the publication of the Vanguard book that we thought we should collect them in a complementary edition, so here we have *Christmas Crimes at The Mysterious Bookshop*.

By the way, it is worth mentioning that "Otto Penzler" appears in some of the stories and, although I am a real person, the characters with my name are fictional.

Have a very merry Christmas and a joyous holiday season.

Otto Penzler

New York

BLACK CHRISTMAS

Jason Starr

I t was the first Christmas since my marriage had ended and I wasn't doing very well. My ex had taken the kids to California, I'd lost my job at Citibank, and I'd gotten a final eviction notice from my landlord. Oh, yeah, and I'd started drinking again. But, worst of all, I couldn't wish Gretchen, my soulmate, a Merry Christmas or tell her how much I still loved her.

I hadn't been in touch with Gretchen since that night last July when I went to see her at NYU Medical Center. We'd been going through a rough patch—I was aware of that—but I knew her sudden change in attitude toward me was only temporary, that I could win her back if I tried hard enough. The problem was she hadn't been returning my phone calls, texts, or emails, and had even unfriended me on Facebook, so how was I supposed to let her know how I felt if I didn't see her in person? I didn't want to show up at her apartment—see how respectful I was trying to be?—so I went to the hospital instead. I went right up to the floor where she worked, down the corridor, and found her in a room, hooking up something with tubes—maybe a catheter—to some old guy.

"Steven, what the hell are you doing here?"

Okay, so she sounded angry, even furious, but I knew she was actually happy to see me. I could see the happiness in her eyes. She was wearing her usual perfume that always drove me crazy, and she looked so beautiful—wavy auburn hair, pale blue eyes, freckled face. *I want to count all your freckles*, I'd once told her at the Hotel Chandler in Midtown, where we used to meet.

"I just want to talk to you." My voice was slurred. I'd had a couple; okay, more than a couple. I added, "For two minutes."

"You have to leave."

"I'll wait," I said.

"I'm so sorry," she said to the patient. Then to me, "No, right now."

"Come on, bear," I said. "Bear" was the pet name we had for each other. "Just two minutes, just to tell you how I'm feeling and—"

2

"Go home, Steven. This is ridiculous."

A doctor—young guy, balding, glasses—came in and said, "There a problem here?"

"This guy barged in here and she wants him to leave," the patient said.

I said, "I just want—" and the doctor grabbed my arm, the son of a bitch *grabbed* it, and said, "You're gonna have to leave now."

I didn't like when people touched me—even when a stranger bumped into me by accident on the subway—but I hated being grabbed.

So I gripped the doctor's arm by the wrist and said to Gretchen, "I don't get why you're acting this way, why you're acting so crazy."

"*I'm* acting crazy?" Why was she crying? Why was she pretending to be so upset? "Are you serious? Are you *serious*, Steven?"

I don't really remember what happened after that. Some more things were said, the doctor threatened me and tried to grab me again, I probably hit him, and then a security guard showed up. Somehow, maybe a few minutes later, I wound up in the lobby of the hospital, restrained by security guards until the police showed up, and then I was arrested, cuffed, and taken away. I didn't really care about what happened to me, though. I just cared about getting another chance to talk to Gretchen. I knew she was seeing things all wrong now, as if she'd been brainwashed, and me showing up at the hospital had only made the situation worse. I knew I could get through to her if I had two minutes, just two minutes, to talk to her. I knew if I could just talk to her one more time I could convince her that she was making a huge mistake, that she had to give it a shot—no, that she had to be strong; yes, be strong—and trust what she had with me. *Just try it*, I'd tell her. *Just give it a shot.* I'd tell her that everybody was afraid of change, but sometimes you just have to jump in and take a risk, that that was what relationships were all about. And I'd tell her that I would be there for her no matter what. I'd tell her I'd go to City Hall and marry her the day she left her husband. And I'd tell her how good she'd feel when she left him for good and was in a healthy, stable relationship with me. Oh, and I'd remind her *again* that we were soulmates, that she'd *said* we were soulmates—that was what this was all about after all, wasn't it?—so what was the point of going through all of this, saying all those things to each other, putting everything on the line, just to wind up like this? *Seriously*, I'd say, *what was the point?*

❄

I'd met Gretchen last year, ironically, I guess, on Christmas Eve. I thought I was unhappy then, but maybe I was just in a bad rut. I had a good job as a loan officer at a Citibank on Broadway and I was living in Battery Park with my wife, Carla, and teenaged daughters Julianne and Jennifer. I used to have a close relationship with my daughters, but lately they were a lot more interested in their friends than in me, and we hardly talked anymore. My marriage had never been great, and Carla and I seemed to fight more than we were nice to each other, but we were still together, hanging on.

That afternoon, though, we'd had a really bad fight—screaming, threatening each other, throwing things. I can't tell you what the fight was about, but did married people ever really fight about anything? We were fighting because we were stuck with each other and sick of each other's annoying habits. I had to get the hell out of the apartment, away from her for a while, so I grabbed my trench coat and took off.

It was cold and windy and there were some snow flurries blowing around the semi-deserted downtown streets. I went up West Street, then went over to where I sometimes wandered to during my lunch hour at work—The Mysterious Bookshop on Warren Street.

It was funny: in high school I hated reading, but when I read those mystery books, I don't know, it didn't feel like reading, it felt like having fun. It was also a nice escape when I was having trouble at home, or my job was bumming me out, or something else was going wrong in my life. I could read about somebody else's problems and my own would go away, like I was, I don't know, taking a vacation from reality.

But I didn't want to get too far away from reality. I liked to read about my world so I stuck to the New York, New Jersey writers—you know, Stella, Stroby, Coben, Spiegelman, Coleman, Fusilli, Rozan, Block—and a bunch more I know I'm forgetting.

Anyway, when I walked into the store this thin, smiley guy I'd seen before asked if he could help me find something and I mumbled, "No, just looking." I knew he was trying to be nice and helpful and all, but I guess it was just the way I was—I liked to be left alone.

Then I saw her. I don't know why I didn't notice her right away because she was hard to miss, and not only because she was the only customer in the store besides me. No, it was because she was so goddamn beautiful. I'd always had a thing for redheads, so I guess that was the first thing I noticed, but she had a great body, too. I mean, she probably needed to lose twenty pounds, but who didn't? Besides, I'd always liked heavier women. I never got why they put those skinny girls who looked like they were starving to death in magazines and in movies and TV shows. Did any guy actually find that attractive? But this red-haired woman with her wide hips and hourglass shape was my idea of perfect. She was in jeans, black leather boots, and a black leather coat. She seemed sad about something, but I don't know how I knew this because she had her back to me and I couldn't see her face.

I wasn't planning to talk to her, but I won't lie, I did want her to notice me. I guess, after the fight with Carla, and another Christmas going by, I was starting to feel my age. I was forty-seven and was starting to think, *Is this all there is?* Was I going to be having the same fights with Carla every day for the rest of my life? Yeah, I guess I was bored—with my life and with my marriage. Carla and I didn't do things together the way we used to and we hardly ever had sex anymore. I tried to spice things up, I really did. I once asked her if she'd consider dressing up sometime, maybe putting on a schoolgirl outfit, and she screamed at me, "*You* put on a schoolgirl outfit!" Now you see what I was dealing with?

But give me some credit. I'd never cheated on Carla. Had I fantasized about cheating on her? Oh, yeah, all the time, but what unhappily married man didn't? If a pretty woman came into the bank, I'd flirt with her a little, and fantasize about other women I met here and there—moms of my daughters' friends, waitresses at restaurants, coworkers, girls on the street, but just because I was thinking about cheating didn't mean I wanted to actually do it. I understood there was a thick line between fantasy and reality, and it was a line I never intended to cross.

As I got closer to the red-haired woman, pretending to look for a book in the S section, I noticed her perfume. I didn't know what it was called, but I'd smelled it before on other women and I liked it a lot.

Then I noticed she was holding *The Heartbreak Lounge* by Wallace Stroby, reading the back cover.

"It's really good," I said.

I don't know why I said this, because I wasn't planning to talk to her. The words had just slipped out.

I'll never forget the first time she looked at me. It wasn't like in the movies where it happens in slow motion. No, she looked at me the way she'd look at anybody else, but there was something there, something different, something special. It was so obvious to both of us.

"Yeah?" she said.

"Yeah, I think he has another one too," I said. "I mean, I read another one once, I can't remember the name of it, though. You like *The Sopranos*?"

I felt like I was rambling, making a fool of myself.

"Yeah, I like *The Sopranos*," she said.

"Oh, then you'll love Stroby," I said. "You know who else is good? That guy Spiegelman. You heard of him?"

"I think I read a review in the *Times* once," she said.

I removed a copy of *Red Cat* from the shelf and said, "I couldn't put this one down. He has this detective guy, Match? No, March. Yeah, March, and . . . Lemme buy these for you."

"Why?" She seemed confused, or maybe just surprised.

"I don't know," I said, "I just feel like it. The Christmas spirit and all. Come on, they're on me."

She kept protesting, but I kept insisting, and finally she caved.

Then something weird happened. I was heading toward the front of the store to pay, when I saw the older guy with white hair and a white beard standing near the door between the wall of bookshelves. I'd seen the guy in the store before, but I didn't know who he was. Maybe he worked there, or owned the place, but he seemed to spend most of his time in a back room. Was there an apartment there? Honestly, I didn't know what he did back there and I wasn't sure I wanted to know, but it was weird because the other times I'd been in the store he ignored me, but this time he was looking right at me and wouldn't look away. It wasn't an angry or threatening look, though. He was looking at me like he knew something, but knew what?

After I paid for the books the red-haired woman and I left the store together. The snow was coming down a little harder now, starting to stick. It was almost dark.

"This was so nice of you," she said.

"You want to get a drink?" I asked.

I didn't know why I'd asked this when I was married with two kids and I was an alcoholic who'd been sober for over seven years. I guess there was just something about this woman; she did something to me. When I was around her, I just couldn't seem to make normal decisions.

"I don't know, it's getting late," she said.

"Come on, one drink won't kill you," I said, smiling.

She smiled back—her teeth were a little crooked, she had an overbite, but I liked it—and said, "Okay, one drink. What the hell?"

We went across the street to the Raccoon Lodge. It was a dingy dive bar that I hadn't been to in years but, I had to admit, it was nice to breathe in the scent of booze.

We both ordered beers. I guess I didn't really realize what I was doing until I took the first sip. It was nice, feeling that surge of relaxation and happiness, but it didn't make me want to go crazy and go off on a binge. I was handling it well.

I was also distracted, entranced by the red-haired woman. We got into a long conversation about books. I'd been reading all these mystery novels for years, but I didn't realize that the actual reading was only part of the fun; it was a lot of fun to talk about the books, too. I couldn't talk about books with Carla, of course, because she didn't like to really read anything except magazines. She'd see me reading and go, "I don't know how you have the patience to read books. It would drive me crazy." And I'd say, "You should give it a try sometime," and she'd roll her eyes and leave the room. It turned out the red-haired woman and I had read a lot of the same books, though, and she told me about some other ones I should read. She said she'd email me a list sometime, which was nice to hear, because it meant we were going to stay in touch, that this wasn't going to be a one-time thing.

After maybe an hour we were still into our first beers—see, I had it under control—when she said, "You haven't even asked me my name yet."

I realized she was right. We'd been so caught up, talking, asking her name hadn't occurred to me.

"I'm Steven," I said.

"Gretchen," she said.

We shook hands and, just like when we'd looked at each other the first time, I knew this would be another experience I'd never forget.

"So," she said, "how long have you been married?"

I was confused; had I mentioned this in conversation? Then I saw her gaze shift briefly, toward my left hand and my wedding ring. I looked at her left hand and saw she was wearing a wedding ring as well.

"Long time," I said. "Maybe too long."

"Yeah, tell me about it," she said.

I told her about what had been going on with Carla lately, how we seemed to be drifting apart and didn't seem to have much in common, and she seemed to be having similar problems in her marriage. She and her husband hadn't been getting along and they'd been in marriage counseling. She had no kids so I wasn't sure what was keeping her in her marriage, why she couldn't just bolt, but I didn't want to ask.

The conversation went on and on. Usually, especially when I was around someone I didn't really know, I had to think of things to say, but with Gretchen the conversation flowed. I told her about my job, how I liked it but how it was boring a lot of the time too, and she told me all about her job as a nurse. Then it turned out we both grew up in central Jersey, just a few towns apart, and that gave us even more to talk about.

At about eight o'clock she said she had to get back, that her husband was expecting her and she didn't want him to get upset. I was disappointed because, even though I knew

Carla was probably wondering where I was, I could've stayed there all night.

We left the bar together and walked. It was snowing harder, maybe two inches on the sidewalk already. At the corner she was going to get a cab up to her place in the east twenties. We told each other that we'd had a great time and how great it was meeting. I wanted to kiss her and, feeling good from the two beers I'd had, there really was nothing stopping me. I knew she wanted to kiss me too, but I didn't try.

"Well, goodnight," I said, already feeling the loss.

Then as I started to walk away she said, "Oh, your email—so I can send you the names of those books."

She punched my email address into her phone and then got in a cab and was gone.

Immediately I feared I'd made a huge mistake. I should've asked for her email or phone number; she'd probably *wanted* me to ask. What the hell was wrong with me? Maybe now she'd think I wasn't interested and she wouldn't bother to contact me. Not trying to kiss her had also been incredibly dumb. I didn't even kiss her goodnight on the cheek, for God's sake.

Back at my apartment, I was miserable. My daughters were out doing whatever so it was just me and Carla. She started a fight with me because I'd left dishes in the sink and then went to bed early. Meanwhile, I couldn't stop thinking about Gretchen, smiling, remembering bits of our conversation at the bar. She hadn't emailed me yet, though, and I was worried I'd never hear from her again.

I stayed up past midnight, checking my email every few minutes. Finally I fell asleep on the couch—I'd been sleeping on the couch most nights lately—and woke up at around dawn and checked my email right away. Still nothing from Gretchen. I told myself that it didn't mean anything, that she still might get in touch, but it was hard not to feel the devastation. I couldn't stop thinking about her eyes, her voice, the smell of her perfume. I really didn't know what I was going to do without her.

I showered in water as hot as I could stand. When I came out, before I toweled off, I checked my phone again. My pulse accelerated when I saw the email:

> *Lovely meeting you, Steven. And thank you again for the books. I was up reading the Stroby book all night. Thanks for the excellent recommendation.*
> *Merry Christmas!*

I read the note at least five times, maybe to convince myself that she'd actually contacted me, that this wasn't just some wonderful dream or hallucination. Then another email arrived:

Maybe this is crazy, but would you like to meet me today?

I wrote back:

Yes!! What time?

We arranged to meet at noon, on the steps of the New York Public Library. I was so excited that I'd nearly forgotten that it was Christmas morning and I still had to open gifts with my family.

When Carla woke up she still seemed angry at me from last night and muttered, "Morning," on her way into the kitchen to make coffee. My daughters had stumbled in around three in the morning and looked hungover when they came out to the living room at about ten. I was craving another drink myself, but not as much as I was craving seeing Gretchen again.

After we opened presents—a few shirts for me from Carla, a couple of sweaters for Carla from me, and gift cards for the kids—we had a family breakfast. There wasn't much talking.

The kids were busy texting and Carla still seemed angry and we didn't have much to talk about anyway. Meanwhile, I was just thinking about how I couldn't wait to get away to see Gretchen.

After breakfast, I put on jeans and a nice pin-striped shirt. I wanted to look good, but not too good, figuring that might get Carla suspicious. When I announced I was going out for a while Carla said, "Have fun," and didn't seem to care one way or another.

Gretchen was waiting for me outside the library, near one of the lions. I was so thrilled to see her that my fears of never seeing her again from just last night seemed like a distant memory. Our conversation picked up where we'd left off, as if we'd known each other forever. As we walked uptown on Fifth Avenue, past all the tourists and Christmas-decorated windows, my arm brushed against hers a couple of times.

We went to see the tree at Rockefeller Center. The area was packed with people but we managed to find a good spot under the tree, right near the ice skating rink.

"It's so magical here, isn't it?" Gretchen said.

Determined not to repeat my regret of last night when I'd blown an opportunity to kiss her, I made my move. It was amazing the way one kiss could change everything, because at the moment my lips touched Gretchen's I was gone. I don't know long the kiss lasted—it may have been a few seconds or a few minutes—but kissing a woman had never felt so right, so perfect. Of course I knew I was taking a big risk. Someone I knew or she knew could've seen us, but I didn't care. I was kissing this beautiful, sexy, amazing woman and nothing else mattered.

We spent the rest of the day together, walking around the city streets and in Central Park, holding hands and kissing. I'd never felt such a strong connection with a woman before. It was hard saying goodbye to return to our spouses, even though we'd already made plans to see each other the next day.

Our second date was at a Midtown bar, but we didn't stay there for long, winding up at a room at the Hotel Chandler on East Thirty-first Street. I guess I should have felt guilty about cheating on Carla, but my feelings for Gretchen overwhelmed everything. It had been years since I'd had sex with anyone other than Carla and I'd forgotten how enjoyable sex could be. Gretchen and I attacked each other's bodies; we couldn't get enough. But it wasn't just the sex that was so intoxicating, it was the closeness. I'd never felt that kind of closeness before.

Pretty soon, Gretchen and I were having a full-blown affair. We saw each other whenever we could—during our lunch hours, evenings, weekends. We lied to our spouses, saying we were going out with friends or had to stay late at work. Lying was hard at first, but I was surprised how quickly I got used to it, how it became normal. The affair wasn't just about the sex and passion, though—we became best friends too. Sometimes when we just met for drinks—yeah, I was drinking again, pretty regularly—we talked nonstop about books, our work, our troubled marriages, and whatever else was going on in our lives. The amazing sex we had was just a bonus of our relationship. It was so refreshing to be with a woman who was uninhibited in bed, who'd do anything to make me feel good. Yeah, she had no problem putting on a schoolgirl outfit and she looked sexy as hell in it.

One night at the Chandler, after we'd been seeing each other for about a month, we were in bed naked, wrapped in each other's arms, and she whispered in my ear, "You're my soulmate, Steven. We were meant for each other," and I told her I felt exactly the same way.

The more time we spent together, the closer we got. Then Gretchen brought up the idea of us leaving our marriages. At first, getting divorced was easier for her to consider than for me because she didn't have kids and her marriage had been in trouble for a long time. She told me that she'd almost left last year and that her husband had even hit her a few times. I knew going through a divorce with Carla would be difficult—one thing she loved was a good fight—and I was worried about how my daughters would take it, but I agreed that Gretchen and I had to be together permanently, that we couldn't continue like this forever.

Finally, one afternoon in early May, Gretchen and I met for lunch at a Chinese place near Union Square and made a pact—that night I would ask Carla for a divorce and she'd ask her husband for a divorce. We knew it wouldn't be easy, that there would be a lot of drama and pain, but we would deal with the fallout together. As long as we had each other, everything would be okay and someday we'd look back at this decision and realize it was the smartest thing we'd ever done.

When I returned home after work, I was eager to get it over with. I didn't want to hurt Carla, but I knew what I'd been doing was wrong and that by ending my marriage sooner rather than later I'd be doing her a big favor in the long run. I expected that my daughters would be upset, but they wouldn't be the first kids in the world with divorced parents. Hell, there were probably more kids with divorced parents than kids with married parents in the world, so trying to protect my kids wasn't a reason to stay in a bad marriage.

The kids were out and Carla was on the couch watching one of the reality shows she always watched so I figured it was the perfect time to break the news. "Hey, there's something I need to talk to you about," I said.

"What?" she asked, staring at the TV.

I pressed pause on the remote and said, "Well it's about us. I guess you've noticed what I've noticed lately, that we aren't getting along anymore. So I think we'd be better off apart, you know, so I guess what I'm trying to say is I want a divorce."

I want a divorce. It was so much easier to say those words than I'd ever imagined. I already felt like a great burden had been lifted. I was finally free.

But Carla didn't have the reaction I'd expected. I thought she'd be upset, crying, or maybe she'd get angry—scream at me, call me names, throw things. What I didn't expect was for her to start laughing.

"You want a divorce." She laughed some more. "I think that's the funniest thing I've ever heard."

I didn't get it. Did she think I was joking?

"I'm being serious," I said. "I don't think we should stay married."

"You really don't think I know what's been going on?" she said. "You must really think I'm some kind of idiot, don't you?"

I knew what she was getting at, but I didn't want to give anything away if I didn't have to.

"What do you mean?" I asked.

"I know about you and your girlfriend, Gretchen," she said. "I saw your texts to her a couple of months ago. I had a P.I. following you and my lawyer got all of your phone records, including all your texts. That's right, I have a lawyer, Steven. I've just been waiting to get as much evidence as I could before I ditched you. *You* want a divorce. That's hilarious."

The divorce was going to be a total nightmare. I was going to get screwed on a settlement and I'd probably be in for a custody battle but, despite everything, I knew I'd made the right decision. Carla was acting like such a bitch; was I really going to miss her? This was the greatest day of my life. I'd been unhappy for too long and it was time to start thinking about myself.

I texted Gretchen:

I did it!!!

I couldn't wait to talk to her, to start planning our future together, but a couple of hours later, when she still hadn't gotten back to me, I was starting to get seriously concerned. She'd said her husband had hit her before—what if he flipped out when she broke the news to him? What if she was injured, in the hospital?

A while later I finally got a text:

We need to talk

I didn't understand what this meant—talk about what?— but I was glad that she seemed to be okay. I texted back, trying to figure what was going on, but she said she wanted to talk to me about it in person.

In the morning she came down to meet me at a Starbucks on Broadway. I knew something was wrong when I went to kiss her and she pulled back.

"What is it?" I asked, sitting across from her. "Did something happen? Did he flip out?"

"I'm sorry." She looked away, avoiding eye contact.

"Sorry?" I said. "Sorry about what?"

"I . . . I couldn't go through with it," she said.

I'd figured it was something like this.

"That's okay," I said. "I mean so you chickened out? So what? You can just tell him tonight when you—"

"No, I'm not asking him," she said. "I decided I don't want to end my marriage. I'm sorry, Steven, I really am. But I gave this a lot of thought yesterday and I still love my husband and I want to try to work things out."

This wasn't happening. Staying with her husband? After she'd been pushing for me to get out of my marriage for weeks? Was she kidding me?

"Are you kidding me?" I asked.

But it was obvious she wasn't. Her eyes were cold and empty and distant.

"I'm so sorry, Steven," she said. "I don't know how this happened, how we got here. It was a mistake letting this happen. A big mistake."

"But you said we're soulmates." This was a nightmare. "You said you loved me. You said you want to spend the rest of your life with me."

"I know," she said. "I know."

I reached out to try to hold her hand, but she wouldn't let me.

"Look, I get it," I said. "You're afraid of your husband. Okay, that's understandable because he's been abusive to you before, so he's manipulating you, Gretchen. That's what's going on here. You just think you want to stay with your husband, because you're worried, you don't want him to get mad at you, but you really want to be with me. I'm the one you really love."

"No." She was shaking her head. "I'm sorry, Steven. I love my husband. I do. I really do."

"No, you love me," I said. "This is about me. Not your husband. *Me.*"

I'd raised my voice and a few people at other tables were looking over, but I couldn't care less.

"We got carried away, Steven. We just found each other at the wrong time and . . . this isn't right, this isn't the way people fall in love. This is just a fantasy, that's all it is, and it's over now. You should try to work out your marriage too. You don't want to just throw your life away for me."

"It's too late for that," I said. "I already told my wife it's over. She has a lawyer."

"Beg her for another chance," Gretchen said.

"I don't want another chance, I want you!"

I banged the table with my fist and her coffee spilled all over her lap.

"Oh, God, I'm sorry," I said.

"No, I'm sorry," she said and rushed out to the street.

I went after her and tried to convince her to come back, to talk about this, but she got into a cab. I chased after her, banging on the window, but she wouldn't even look at me as the cab sped away.

I knew she didn't mean anything she'd said. She was just panicking, that was all, but soon her panic would end and she'd come back to me.

I must've sent her fifty texts that day and left a dozen voicemails, telling her that I loved her and I wanted to talk to her, but she didn't get back to me. I didn't hear from her the next day, or the day after that, or the day after that. Then I called and got a recording that her number was out of service. I couldn't imagine that she'd changed her number because of me. Why wouldn't she want to talk to the man she loved, to her soulmate? Her husband must have forced her to change her number.

Meanwhile, Carla insisted that I move out of the apartment and my daughters—who knew I'd had an affair—wanted me out, too. So I found a tiny place on the Bowery near Chinatown. I figured I'd live there temporarily until Gretchen came around and then we'd move in together. Maybe once she kicked her husband out of her place, I could move in with her.

The only problem was Gretchen wasn't coming around. I hadn't heard a word from her since that morning at Starbucks. I discovered that she'd unfriended me on Facebook—probably her husband's doing—so I had no way to contact her or to find out what was going on in her life. My first night in my new apartment, I woke up in the middle of the night, after a happy dream with Gretchen in it, and then I thought, *Gretchen's gone*, and felt a sick, empty, awful feeling in my gut.

I thought about telling her husband, getting it over with for her, but I knew she'd be angry with me if I did that and I didn't want to hurt her. I loved her too much to hurt her. I didn't want her to feel the pain I was feeling. I wanted her to be happy.

Trying to numb my pain, I was drinking heavily. One morning I woke up with bruises all over my body and I had no idea what had happened. Then I made a huge mistake, showing up for work drunk and causing a big scene, and I got fired. My life was in freefall and I was all alone. It wasn't supposed to be this way. I was supposed to be with Gretchen. We were supposed go through our pain together.

Finally I had to see her, I couldn't take it anymore, so I showed up at NYU Medical Center and fought with the doctor and the security guards which only made things worse. The police claimed I'd broken a security guard's nose, which I don't remember at all, not that it mattered. My lawyer managed to get the charges dropped but this had happened at the worst possible time, in the middle of my divorce, right when the lawyers were getting into the nitty-gritty and Carla was at her angriest and most vindictive. Her lawyer used my arrest and recent binge drinking and other violent outbursts as examples of why I shouldn't have custody of my kids, and my lawyer advised me to give in and make a deal because I wouldn't stand a chance in court. So Carla got full custody and was allowed to move the kids out of state, and I was only allowed to see them once a month with a social worker present. Meanwhile, Gretchen had gotten a restraining order against me and I wasn't allowed to have any contact with her for at least five years.

Now it was Christmas Eve again. Gretchen and I should've been celebrating our first anniversary, but I was alone in a tiny apartment, thinking a lot of bad thoughts, and I had to get out, to get some air.

The weather wasn't very Christmaslike—damp, drizzly, about fifty degrees. I figured I'd go to a bar or just buy some booze at a liquor store, but then I had another idea and I walked over to The Mysterious Bookshop. Mystery novels were always a great way to escape from my problems and I needed that more than ever.

A stocky bearded guy was at the cash register, reading *Moonlight Mile* by Dennis Lehane. He said "Merry Christmas" to me when I walked in but I didn't say anything back.

Then I saw her. It wasn't Gretchen, it was another woman. She was kind of short, thin, probably too thin. She wasn't really my type and I probably wouldn't've noticed her at all if she wasn't browsing in the S section, holding Stroby's *The Heartbreak Lounge*.

Was this a coincidence or an omen?

I went over to her and said, "It's really good."

We started talking. It wasn't an instant connection like I had with Gretchen, but she seemed nice enough. I insisted on buying her the Stroby book as a Christmas present. On my way to the register, I saw the man with the white hair. He was standing exactly where I'd seen him last Christmas, staring at me in the same knowing way. It was starting to freak me out and I was relieved when the woman and I left the store.

"Thank you again for the book," she said. "You really didn't have to do that."

"Oh, it's no problem, I wanted you to have it," I said. "I'm Steven, by the way."

"Linda," she said.

"How about a drink across the street?" I asked.

"I'd love that," she said, "but I have to walk my dog, he's been inside all day. Another time would be great, though."

We exchanged phone numbers and then said goodbye and walked off in opposite directions.

Back at my apartment, I tried to get excited about the future. Linda wasn't really my type, but she seemed nice enough and she liked mystery books, so those were two pluses right there. She hadn't been wearing a wedding ring, so there was nothing keeping us from dating like a normal couple. Yeah, my life was in the toilet now, but the truth was my marriage hadn't been good for a long time, so I was probably better off divorced. It sucked that my daughters were so far away but they'd be in college soon anyway and I'd be able to see them more often. I could go back to AA, get sober, and work on my resume and rebuild my career.

I could have a happy life, I was sure of it, but it hit me that I didn't want a happy life with somebody else—I wanted a happy life with Gretchen. She was my soulmate and you only get one chance in life to be with your soulmate, and when that chance comes along, no matter what situation you're in, you have to seize it, do anything in your power to make sure that person doesn't get away.

Suddenly I knew exactly what I had to do. It was all so simple.

I texted Linda:

> *It was great meeting u today, but honestly there's somebody else in my life I'm in love with so meeting u again wouldn't be fair. Hope u meet your soulmate someday 2. Merry Xmas Steven*

I felt better already, convinced I was doing the right thing. I had a few swigs of whiskey for some extra encouragement then headed uptown.

I'd never been inside Gretchen's apartment, but I'd been by the building a bunch of times recently. Yeah, I knew I'd been violating the restraining order and could go to jail, but sometimes I couldn't stay away from her and I had to see her face and make sure she was okay, that her son of a bitch husband hadn't hurt her. There was something pulling me toward her, something I couldn't control or explain. It wasn't my fault I was in love with her.

She lived in a prewar walk-up. I knew she wouldn't buzz me up to her place, so I waited, maybe an hour, until some guy left the building. I pretended that I had just rung an apartment and was waiting to be buzzed up, but when the guy left, I slipped my foot in front of the closing door and I was in.

I went right up to her apartment on the fourth floor and rang the bell. A few seconds later, I heard footsteps, and then the peephole opened.

"Can I help you?" It was her prick husband.

"I live across the hall, I think there's a fire," I said urgently.

When he opened the door, I pushed my way inside.

He was in boxers, no shirt. "Hey," he said, "what the—"

Imaging him hitting Gretchen in the face, making her cry, I stabbed him in the center of his chest or maybe a little closer to his neck. I didn't want to hurt him but he was the obstacle keeping me from my soulmate, so what choice did I have?

Then Gretchen appeared. I expected her to be happy, to kiss me the way she had under the Rockefeller Center Christmas tree, but I was confused because she was screaming, trying to save her prick husband's life. Why wasn't she relieved that I'd ended her misery?

But was she *really* trying to save him? Maybe she was still under her husband's control, afraid to let go of him, but once the reality set in that he was gone for good, that he couldn't hurt her anymore, her attitude would change. She'd realize that I'd given her the greatest Christmas gift of all—freedom—and that there was nothing holding her back from being with her true soulmate now. I knew there would be a police investigation but if we left immediately, rented a car, got across the border and into Canada, we could change our identities, and live the rest of our lives happily ever after.

"I love you so much, bear," I said.

She was still screaming, wailing, calling me horrible names. Maybe she needed a drink to relax? I went into the kitchen, to see if I could find some wine or something, when I felt the blow to the back of my head. I managed to turn for a second, saw her holding the large vase, and a moment later I was on the floor, the pain overwhelming.

Then the white-haired guy from The Mysterious Bookshop appeared, and he reached out and helped me to my feet. Now I understood what that knowing look he'd been giving me meant. He'd been waiting for me all along.

As he led me away into the darkness, I wanted to tell Gretchen that I forgave her, and that she was still my soulmate, and that I loved her more than anything, but it was too late for us.

Well, in this world anyway.

A MIDNIGHT CLEAR

Lyndsay Faye

T here is a bottle three-quarters full of Jeremiah Weed ninety-proof bourbon sitting on Tom's crumbling Formica kitchen counter, and that is important.

There are four more full bottles and a fifth bottle that is nearly empty in the space under Tom's bed between lint-draped free weights and dusty dress shoes, and that is important.

Tom, after pouring two fingers from the bottle on the kitchen counter into a coffee mug, fetches the nearly empty bottle from under the bed and restores the kitchen bottle to three-quarters full using a white plastic funnel.

The kitchen bottle of Jeremiah Weed must remain at three quarters at all times. The others, purchased in two-packs from that warehouse up Broadway near Astor, must remain under the bed.

Tom crosses the living space of his tiny one-bedroom, glancing out the window at the snow hovering like a locust horde and the swaddled strangers hastening down Murray Street in the gloom. Below his fire escape, the pizza joint chugs greasy drafts into the night, and the bouncer outside the New York Dolls Gentlemen's Club smokes a cigarette for lack of better occupation. Christmas lights draped over the neighboring fire escape, blinking and relentless, stain Tom's wall pink, then sapphire, then a poisonous electric green.

Tom had expected to grow fonder of Christmas as an adult, the way he'd expected to have children and maybe season tickets to see the Mets. But the lights send his teeth scraping across each other. And there isn't anyone here but Tom.

After another sip of bourbon, Tom checks his cleaned and loaded gun. He is not granted a gun by virtue of his private security position for a very tall skyscraper filled with very glib men. They would just as soon Tom wander the halls of the building by night equipped with a whistle and a glare. But Tom hadn't trusted the neighborhood when they'd first moved in, had he, and he'd wanted more than anything for

Beth to be safe, hadn't he, and that hadn't panned out well, had it, but he still owned the squat, ugly hunk of sour metal that could kill anyone if aimed at the right spot, the heart for example, the heart would be perfect under the circumstances, and after checking the gun Tom allows himself a terrible moment of imagining his wife might even now come walking through their front door, shrugging her coat onto the table and setting down a bag in which a small gift is hidden away for next week's holiday.

Beth would set her keys down and call out, "I almost died eight times between here and the train, the street is so slick," and Tom would put his hand behind her neck, where the brown woolen cap would begin to trickle snowmelt into her long blonde hair, and she'd say, "We should invest in winter skis," and Tom would kiss her until she laughed, because he was hungry but it wasn't for dinner. It was for the starglow in the little crystals stuck to her eyebrows.

The bourbon slides neatly down Tom's throat as he stands. Heading for the kitchen, he pours another drink. Then he kneels by the bed and finds the nearly empty bottle and replenishes the countertop whiskey and leaves the now-empty bottle next to the front door.

The empty bottles are taken at once to the recycling bin as they are created, and that is important.

Pausing, Tom lifts a picture of himself and his wife Beth, smiling above thick woolen scarves on a spontaneously taken trip to Coney Island. Their faces are flushed from cold and from vodka sipped at one of the fluorescent-lit Russian restaurants where the tables boast plastic flowers and the menus are in Cyrillic but the paunchy waiters understand *vodka* even when poorly pronounced. The picture from another Christmas season, from before.

Before Eddie Adamo.

Before Tom thought of the perfect use for his gun.

Tom replaces the photograph and his fingers come away grainy with dust.

Beth had leaned over, glancing around as if anyone cared what was said in English in that restaurant, whispering, "Everyone here is eating things that have been stuffed into cabbage. Are Russians allowed to cook food without stuffing it into cabbage afterward? Can it be delivered in a non-cabbage vehicle?" Then she'd flicked her wrist and the vodka was gone, and Tom had said, "Be careful, I don't want to have come all the way out here and then have to carry you home," and Beth had said, "We won't go home for hours and hours. Maybe we'll never go home at all."

Before leaving his apartment, Tom pulls a much-thumbed note out of his wallet. The note lives there, it has ever since he found it on the coffee table, and he rereads the section that burns his eyes. The few lines Beth wrote that make him feel capable of murder.

I've been frightened for such a long time. I'd have told you before, but I thought that you might blame yourself if all goes to pieces anyhow and you can't prevent it. I'm terrified of Eddie, what he might do, of my life, terrified everything is ruined. But I always loved you, and I'm sorry if there were times you didn't know that. Because I felt it, every day.

Tom takes a last look at the buckling floor and the weeping sink and the grime embedded into the tile around the fridge. They hadn't meant to end up living in a dump, but that's what happened. He had meant to find better work than the security job, but that was when everyone thought unemployment was a temporary problem. And when Beth was still here. He puts the empty bottle of Jeremiah Weed into one of the black bags from the liquor store, puts his gun in the inner pocket of his fraying winter coat, and departs.

Outside, Murray Street is deserted but oddly tense, that feeling of holiday mania that rushes a man along even when he's navigating near-empty, snow-slick intersections. Tom knows where Eddie Adamo is just now, and the thought makes his fingers tingle with purpose beneath their nail beds. Weeks of planning, days of cold palms preluding night sweats, an extra trip to the liquor warehouse when he only generally needs to visit it every week. His hands are steady as he steps into the recycling area and disposes of the bottle.

The bottles that are empty are taken outside and recycled, never left lying about the apartment, and that is important.

Almost as important as Beth had made Christmas seem. Tom can nearly see her, turning the corner just ahead of him from Warren Street, returning to their terrible apartment after stopping by that bookstore she said always made her feel as if she were in a scene from *Harry Potter*. The Mysterious Bookshop.

She would round the corner and she would say to Tom, "I just read the best paragraph. Don't you love picking up a book, reading the first paragraph, and feeling as if you're about to get on a plane or something? Leave your life? I read the first paragraphs of five of the books on the front shelf, and they don't mind there, you know, they never mind, and I didn't buy any of them yet, I promise, but do you think—"

No.

Tom doesn't think about the money Beth wished they had, because he doesn't think about things he can't change, and that is important.

She would round the corner and she would say to Tom, "I just read the best paragraph. Don't you love picking up a book, and reading the first paragraph, and feeling as if you're about to get on a plane or something? Leave your life? Eddie found a stack of books in the common area yesterday, just left there like trash, he put them in his apartment, and he said if I wanted I could stop by and—"

No.

No, no, no.

Tom shoves his hand against his lips, as if being unable to speak will make it easier to think. It doesn't help, but it's a distracting sensation, and it doesn't hurt either.

She would round the corner and she would say to Tom, "I just read the best paragraph. Don't you love picking up a book, and reading the first paragraph, and feeling as if you're about to get on a plane or something? Leave your life? Christmas always makes me feel like that, though. As if I've traveled somewhere else when the lights go up and there are trees in all the restaurant windows. Don't you want a tree this year? Don't you remember how good a tree all lit up made you feel as a kid?"

But Tom doesn't remember that at all. He can't remember much of anything good happening until Beth came along.

The gun in Tom's coat feels heavier now than it did when he hid it away. He turns onto Warren and looks up at the red light of the Raccoon Lodge, the dull green and black paint of its building lost in the fiery glare. Tom checks his watch and then curses quietly to himself.

Early. The sun sets so fast now, runs without a backward glance, as if it couldn't bear to look at New York for a moment longer, and Tom is early. He took his time with the first drink, was careless with the second, clearly hadn't been paying attention.

The first drink of the night is savored for at least half an hour, and that is important.

The second drink of the night is enjoyed for at least twenty minutes, and that is important.

The third drink of the night—

"Enough," Tom mutters to himself.

Eddie Adamo won't have arrived at the Raccoon Lodge yet. Eddie, with his button-down shirts and his rat's smile and his too-small ears and his dark, dark hair. Eddie, who is presently selling worthless engagement rings and fake Rolex watches at the jewelry store five blocks away that claims to be a diamond importer but is really an exporter of crap. Eddie will be open an hour later for the holiday season, foisting gold chains on people who buy bulk Cup-O-Noodles to sustain them through their part-time retail jobs and introduce culinary variety with frozen bags of peas.

People like Tom.

Tom sucks in a breath of burning winter air. He is going to shoot Eddie Adamo, shoot him right in the heart that didn't care that Beth was Tom's *wife*. Eddie who bought Beth drinks and little gifts, Eddie who took her from Tom and then tired of Beth's warm smile and sharp, easy remarks and killed her and quietly disposed of her remains.

Eddie, who is counting his dirty till and congratulating himself on making Christmas about buying ten-karat hoop earrings.

Eddie, who is the reason Beth can never come back.

Tom will ask Eddie, just once and calmly, where Beth is buried. If she is buried. So that Tom can visit her small bones, and tell them that he loved her.

If Eddie confesses where Beth is buried, Tom will take certain steps.

If Eddie doesn't, Tom will take other, more dramatic steps. Right there in the middle of the Raccoon Lodge.

Hurriedly, Tom crosses the street. He can't be lurking when Eddie arrives. He lands in front of the bookstore on the opposite side of the road and sees his reflection staring back from the glass of the window display. Tom's face is gaunt and doughy, his eyes laced with thin pink veins, his smile that Beth called *evil* when she was teasing him nowhere in evidence.

On a whim, Tom shoves his hands in his pockets and enters The Mysterious Bookshop.

A bookseller sitting at a computer station to his left greets Tom and he nods, the nod of a man who wants no help and just stepped in to thaw out the tips of his ears for a moment. The store, which he hasn't ever set foot in alone, only with Beth's hand tucked into his elbow, is like a library as imagined by a kid on Santa's knee. Bookshelves from floor to ceiling on the three walls, and every shelf stuffed full. It smells of paper in here, of rainy January nights. Tom knows that many are signed, because Beth told him so, and there she is in his mind's eye emerging from the door at the back of the shop.

She would rub her hands up and down her forearms like she always did when she was delighted, laughing half to herself, saying, "Couldn't you just put a cot over there and stay forever? Couldn't you? And never hear house music via blown speakers through the bedroom wall again?"

At the back of the bookstore, Tom stops, eyes scanning titles. He needs to kill fifteen minutes thanks to his foolish inattention to the mugs of bourbon and Eddie's greedy Christmas hours. Lacking anything better to do, he pulls down a collection of the detective adventure stories he'd read as a kid, hiding out in the musty local library from school and home and worse. There are chairs in The Mysterious Bookshop, generously padded chairs, as if people ought to just walk in and read books. As if that's civilized instead of cheap. Tom is starting to see why Beth liked it here, why she always made a point of stopping by when the window had changed or the weather was less than perfection.

Bones creaking, accustomed to long shifts of standing and walking and not a thing else—none of those thrilling chase scenes you see in movies, the struggles and near-deaths and triumphs, the bit part of the hapless security guard caught up in a mortal struggle with the snide British-accented terrorist—Tom sits down with the book. Flipping through story titles, he finds one he remembers liking when he was thirteen, and starts reading. The setting is appropriate, during the festive season he wishes were over and done with, and the brilliant detective ruminates over a lost hat.

He picked it up and gazed at it in the peculiar introspective fashion which was characteristic of him. "It is perhaps less suggestive than it might have been," he remarked, "and yet there are a few inferences which are very distinct, and a few others which represent at least a strong balance of probability. That the man was highly intellectual is of course obvious upon the face of it, and also that he was fairly well-to-do within the last three years, although he has now fallen upon evil days. He had foresight, but has less now than formerly, pointing to a moral retrogression, which, when taken with the decline of his fortunes, seems to indicate some evil influence, probably drink, at work upon him. This may account also for the obvious fact that his wife has ceased to love him."

Tom frowns at the minute hand of his watch. He has become engrossed, dragged into a wild era with which he is familiar only thanks to the narrator's knack with words. He recalls being glued to this book as a punk kid, dreaming of pipe smoke and clattering horse-drawn chases through ancient streets. The light in The Mysterious Bookshop is a soft lemon color, gleaming like gaslight or the glow of tallow candles. Maybe it wasn't so smart to pick this book up again, he reflects.

But he can read the rest quickly. And then cross the street. It isn't as if his quest will be a long one tonight.

One question, one answer, one bullet.

Simple. Final.

Tom feels something painful gnaw at his gut before he shoves it back down and finishes the short story. He doesn't remember the ending before he reaches it, but it pleases him in a nostalgic way. Tom slots the illustrated hardcover back into its place on the shelf.

"Have a good night, sir," offers the bookseller when Tom nears him.

Tom doesn't know how to respond, his tongue gone starchy, glued to the back of his throat, so the soft *swish* of The Mysterious Bookshop's door is his only goodbye other than the gun in his coat growing heavier still.

It was stupid to go in there.

It was crazy to allow himself to be seen.

But then again, mustering the energy to care is growing increasingly difficult.

The Raccoon Lodge isn't getting much foot traffic—just regulars stumping their way home from the too-hot subway cars and the too-cold wind, the snowflakes still falling, scattered and breathtaking.

Tom suddenly doesn't want to do this.

He propels his legs across the street, one scarred boot at a time. Beth deserves this. Beth deserves everything Tom ever gave her.

Beth deserved much more than that.

If the world worked as it should, Beth would emerge from the Raccoon Lodge mere feet away from him, and why can't it happen, why not, and Beth would be laughing too brassy from the drinks she and Eddie had shared and the company they'd kept while Tom was busy walking the corridors of a skyscraper no one was trying to break into—and if anyone had attempted a break-in, Tom couldn't have stopped them, weaponless and stiff-kneed as he was—but, no, focus, breathe, you have to focus, Beth would come out of the Raccoon Lodge laughing too high and too fast and Eddie's musk would sit on the curve of her shoulder and she'd be wearing a too-yellow chain that caught the street lamp as she—

Tom stops.

There is a mini bottle of bourbon in his coat pocket, as there always is, and that is important.

Tom drinks it in the middle of the sidewalk.

He then swivels, identifying the nearest trash can, before recognizing that no one is there to see him. He throws the scrap of plastic in the gutter.

Empty mini bottles never stay in his coat, and that is important.

Tom continues on his way.

Inside the Raccoon Lodge, under the colored glass lamps and the many shelves of liquor and the fading firemen's pictures, maybe thirty people are gathered. It isn't many, for this place. Tom recalls when he and Beth had been angling for their horrible apartment, when the air here reeked of smoke and chemicals and twisted metal, and he'd been able to pay three months down on a place that no one in his right mind would want, and they'd discovered the Raccoon Lodge. All the firefighters.

Dozens of them, tired, limping, determined, hopeful, brave. He'd admired them as if they were elder brothers. Gods. Untouchable. Tom had wanted to reach out, as a lowly security guard new-hired in a blessedly unscathed building ten blocks north, to feel their ashy coats and tell them *I am one of you. I protect people.*

Tom recalls later, when the firemen started coughing.

Tom loves them almost as ferociously as he had Beth. Because they meant something *achievable*, and yet something *divine*, and he'd never done anything in his life worth special notice apart from maybe writing a good enough note to convince Beth to leave the club he'd found her in and agree to a cup of diner coffee in the middle of the night. The cheapest date in the history of love.

There is Eddie Adamo.

He sits on a bench at the back behind the pool table, looking worn and wary. His slender shoulders seem birdlike in his thin grey sweater, and Tom is reminded again of how active Eddie always looks, how charmingly alive, and Tom's mouth waters to wipe Eddie off the face of the planet.

"What can I get you?" asks the bartender, who is buxom enough to be striking but not unattainable. She has a way of not-smiling that looks like showing respect. Tom likes her, but he can't recall her name.

"Bourbon, neat," he answers, stomach churning, and hands her a twenty.

Bar tabs are always paid in cash, and that is important.

Tom drinks half the whiskey at a go and then realizes Eddie is cautiously watching him. It would be more menacing, Tom thinks, to walk up to Eddie with a glass held casually in his hand. But he is trembling with anticipation now, and so he finishes and sets the tumbler on the bar.

Tom walks to the back of the room past the pool players. His gun has never been heavier. It weighs a thousand pounds now if it weighs an ounce.

When Tom stops before Eddie, Eddie looks up. Something about his face is very strange. Eddie is a sly, secretive sort, with a sharp chin and brooding eyes, but just now Tom feels as if he is being x-rayed. As if Eddie can hear his innermost thoughts, can see the bullets inside the gun inside the coat. Eddie is drinking a beer and after taking a sip, he drops his elbows onto his knees and stares up into Tom's face, brows raised.

Does Eddie know about Tom's plan? Is Tom so transparent? Can Eddie read minds?

Sweat prickles along the back of Tom's neck.

"You want to know where Beth is," Eddie says. His voice is flat. Sad, almost. Regretful? No, Eddie is too cruel to be regretful. "The fact of the matter is I can't tell you. I don't know, Tom. If I knew, I would tell you. Less risky for me, isn't it? Telling you. But I don't know."

Tom backs away, mouth open. How could Beth's killer not know where she was?

"I'm going now," Eddie sighs, standing. "But I have a feeling I'll be seeing you around."

Breathing is difficult for Tom in the wake of Eddie's departure. There is a knot in his chest like a fist. The pool players, a man with a grifter's beard and a construction worker just off work, are arguing with plentiful good-natured obscenities about politics. Tom feels dizzy.

What just happened? And why?

A black rage descends.

Of course Eddie had it all figured. This is why Beth allowed herself to be seduced by Eddie, to be lured into his net, because Eddie is one step ahead of Tom in every way.

The gun feels considerably lighter now.

Lurching, Tom stumbles out the door.

The snow is sparse before The Mysterious Bookshop beyond, but the wind howls. Tom retraces his steps, panting a little in haste and a vicious sort of excitement.

This is how it feels to chase a terrorist through a skyscraper.

This is how it feels to fight a fire.

This, right now, is how it feels to matter.

Tom shoulders open the door to his own apartment building and runs up the dank stairs.

He doesn't go to his apartment, however. He heads for his neighbor's place, where the door is open, and the lights flicker *pink-sapphire-green* in a way that nauseates him. He draws his gun.

Tom's neighbor Eddie Adamo has opened another beer, and is sitting in a reclining chair looking haggard. The gun in Eddie's hand is steady but not aimed at anything in particular. Tom can't remember when Eddie got this thin.

"I told you last year it was the final straw," Eddie says, a high note of anxiety in his voice. "It's been a rough patch, I know, man, but I can't keep letting you threaten to kill me every Christmas. That would be, like, suicidal on my part. You need to get a hold of yourself, Tom, before you do something nuts. I'm really worried. She left us *both*, you get that, right?"

Tom doesn't answer. So Eddie keeps talking.

"She left *both of us*. Three years ago. She hasn't returned any of my calls. I can't keep doing this with you like it's some kind of crazy holiday ritual. Look, I bought a gun. I don't even *want* a gun. God."

Tom closes his eyes. He needs to think about something, anything else. The gun he is holding falls to the floor.

The picture of you and Beth was so dusty when you picked it up earlier, dustier than—

The bottle on the kitchen counter is always at three quarters, just like it was on the last day you saw her, and that is important—

A detective sits on a sofa staring very intently at a battered old hat that means a man's wife has ceased to love him—

But she was frightened, she said in the note she left behind that she was so frightened, and that's why you—

"This is all your fault," Tom hisses at Eddie, fists clenching.

"I *know*!" Eddie shouts. "Don't you think I know that? I know! When I think of how close we all were . . . it's awful, you gotta realize that. You have to. You were gone such long hours, and . . . I don't even know how you found out about us. Not after all this time. You've got to talk to me, Tom. We've been through this. She left me a note saying goodbye, and that she was safe, and that's all. Then you start in with this lunatic conspiracy theory, and god knows I felt horrible enough not to have you arrested. Anyway, who knows what you'd have said to them about me, the last thing I need is to be accused of murder to the sort of cops I deal with, but this has to stop. Right now."

Tom feels on the verge of tears. He thinks about Beth, her face lit up at the strains of a bad eighties song, dancing with a

LYNDSAY FAYE

broom handle. He thinks about a detective with a hawk nose and a pipe, and about days when Tom was better.

Clearer.

Tom opens his wallet and, hands shaking, pulls out Beth's note. He reads it first, carefully now for the first time in a long time, and then passes it to Eddie.

Dear Tom,

I hope when you find this you can forgive me for not saying everything in person. I want to, so much. But it's been harder and harder lately, and I started to think I couldn't make a change at all if I had to face you—that I'd run myself into the ground before hurting you. This will hurt you too, but I won't be there to see it. That makes me a coward, I know, but I want to be better and I don't think I can be better here in New York.

When we got married, I didn't picture this life. Didn't picture the noise or the smells or the dirt that won't scrub out of the bathtub. Or the sort of creatures I find in the bathtub, for that matter. That isn't your fault, but we were so young, and I turned selfish. I wanted distractions and I found them, and they weren't distractions I shared with you. And now I feel as if I can't bear the sight of this place, or myself, any longer.

I told you Eddie and I were only friends, and that was partly true. I don't love him. But I did make mistakes with him, stupid ones, ones that I hid from you, and I'll never forgive myself for that. For the hell you must have been through if you already knew before reading this. It's like I can't recognize the girl you married, and I think that scares me most of all.

I've been frightened for such a long time. I'd have told you before, but I thought that you might blame yourself if all goes to pieces anyhow and you can't prevent it. I'm terrified of Eddie, what he might do, of my life, terrified everything is ruined. But I always loved you, and I'm sorry if there were times you didn't know that. Because I felt it, every day.

I'm going back to Connecticut to stay with my parents. Away from the mess I've made, the awful person I turned into, to try and feel like myself again. I hope you come to forgive me, and want to talk to me, to see me sometime even. Now that all is out in the open . . . I failed us, and even so, I hope

*you call me. Or write, or email or something. But
I'll understand if you can't.*

Love,

Beth

Eddie takes a deep breath. "Okay," he says. Then, "Okay."

Tom sits down on the ratty couch next to Eddie's recliner. His knees don't feel strong enough to hold him up. The silence is cut by the faint rattle of the radiator, by the hiss of the steam pipes. Tom can't remember how he came to be here, but he knows he can't stand *here* any longer. Wherever *here* is.

Tom suspects he invented *here*.

He's going to have to think some things through.

"You suppose she feels better now?" Eddie says dully.

"Yeah," Tom whispers. "Yeah. I haven't . . . called, or . . . or anything. But she's a strong girl."

Eddie doesn't answer. For a while, he frowns, both men listening to the clanking of old pipes.

Eddie's place is pretty terrible too, Tom realizes. There are houseplants, and a quilt over the couch. Otherwise not discernibly better than Tom's apartment. Tom feels as if he's seeing things, actually looking at them, for the first time.

"She never called you back, when you tried to reach her, huh?" Tom asks Eddie hoarsely.

Eddie shakes his head. The lights on his fire escape blink through their hellish carnival rotations. "She wasn't in love with me."

"No," says Tom.

"You ought to call her," Eddie says.

"Yeah," says Tom.

He closes his eyes again and pictures the detective and the words he read in The Mysterious Bookshop. Tom tries to recall what it felt like to be thirteen, and to believe that he could grow up to be anything in the world. To be a fireman or a spy or a master sleuth. To choose his own life.

I am not retained by the police to supply their deficiencies. If Horner were in danger it would be another thing; but this fellow will not appear against him, and the case must collapse. I suppose that I am commuting a felony, but it is just possible that I am saving a soul. This fellow will not go wrong again; he is too terribly frightened. Send him to jail now, and you make him a jail-bird for life. Besides, it is the season of forgiveness. Chance has put in our way a most singular and whimsical problem, and its solution is its own reward.

It isn't going to be perfect, Tom thinks, and it isn't going to be easy either. Getting rid of the bottles, growing friendly with facts. Maybe he won't be able to do it in the end. But trying will be better than nothing, and it will be something he wants for himself.

"You hungry?" Tom asks, opening his eyes.

Eddie glances at the gun in his lap, and at the gun on the floor. Tom reaches down and shakes the bullets out of his pistol onto the rug. Eddie, blinking slowly, does the same and then rests his gun on the card table next to him.

"I could eat, sure," Eddie says.

That's good, Tom thinks. He can remember other nights here at Eddie's, nights of cheap pizza and laughter and the windows all open in the jungle heat of August. He can remember Chinese takeaway and baseball games on the TV.

"Can . . . can I use your phone in a minute?" Tom asks next.

"Yeah," Eddie says. He smiles a sad smile. "Yeah. You can use my phone."

WOLFE TRAP

A CLAUDIUS LYON MYSTERY

Loren D. Estleman

When you looked in the dictionary under "tough cop," you never got as far as the picture, because Captain Stoddard of the Brooklyn Bunko Squad would tear out the page and shove it down your throat.

So when I saw that craggy, bitter-almond face through the two-way glass in the front door of Claudius Lyon's brownstone I knew the day could only get better from there.

Turned out I was wrong.

"I know you're in there, Woodbine. That little gob of goo never leaves the place and you're too busy bleeding him dry to go out for a pint of Old Overshoe."

"One moment, please." I skedaddled to report the glad tidings to my employer.

He was sitting in the overstuffed green chair that was too big for him behind the desk that was too big for even Nero Wolfe, his hero and role model in the office he'd copied from a photo spread on Wolfe's place of business in *Knickerbocker*. I caught him reading Encyclopedia Brown before he could stash it behind a hefty copy of *Crime and Punishment*. The short, fat faker never gave up the ruse.

He squeaked, turned a paler shade of boiled turnip, and said, "We don't have to let him in, do we? He doesn't have a warrant or anything, does he?"

"I couldn't tell from just his face. I don't think even a police dog like him goes around carrying them in his mouth."

"Tell him to go away." He reburied his nose in his book.

"Not me, boss. I'd sooner punch a grizzly on the snoot. He'll just come back hungrier."

He set aside the literature and hopped down from the chair. "I'm in the plant rooms and can't be disturbed."

"Not for another twenty minutes. He knows Wolfe's routine as well as you."

"A man's home is his castle, confound it!"

"That's the thing about castles. Somebody's always storming them. Look, we're not working on anything right now. He can't bust us for conducting a private investigation without a license, which is his only beef with us. Let's just swallow the hemlock and get it over with."

He screwed up his round baby face, but he never got quite to the point of actually bawling. "Very well. Give me a moment to prepare."

I left him while he was slipping Encyclopedia Brown page-ends foremost on a shelf of weighty classics he got as much use out of as a stationary bike. He never read anything but whodunits and *The Vine*, the monthly newsletter of the Empire State Tomato-Breeders' Association.

"Season's greetings, Captain." I opened the front door.

It *was* that time of year, but no one at headquarters would dare tell him.

Stoddard shoved past me and into the office, sneered at the framed label from a can of Chef Boyardee, the big globe that still maintained there was a Soviet Union, and the day's display on Lyon's desk: a dwarf tomato plant with fruit the size of buckshot. The boss flattered himself he'd developed a new subspecies, the way Wolfe is doing all the time with orchids, but it was just an undernourished specimen of cherry tomato. His idol's botanical interests are exacting and difficult, but tomatoes practically grow themselves, giving Lyon plenty of time to goof off and read

The Hot-Cha-Cha Murder Case during his daily four hours total on the roof.

I'll give him this much: the tyrannical cop made him as nervous as he did me—which given my arrest record is no mere qualm—but unless you were sharp enough to catch the slight tremor in his pudgy hands gripping the edge of his desk, you wouldn't know it. He even managed to dial down his frightened treble to a decibel below a dog whistle.

"What can I do for you, Mr. Stoddard?"

The captain, of course, never missed a sign of weakness in others, but for once kept the sadistic note from his snarling baritone.

"Normally I'd say come clean and confess to violation of the New York State Code prohibiting snooping without a ticket on file in Albany, but I'll leave that to another time. You're coming with me to Manhattan."

Sickly green crept into Lyon's cheeks, turning them from Macintoshes into Granny Smiths. But he kept his even high pitch. "Out of the question. As you know, I never leave my house on business."

If anything, when our guest smiled he was even more unnerving. "Who said it was business? Never mind. It is."

Without waiting for an invitation, which was customary to him, he plunked himself into the pinkish-orange leather chair facing the desk. It was supposed to be red, like its model across the river, but the upholsterer was colorblind.

"It's my niece," he said. "My brother's daughter."

For once I was more suspicious of him than he was of us. The thought that there should be two Stoddards in existence, and that one of them had procreated, was about as easy to swallow as a tomato-butter sandwich, one of my esteemed employer's more notorious failures.

"Stella's a smart cookie," he went on. "She talked herself into a job in a successful bookstore when she was sixteen, and she's worked there four years. Now her boss suspects her of stealing two hundred dollars from the desk in his office during a Christmas party at the store. I wouldn't be any kind of cop if I thought anybody was above suspicion, but Stella's got too much going on upstairs to risk her job and her freedom over a couple of hundred bucks."

"You are, as you say, a police officer," Lyon said.

"You know damn well I'm a captain."

"As you say." His tone wavered between a high tremolo and a vacuum cleaner. "Why not investigate the case yourself?"

"It's a mystery bookshop. I don't read the things myself; last thing I want to think about when I get home is work, and from what I hear most of them bollix up the facts, putting silencers on revolvers and such. You gobble the things up like candy, so I thought you could shed some light on the nature of the business. The money came from a customer who bought a rare book, in a dust jacket. The owner says that's important. Me, I throw 'em away as soon as I bring home a book."

"Amazing."

Stoddard's normal congestion deepened a shade, but he couldn't tell any more than I could if the chubby little sparrow was referring to the habit or the thought of the captain bringing a book into his house. I figured it was *1,000 Ways to Beat a Suspect to Death*.

"It's got a foreign title." He dug out a fold of ruled paper and squinted at his ballpoint scrawl. "*Fer-de-Lance*, first edition."

Lyon squeaked.

"Thought you'd be interested. Penzler says it was the first book about your god."

"*Otto* Penzler?"

"You know him?"

"We've never met, but I've ordered some items from his shop, and we've spoken on the telephone." Lyon, plainly hooked (he even forgot to be afraid of his company), shook his head. "Something's amiss. Two hundred is far too little for a first edition of that book, which began the Nero Wolfe series, and Mr. Penzler is far too well-versed in his trade to let it go for pennies."

The captain looked again at his notes, rubbed his nose. "Okay, I misread my own chicken scratches. It's a first *movie* edition, with pictures of the actors on the cover and stills from the film inside. That help?"

Lyon nodded, folding his hands across his middle. The fingers just met.

"*Meet Nero Wolfe*, starring Edward Arnold and Lionel Stander. They changed the book's title at the time of release, and almost everything else inside. I have a fair copy myself, but, dear me, I never paid anything approaching two hundred dollars for it. The first, of course, would be worth thousands."

"So somebody got suckered."

"Doubtful. Penzler's reputation is spotless."

"Anyway, he swears Stella was the only one who went into his office between the time he locked the money in the drawer and he discovered it was missing; she'd gone there on some errand or other. What's got me buffaloed is how whoever did it managed to unlock the drawer, take the money, and relock it afterwards. Penzler claims to have the only key, and it was on his person the entire time. Stella's good at a lot of things, but second-story work isn't one of them."

I figured if Stella lived up to half the hype, she was adopted.

Lyon actually clapped his hands. "A locked-room mystery!"

"It was a drawer, not a room."

"One takes things as they come."

I leaned across the desk and whispered in his face.

"It's a trap. He'll find some way to make you accept payment, and then he'll have you on that practicing-with-out-a-license rap."

"Fortunately, I'm independently wealthy, and never need to." He raised his voice. "Arnie, we're going to the big island."

I screwed up my nose. "'Book 'em, Dan-o.'"

Well, the mountain came to Muhammad, the continents drifted apart, and twenty minutes later Lyon finished prying himself into a bilious green overcoat and a Tyrolean hat with a green feather in the band. (Wolfe prefers yellow; the little blob of cholesterol was bound to have an independent streak somewhere.) I'd swear he'd kept the coat unused since before I came under his roof if I didn't know for a fact he kept contributing to his girth like Methuselah kept having birthdays, and the damn thing fit.

Sitting next to the captain in the front seat of his unmarked Winston Leviathan, Lyon kicking his feet in back, I watched the man behind the wheel scowling at all the decorated windows and bundled-up pedestrians lugging bright packages past decorated windows. He was by Scrooge out of the Grinch by way of the ACLU.

The store was in Tribeca. A hand-lettered sign in red and green announced that the shop was closed for a Christmas party. A burly young employee with a beard buzzed us into a big, hollowed-out, well-lit cube walled with books starting at the floor and reaching fifteen feet to the ceiling, with rolling ladders attached to metal rails. Green, red, gold, and silver streamers festooned the place and there was a punch bowl the size of a witch's cauldron and the usual scattering of bottles, partially filled glasses, and abandoned soda-pop cans, along with trays of cookies shaped like Santas and snowmen and Christmas trees that looked like air fresheners, the requisite bowls of untouched nuts, and a basket half-filled with poppy-seed buns. A trimmed tree lorded over all in glorious bad taste, in tune with the season.

"Mr. Lyon?" greeted a compact man in an argyle sweater and slacks, wearing gold-rimmed glasses, white hair neatly brushed back, and a snowy, well-trimmed beard. I don't know what I'd expected; a character in a ragged sweatshirt who smelled like old magazines, maybe. All I know about books is the odds at Pimlico. This guy resembled the German scientist who's always explaining Godzilla. "By golly, you look like Archie Goodwin washed Wolfe in hot water and threw him in the dryer with the setting on Normal."

"Mr. Penzler, I presume." Lyon's response was cool, and he ignored the proprietor's outstretched hand; I knew him well enough to know he wasn't offended by the comparison, only by the way it was put. "What is this I am told about someone paying two hundred dollars for a movie edition of *Fer-de-Lance*?"

"It's ridiculous, I agree. But as a collector you must know that when a true first edition prices itself out of most people's market, they turn to the next one down, and yet the next, increasing the value of each in its own order. When I opened this shop, I couldn't give away movie tie-ins; ten years ago, I'd have been lucky to get twenty dollars for one in fine condition. As it was, I made this buyer a bargain, seeing as how he's a loyal, long-time customer. I should add that it was inscribed by Lionel Stander, when he was appearing on *Hart to Hart*."

Lyon asked the customer's name.

"I'm sorry, but that's confidential."

"At least he's intelligent enough not to show himself a gull to the world. Have you another copy? I'd like to refresh my memory."

Penzler scaled a ladder without hesitating and came back with his prize. He'd committed his stock to memory.

"This is a fair copy, with a closed tear in the jacket and a library stamp on the first page. Would you believe I expect to get sixty for it?"

I looked at it over the boss's suety shoulder. A black-and-white photo of a fat, distinguished-looking party and a taller, younger man with a face like a shaved gorilla's decorated the cover.

Lyon tried to say, "Pfui!" Fortunately for the jacket, it was sealed in plastic; the amount of spraying involved, and the attempt to avoid it, distorted the exclamation so much even Nero Wolfe couldn't have sued him successfully for copyright infringement. He wiped the book on his sleeve. "It's no wonder Rex Stout, acting on Wolfe's behalf, refused to allow any films to be made after the first two-picture contract ended. Edward Arnold was an acceptable Wolfe, but Lionel Stander bore as much resemblance to Archie Goodwin as—"

"Woodbine," Stoddard finished. "Give him the rest, Penzler, just as you gave it to me."

The bookstore owner explained that Stella, the captain's niece, had placed herself in voluntary police custody after the theft was discovered. Penzler had closed the shop early for the party, and as he was too busy to deposit the two hundred cash he'd just gotten for the book and reluctant to deprive any of his hard-working employees of party time by making them run the errand, he'd simply locked it in the top drawer of his desk. An hour or so later, he sent Stella into the office to bring back more refreshments. As the celebration was winding down, he returned to put the money in his wallet so it wouldn't be left unattended overnight, and that was when he discovered it was missing.

Lyon asked if she was searched.

"NYPD searched the entire staff," Stoddard said. "The money wasn't on any of them; but anyone could have stashed it anywhere. I've asked the locals to toss the place, but with all these books to look through it'll take days."

"May I see the scene of the crime?"

Penzler smiled. "In all the years I've collected, sold, and written about mystery fiction, that's the first time I've ever actually heard anyone use that phrase."

In the office, our host produced a key and unlocked the top drawer of a graceful-looking antique desk. Inside was the usual desk stuff.

"It was on top of that pad: four fifties folded and loose. Don't bother searching the drawer. I've had everything out of it several times."

Lyon pointed at a scattering of tiny brownish-black fragments. "Were those here when you put in the cash?"

Penzler frowned. "I can't say I noticed them."

I had a brainstorm. When you've been a crook all your life, it's not hard to think like a detective. I licked a finger, touched it to one of the fragments, and put it on my tongue.

"Poppy seeds," I said. "Not very tasty ones. I saw a bowl of poppy-seed buns in the shop. Whoever broke into the drawer must have been eating one at the time."

"Ha!" I know in print it looks like ordinary laughter, but what came out of Captain Stoddard's mouth bore no resemblance to human mirth. "That proves she's innocent. Stella's allergic to gluten. She'd no sooner eat a bun than gobble down poison."

Penzler cleared his throat embarrassedly. "I knew that, Captain. It's why I bought them from the gluten-free section of the bakery."

What came out of the cop's mouth next wouldn't read like laughter even in print.

Penzler said, "I don't intend to press charges, or even dismiss Stella; this is the season for forgiving, after all. However, I do think I'm entitled to reimbursement."

"Meanwhile my niece's reputation is destroyed."

Lyon stuck a finger in his ear and commenced to rotate. When it was his right ear, he was just after wax, but when it was his left, as now, he was stroking an idea to the surface of his brain, like a needle coaxing a splinter out of his thumb. So far it had never failed to amount to something just as satisfying. He asked Penzler if he had a magnifying glass.

"I thought all you amateur dicks carried one," Stoddard barked.

Penzler opened another drawer and drew out a square lens in a black metal frame with a handle. For some time, Lyon studied the inside of the drawer, then dropped to the floor.

I knew it, I thought. The short, fat nothing had blown an artery at last; all those greasy gefilte fish his chef Gus shoveled into him had taken their ichthyological revenge. But as I was stooping to test his tonnage and calculate the ability of my back to support it, he began crawling across the carpet on his knees and elbows, holding the glass in one hand. It was more physical activity than I'd seen him engaged in ever; the sawed-off porker went begging for a coronary just pushing the button to his private elevator.

He applied the glass again when he reached the paneled wall behind the desk. While the rest of us goggled—Penzler with bemusement, Stoddard with raw-boned contempt, and me wondering if I should give notice or just walk out in search of someone *compos mentis* to work for (provided he didn't keep too weather an eye on the business accounts)—he crept along like an obese inchworm, training the lens along the baseboard.

At length he indicated triumph (I'd worked for him long enough to interpret all his chirps, squeals, and yelps the way a zoologist learns the language of monkeys), flattened himself on the floor, made a rooting motion I couldn't identify because of the fat obstacle he made, and with a noise like a rusty hinge pushed himself back onto his knees and rested his buttocks on his heels, holding up some colored strands between thumb and forefinger. If he could grow a tomato as red as his face at that moment, he'd be Mr. December in *The Vine*.

"Mr. Stoddard, I think the experts in your laboratory will find little difficulty tracing these samples back to the United States Treasury."

"Treasury!" We all said it at once.

"I could be wrong. The new bills are so much more colorful than the old that I may be mistaking Christmas confetti for currency. However, I doubt it. Your culprit is a female, hair brownish gray, weighing a few grams at most, measuring perhaps two and one-half inches from nose to tail, and she has accomplices. A mate, for one, and what is doubtless a squirming brood." He thumped the baseboard, calling our attention to a hole the size of a half-dollar.

"A mouse!" Stoddard's tone was disbelieving, but then he'd have demanded a paternity test in the manger in Bethlehem.

"You mean she's shredded my money to build a nest for her young?" Penzler's tone was wounded. Even someone as esoteric (I'm pretty sure of the word; I Googled it) as a bookseller is still a merchant, and a dollar destroyed is a heart broken.

"I lost the jacket off a nice copy of Graham Greene's *Brighton Rock* to a rodent with a family, cutting the book to a fraction of its value. New York is an old city, and no matter how many times it rebuilds itself or how clean the neighborhood and its residents, the creatures' bloodlines stretch back to Peter Stuyvesant."

"I didn't know the little bastards could pick locks," I said.

"The Greene was in a chest of drawers, and although it wasn't locked, all they need is a gap in the joints the size of a pencil to gain access. The chest wasn't nearly as old as this fine desk, but time is patient. It will unfasten what is fast and loosen what is snug, no matter how long it takes."

Penzler strode over, helped Lyon grunting to his feet, and stared at the shredded remains of four half-century notes. He gave them to Stoddard, who produced a glassine bag from an overcoat pocket and sealed them inside. "I'll send forensics to scoop out the rest. If you're lucky, Penzler, you may wind up with enough for Treasury to replace the pieces with whole bills."

A weight even heavier than Lyon's seemed to lift itself from the shoulders of the bookseller, who apologized to the captain. "Stella has a raise and a bonus coming, and a public apology in front of the staff."

"Just be sure of yourself next time. Locked rooms and locked drawers. Pfui!"

Lyon was still sputtering at Stoddard's correct pronun-
ciation of the word when Penzler opened the glazed door
of a bookcase that matched the desk and handed him
something: a book, its jacket sealed in stiff plastic, with a
frightened-looking adolescent girl painted on the cover and
the title *The Secret of the Old Clock*.

"Ha!" Stoddard bellowed again, nastier than before.
"Claudius Lyon, I arrest you for practicing investigation
without a license, for profit." The ungrateful S.O.B. took a
pair of handcuffs from another pocket.

"Told you it was a trap!" I said.

I expected another high-pitched noise from Lyon, or at
least pallor. Instead, he held the book out to the arresting
officer. "You'll need evidence."

Stoddard snatched it from his hand as if he thought he was
getting ready to throw the evidence out a window.

"Please examine the flyleaf."

Grinding his teeth, the captain snapped open the cover.
Instead of Lyon's, it was his face that faded to a mild shade
of mauve. Craning my neck to see past his shoulder, I recognized the leafy tomato plant printed on the bookplate:

EX LIBRIS
Claudius Lyon

700 Avenue J
Flatbush, NY

"In addition to being a bookseller and a scholar, Mr. Penzler operates a number of small presses, one of which produces facsimile copies of great mystery first editions, which he offers at popular prices. When he called to say he'd heard I possessed a first of the inaugural Nancy Drew mystery and asking to borrow it so he could reproduce it, I sent it over by special messenger."

"It came out beautifully," Penzler said. "You'll receive a copy of the first one off the press, inscribed by the publisher. It's the least I can do, since you wouldn't accept remuneration."

"I'll buy it. I wouldn't want to risk Mr. Stoddard's disapproval."

The captain thrust the book back into Lyon's hands and stamped out, leaving us without our ride. Penzler lifted the telephone receiver off his desk and called for a car.

I said, "Wait a minute. What about the poppy seeds?"

Claudius Lyon blinked at me. "Not seeds," he said. "Mouse droppings."

I had our cab stop at a drugstore on the way back and gargled with Listerine all the way home.

SECRET SANTA

Ace Atkins

Christmas Eve, 1985

H e'd been a big deal twenty years ago. Or at least that's what he told me.

The Writer said no one cared about hero books anymore. "The hardboiled hero is dead," he said, slurring his words. He smelled of mothballs and Scotch. "People want to read about spies or vice cops. Policemen in pastels, busting Colombian coke dealers. The idea of one man walking down the mean streets is now considered old fashioned."

"So you were big time?" I said. "Right? I mean, back in the day?"

"In '68, the only book that outsold me was that asshole Arthur Hailey," he said. "*Airport*. Do you remember that piece of crap?"

"To be honest," I said, "I don't read much. My work keeps me pretty damn busy."

"Do you remember those ridiculous movies with all those has-been movie stars?" he said. "In one, I think there were five or so, some hijackers take over a 747 and Jack Lemmon and Lee Grant have to save the day. Or maybe it was food poisoning? I can't keep them straight."

"Oh, sure," I said. "*Yeah. Yeah.* They crashed into an oil platform or something because they were flying under the radar."

"Well, that's Hailey," the Writer said. "He was huge. Writing about big hotels, big business, and bullshit. Now he's dead. Or not. Might as well be. Out of print. No one wants the Big Book. No one wants the real hero. A red-blooded American man who fights the bad boys and beds the bad girls. You really never read?"

I peered back in the rearview as I headed toward downtown from LaGuardia.

The Writer was a small, wiry guy dressed in a faded gray three-piece suit. He had a full head of white hair and a closely clipped mustache. He wore huge black eyeglasses that covered most of his thin face. When I'd picked him up at LaGuardia and spotted him lighting up a long brown cigarette, I thought he might be Dr. Seuss.

"I read books in school," I said. "Those Bronte sisters. Mandatory reading. But between us, not one good sex scene between 'em."

"I could write a sex scene," the Writer said. "I could write pages upon pages of sweaty, panting hellcats that would make a grown man suck his thumb. All my women had big feet and strong shoulders. They didn't get made love to. They took charge and punished the man. It was my trademark. Robert McGinnis always did my covers. I bet you don't know McGinnis, either."

"Sorry," I said. "Like I said. Few books. Not a lot of art where I grew up."

"McGinnis was a master," the Writer said. "Very underappreciated. A foot man, too."

"Well, I heard you were real famous," I said. "And to treat you right."

"What else did they tell you?" The Writer launched into a hacking cough while he smoked another long brown cigarette and settled into the back seat of the Town Car.

"Someone has threatened to kill you," I said. "And that you needed protection while at your event."

"On Christmas Eve," he said. "Isn't that in poor taste? Someone wants to harm me at my annual Christmas Eve book signing? It sickens me."

"Don't worry about any of that stuff," I said. "I got you covered."

"But you will let me know if anything is amiss," the Writer said, spewing smoke from the side of his mouth. "Go in first and tell me if it's safe to sign books. My friend Otto knows a great many cops. If there are any problems, Otto will know exactly what to do. He can talk. *And I'll tell you right out, I am a man who likes talking to a man who talks.*"

"Yeah, sure, sure," I said. "Why would someone want to hurt you?"

"Jealousy," the Writer said. "Anger. Rage. Revenge. So many motives. I know you said you're not a reader, but you are aware that this is the book in which I finally kill off Mitch Wilde. There was an item about it in *Publishers Weekly*."

We headed out of the Queens Midtown Tunnel and into Manhattan. It was gray and cold, sleet pelting the windshield. Lots of Christmas lights, holly, and gold tinsel twinkled behind window displays. I reached for my paper cup of coffee before I said it: "And who's Mitch Wilde?"

"Oh, for Christ's sake," the Writer said. "Mitch Wilde is the star of more than sixty-two novels. He's an ex-Marine, playboy, problem-solver. He speaks four languages, skin dives, prepares Indian food, and is a master of Kung Fu. Really? You must be kidding me!"

"Can you name some of your books?"

"Can I?" the Writer said. "*Wilde Blood, Wilde's Paradise, Wilde's Ways?*"

I didn't answer, just kept on trying to get around traffic and get this guy to his gig on 56th Street at The Mysterious Bookshop. Midtown was lit up like a Times Square hooker. Something about Christmas made the town look desperate and cheap. Everyone wanted to pick your pocket this time of year. I had three kids at home who thought money grew on trees—the reason I took the job.

"Ever heard of Sherlock Holmes?" he said.

"Of course," I said. "Sure. Everybody knows that guy."

"Mitch Wilde was America's Sherlock Holmes," he said. The Scotch smell on his breath and the smoke filled the entire car. I cracked a window. "Anthony Boucher once wrote that in the *Times*. It adorned countless Fawcett Gold Medal paperbacks."

"And then what?" I asked.

"And then my readers quit me or died off," he said. "That's why I'm killing Mitch off now. My young agent says it's a smart career move. I have a stellar idea for a new series. A woman spy who is every bit as nasty and mean as a man. No feelings. No feelings at all."

We pulled up in front of The Mysterious Bookshop and I double-parked, leaving the motor running. The store was a well-known place, although sometimes hard to find, down a couple of steps below street level. I got out of the car and held the door open for the Writer.

"I suppose you want me to just stroll right in and get shot in the heart?" he said. "I was told I would get adequate security. If I only needed a ride, I would've called a yellow cab."

"Yes, sir."

I closed the car door and walked down several steps and into the store.

A bell rang overhead, the space looking like an old time speakeasy, tight and clustered, endless bookshelves and books on tables. A spiral staircase leading up high into the ceiling. All the books were about crime or murder.

As I picked up a copy of a novel called *Take a Murder, Darling*, a middle-aged man with a lot of salt-and-pepper hair and a matching beard and mustache circled down the small staircase. He had on a blue blazer with brass buttons, a maroon tie, and a matching show hankie. The owner of the store, Otto Penzler, always looked like he should be at the helm of some yacht. But he was a good guy and gave me work at the store when he could.

"Jesus, Rick," he said. "How's he look?"

I told him the Writer was stinking drunk and was damn sure someone wanted to kill him.

"Every year." He made a circular motion around his head with his forefinger. "It's the same. What a grand tradition."

"Then why do it?" I said. "I mean, why not just say no?"

"Because I owe him," he said. "And let's leave it at that."

Penzler pointed to a linen-covered table topped with a drugstore Christmas tree surrounded with a bowl of crackers, a plate of soft cheese, and an open bottle of white wine. No one else was in the store. I heard some kind of Hallelujah chorus really belting it out from up above the staircase.

Penzler kept an office up there lined with priceless classics, first editions of Raymond Chandler, Dashiell Hammett, Richard S. Prather, and almost everyone else.

"Was this guy really a big deal?" I said. "Or is he just yanking my chain?"

"Back in '66, he would've had them lined up around the block. But it's 1985. Time changes while some people stay the same."

"I'll take care of him," I said, walking toward the door. "Don't worry about nothin', Mr. Penzler."

"How drunk is he?"

"I seen skunks in better shape."

I walked back up to the street and opened the back door. I helped the Writer ease out of the car. The steps were icy and hard for him to navigate. Inside, Penzler sat the man at a small desk piled with dozens of books waiting to be signed. The book was called *Deuces Wilde*. The cover had twin naked women holding playing cards over their breasts. A man with a gun stood in silhouette behind them.

Penzler offered the Writer a glass of wine. The Writer declined and pulled a silver flask from his coat, which smelled of mothballs. He took a long swig and then held out his hand. Penzler presented him with a pen and stepped back.

The Writer furiously started to scrawl in dozens of books.

"Otto, Otto, Otto," the Writer said.

Penzler smiled and nodded.

"Oh, yes," the Writer said. "So good to see you. Such a wonderful time in San Francisco. The veal. The veal. Otto, Otto, Otto."

About halfway through the stack, the Writer keeled over and fell to the floor. I felt for a pulse and made sure he was breathing. He began to snore. A radio upstairs began to play "Hark! The Herald Angels Sing."

"Now that's a record," Penzler said, rolling his eyes. "He's down for the count."

"Don't worry about it," I said. "Your friend is safe."

"Oh, he's not my friend," Otto said. "He once tried to punch me out at Bouchercon. All I said was that Mitch Wilde was a hard man to believe in. You know, with the cooking and scuba diving and all that? He even had the nerve to write that his hero's phallus was not unlike an uncoiled python."

I lifted the Writer into my arms and slung him over my shoulder. He couldn't have weighed a hundred pounds. His gray suit smelled like it had been shut up in an old closet a good long while. "How bad are his books?"

"His plots were outrageous," Penzler said. "His characters simplistic and silly. But I will admit he could really write a great sex scene."

"That's what he said!"

"It's true." Penzler held the bookshop door wide and we all walked back up to the car. I opened the door to the back seat and tossed the Writer in. Penzler had told me he was staying at the Marriott, near Times Square.

"Mitch Wilde really screwed some amazing women," Penzler said. "They were always muscular and athletic. He'd always find a reason for Wilde and a girl or sometimes several girls to end up on an island somewhere. All their clothes would be destroyed by bullets or bandits and they'd have to hang banana leaves from their waists or walk around completely nude. And the feet. Oh, my God. The man had a thing for feet."

"I don't get it."

Penzler stood out in the cold without an overcoat and blew out a long cloudy breath. He shrugged, reached into his pocket, and handed over the money he'd promised. After a few moments, he said, "If he sobers up, I want you to see danger."

"You got it."

"Danger. Excitement. Possible death. Everywhere," Penzler said. He smiled. "Give the poor son of a bitch a real thrill. See an assassin around every turn. Hit women on scooters. Snipers on balconies. Shifty-eyed bartenders who might poison his cocktails. You know. Scare the crap out of him if you can. He'll love it."

"It's your dime," I said. "I was just going to dump him at the hotel and then get back to Brooklyn. When do you need those boxes moved from the warehouse?"

"That can wait," he said. "This is about doing some good in the world. Good luck."

Thirty minutes later, the Writer came awake and righted himself in the back seat while I drove.

"Lay back down," I said.

"Excuse me?"

"Lay back down," I said. "Someone followed us from The Mysterious Bookshop. I canceled all your other events."

"Who?"

"I don't know." I looked in the rearview mirror of the Town Car. "Two women in leather on a motorcycle. I believe one has a gun. You need to do as I say."

The Writer lay prone in the backseat. I smiled. I drove down to Battery Park, stopped for a few minutes to check out all the scaffolding on the Statue of Liberty, and then U-turned back uptown. I stopped again at a payphone at 10th and 17th Street to call my wife. I told her to leave the meatloaf in the fridge and a bottle of rye on the counter. It'd be a few hours, but we'd still make Mass. Not to mention that we now had money for January's rent.

"Women," the Writer said. "I knew it would be a woman. Women are my biggest readers. They are more emotional, prone to take Wilde's death personally. I was once at the ALA in Chicago and I had a librarian from Topeka perform a sex act on me in a phone booth. She thought of me and Mitch Wilde as one and the same. Which is silly. Mitch Wilde is two inches taller!"

"Are you married?"

"Five times."

"Divorced?"

"They couldn't cut it," he said. "Cowards."

"I think we lost them," I said as we pulled up to the hotel and let the valet open the door. "Let's walk into the hotel together and take a seat at the bar."

"Won't that make us vulnerable?"

"They won't attack you in a public place," I said. "I'll help you get checked in and make sure your room is safe."

It was stuff I'd heard on TV, but I said it with confidence.

"They always wait for you there," the Writer said. "Don't forget to look under the bed. In *Wilde's Game*, a Russian killer cut a space into a box spring and waited for Mitch. Don't be a fool. Assassins never hide in closets. Or behind shower curtains. That's amateur hour."

The Marriott had a wide open lobby with lots of thriving green plants and great glass elevators that rocketed up and down every few minutes. I set the Writer at the bar and told him not to worry. I'd take care of everything.

"Glenfiddich," he said to the bartender. "Pin neat."

I walked toward the front desk to get the man checked in. I was thinking how long I'd have to keep playing games with the Writer when I spotted a strange guy waiting by the elevators. He looked away, but I could tell he'd been watching the Writer.

The man had on gray Sansabelt slacks and a sloppy red sweater with snowflake patterns across the chest and sleeves. He was medium height, paunchy in the stomach, and soft in the face. He had thinning blond hair that he'd apparently sprayed down across his head.

Something black was in his hand. He caught my eye and turned away. At first I thought it might be a gun but, on second glance, it was a book.

I turned away from the registration desk and went back to the bar. The Writer had made quick work of the Scotch. He snapped his fingers at the bartender.

"When did you start getting these notes?" I said.

"The new ones?" he said. "Last year. Right after I'd announced the end of Mitch Wilde. I did tell you it was in *Publishers Weekly*?"

"And what did these notes say?"

"They said that a writer has no right to kill his creation," he said. "I was told Mitch Wilde no longer belongs to me but to his fans. At first I thought it was quite flattering. And then I read the part where this person suggested I die instead. Say, where are those women in black following me? Were the outfits skintight leather? With perhaps a zipper in front? Thigh-high boots?"

"I was wrong," I said. "Finish your drink. And let's take a walk."

He slammed back the Scotch and we were back on the street, moving toward Times Square. He pulled out another long brown cigarette from the fancy silver case and walked a little better than he had earlier. "So festive and lovely," he said. "I think I'll order up a bottle of dago red and a steak and send the bill to the publisher. Farewell, Mitch Wilde. Farewell to all the heroes. This decade has all but neutered us."

We passed the Kitty Cat Theater, showing a film called *Hindsight*, a movie starring Heather Wayne that promised that it looked great from the rear. Panhandlers, bums, and whores held out their hands or opened their coats. The Writer seemed to soak it all in, loving it as he shuffled along, powered with the Scotch and cigarettes.

"How about some pie?" he said. "How about some pie? What's your name again?"

"Rick."

"Yep," he said. "Blueberry pie for us all."

I stopped to look into a window of a place called Fascination that offered video games, poker, and pool. The big billboards for Panasonic, JVC, and Coca-Cola flashed high in the cold night. I turned to look over my shoulder. The pudgy guy in the reindeer sweater was about forty feet back staring into the window of the peep show. He held the book close to his side like a reverend with his Bible.

I grabbed the Writer's arm and we kept on walking. Besides a few Christmas trees in pawnshop windows, the only sign of the season was a marquee for a movie called *A Coming of Angels*. A Teenage Dream. I was pretty sure it wasn't a Frank Capra picture.

"I love it," the Writer said. "Humanity. Damn! All of it in a fetid punchbowl."

He sounded even drunker than before. He smiled big and again asked about the women on the motorcycle and wondered if perhaps I had dismissed them too quickly. Maybe if we headed back and searched for them.

"I want you to stop at the next window," I said. "At that camera shop and then look back the way we came. Tell me if you've ever seen the guy in the red sweater. Think on it hard."

The Writer walked along the wet street, bypassing the slush, greeting the working girls in cheetah print coats. He tossed down the cigarette and reached for another. He laughed for a bit, smoke coming out of his nose. "You do know this is a little private joke," he said. "Between me, Otto, and my publisher. We do this every year. I get drunk, play Mitch Wilde, and fly home happy. Twice I've gotten laid. Quite by accident. But that's a long time ago. I don't know if they know. But I know it."

"Look back," I said. "Behind your shoulder."

"I'd rather not," he said. "Let's drop this business. Yes, I remember. It's the damn Howard Johnson's that has the pie. Can I buy you some pie and then you can point me in the right direction of the hotel? I may even seek a bit of company on my trek back."

"Do you see him?"

The Writer looked annoyed but glanced back down the row of shops and movie theaters. He turned back and shrugged. "The man in that hideous sweater?"

"Yes."

"I don't know him," he said. "I don't want to know him. Why?"

"He's following us."

"Oh, come on now," he said. "I admit to the game. I really wish you'd kept up with the girls. Couldn't you have hired a girl to follow us? Now that would have been fun. Not some fat guy in a sweater."

"I believe he's carrying one of your books."

"Oh, Jesus," he said. "You are committed."

"I don't know," I said. "Let's get back to the hotel. Screw the pie. I'll call security."

"I thought you were security," the Writer said, smirking. "Personal protection for the holidays. Another piece of Otto's free cheese and crackers and putrid wine."

"I'm a baggage handler at JFK," I said. "I work for Mr. Penzler when he needs some extra muscle. Loading books and stuff."

"Of course," the Writer said. "Pie. Onward pie."

One of the hookers gave a hopeful sideways glance, hand to hip, but the Writer moved on toward the bright orange-and-blue glow of the Howard Johnson's. Reindeer Sweater kept on coming, closing the gap between us.

"Sir," I said.

"Oh, for Christ's sake."

"Sir."

"Yes, I got letters," he said. "But who would want to kill me? Really? It took my new agent three months before he'd read my latest novel. And I suspect the notes came from his teeny-bopper assistant. They only want the backlist when I'm dead. We can stop all the cloak and dagger. Tell Otto it's been fun. I'll eat the pie myself."

The sweater guy was on us. And he held out a pistol in his shaking hands. He called the Writer a lot of rotten words and then started to cry. The Writer narrowed his eyes, took a puff of the shortening brown cigarette, and turned to me. "You must be kidding. Where did you get this creep? A reject from the cast of *Mack and Mabel*?"

"You had no right," said the man in the reindeer sweater.

The Writer again looked to me.

I looked back. I shrugged. "He's a legit nut."

"Amazing." The small, wiry Writer stepped up toe to toe with the man with the gun. "I had every right. I lived with Mitch Wilde for decades. He has made me a successful man and an absolute failure. He has been adored by so-called fans like you and then cast off. I will not float to the bottom of the literary sea with him."

"You selfish bastard," the man said.

The Writer blew smoke in the man's face. "Mitch Wilde is dead."

The sweater guy wrinkled up his face and pushed the pistol into the Writer's ribs. I didn't know what to do other than maybe pick him up over my head like a piece of Samsonite and shake some sense into him. But since he had a gun, I waited.

The Writer plugged the barrel of the gun with his index finger.

"Can I ask you something?" the Writer said.

The sweater guy nodded.

"Why do you even care?"

"Mitch Wilde got me through my divorce," he said. "He saved my life. You kill him and I don't know. What will happen to me? I just don't know nothing about nothing."

"Wonderfully put," the Writer said, pulling his typing finger from the gun. He looked to me and shrugged. "And you would kill me for that? Mitch Wilde is worth you going to prison and ruining your life? You believe in him that much?"

"Yes," the sweater guy said. "Absolutely."

The Writer stood there in the middle of Times Square with the flashing signs, neon, and porno marquees and placed both hands in his coat pockets. "He's not part of this?" he said, turning to me.

"No, sir," I said.

The Writer removed his coat, loosened his tie, and rolled up his sleeves in the cold night. He placed his arm around the sweater guy and began to walk him toward the glowing box of the HoJo. I stayed put and watched the guy take the pistol and hide it in the rear of his Sansabelt slacks as they wandered off.

"How do you feel about blueberry pie?" the Writer said.

"I like it," the man said. "Sure. OK."

"*Wilde's Law*," he said. "Corruption, greed, sex, and redemption in the center of New York. How does that sound to you?"

THE GIFT OF THE WISEGUY

Rob Hart

Eric Calabrese stood at the back of The Mysterious Bookshop, surveying the crowd that was nearly spilling out the door and onto the sidewalk. Snow fell in lazy circles outside the tall windows and the space was permeated by the smell of his grandmother's lasagna.

She died years ago, but his sister Christine resurrected the recipe. She made five trays. Eric thought it was a bit much. But that's Italian hospitality: There's not enough food unless there's too much food.

He'd brought Tupperware containers so people could bring home leftovers, a scenario growing less likely every time the heavy doors swung open and a burst of cold air whipped through the store.

He had been warned continuously—by his agent, by his publisher, by his writing pals—that book release parties were exercises in frustration. Especially for a first book. Even more especially during the holidays, with so many people out of town. That he might see a couple of friends, maybe a few stragglers off the street, but that's it.

But then the *New York Times* review hit.

The writer called his book "thoughtful" and "precise" and "heart-rending." Suddenly it was everywhere. NY1, the *Daily News*, and the *Post* covered it. Buzzfeed shot a short video, in which a writer for the site, who looked like he was playing dress-up as a lumberjack, raved about it. Tomorrow morning he had to be in Times Square at 6:00 a.m. for *Good Morning America*.

The plastic cup of red wine in his hand, the first of the night, would also be the last. No sense in being hungover for that.

Someone broke through the crowd and approached the spot Eric had staked out by the coat rack. It was Ian, the lanky bookstore manager.

"You ready to get started?" Ian asked.

"Sure," Eric said. "What's the plan?"

"I'll do a quick introduction, and then you can have the floor. Otto isn't a big fan of authors reading from their books.

Usually we just do discussion and questions. But with a crowd like this . . ." He gestured at the packed room. "You can do pretty much whatever you want."

"Could I have a minute?"

"Sure," Ian said. "Just give me a wave."

Eric finished the last sip of his wine and set the cup on a shelf heavy with Sherlock Holmes books. He ducked into the back room, and then the bathroom, shutting the door and locking it behind him. He put down the toilet seat and sat, running his fingers over the glossy cover of his book.

White Sheep: Growing Up in the Calabrese Family.

There were a hundred more copies in the store—after the *Times* review, Ian said he upped the order. This was one of the first off the press, filled up with sticky notes, marking off passages Eric thought might be good for live readings.

He wasn't thrilled about a discussion. Because there wasn't much about this he wanted to discuss. Everything he wanted to say about his childhood was in black-and-white, between his hands. Writing about it had excised it, and it felt perverse to dwell.

Eric looked at himself on the cover of the book. The photo the designer chose was in color, but faded. He was standing in front of the Wonder Wheel in Coney Island. His mother, short and pear-shaped with big eyes and a stern smile, had her arm draped over his shoulder. Next to them was his father, holding Christine, wrapped in a swaddling blanket. She was only six months old.

He hated the photo.

He was chubby and his ears stuck out. He was wearing that god-awful *Star Wars* t-shirt, which had been black once, but had stretched and faded to gray. His white tube socks came up to his knobby knees.

Worse than that, his father was in it.

But his publisher, Jason, insisted. The story was about them, and the photo lent it an air of *verisimilitude*. That's the word Jason used.

It meant "honesty." Eric was pretty sure Jason was trying to bury the debate under a ten-dollar word. It worked. He handed over the photo and here it was, staring back at him like a bad memory that keeps a person up at night.

When Eric could put aside the weight of it pressing against his chest, when he could separate the memory of his dad disappearing from their lives only a few months after it was taken, he had to acknowledge it did look pretty nice on the cover of the book.

Eric wondered what his father looked like now, twenty years later.

Wondered if he was even alive.

He was a stout man, thick in the shoulders, but in a healthy way. He played football in college and looked like he could still hold his own in a pickup game. Dark, curly hair that got passed to Christine, whereas Eric inherited his mother's light and fair complexion.

There was a knock at the door. Eric got up and flushed the toilet, so whoever was outside wouldn't wonder why he was just sitting around in the bathroom.

He opened the door and stepped into the back room.

Straight into his father.

Manetto Calabrese.

Eric drew in a breath, held it, found he couldn't let it out. He nearly dropped the book, but caught himself.

He knew it immediately. Those pale blue eyes, the dark hair gone gray but still curling in ringlets around his ears. Except, he looked so different. Like the air had been let out of his body. A Thanksgiving Day balloon at the end of the route, caving in on itself.

"Hello, Eric," his father said, his voice weak, but still reverberating the way it did, so you could always tell where he was in a room. He was wearing a tan coat, a red scarf, and black leather gloves. His face freshly shaved. Impeccably put together, always and all these years later.

"Dad?"

His father smiled. The smile stretched his face into something akin to a grimace.

Eric's first instinct was to ball up his fist, throw it into his father's face.

He took a deep breath. Reminded himself that he was not like his father.

"What are you doing here?" he asked, lowering his voice.

"My boy writes a book," he says. "I wanted to wish you well."

Eric felt his temperature and pulse rising in tandem. "So you just show up? You're in witness protection. You can't do that."

"It's too late now, isn't it," he said with another smile, showing a little more strength. "How've you been, kiddo?"

"Don't do that," Eric said, stepping back toward the bathroom door. Wanting there to be space between them, which was difficult in the back room, full of books and shelves that had been pushed off the floor to make room up front. "You missed so much of my life. You missed *Mom's funeral.*"

The smile disappeared. "She wouldn't have wanted me there."

"We would have wanted you there. Just some kind of acknowledgement that you even cared."

"I do care," his father said. "I care very much. There are still people in this town that want me dead. You think I do this lightly?"

Eric started to say something, but stopped himself. What was there to say that could sum up twenty years and every conceivable emotion?

Except: "You shouldn't have come."

"C'mon, I know I've made a lot of mistakes," his father said. "And I have to admit, I was a little upset when I first read the book. There's a lot of dirt in there. But it's mostly all correct . . ."

"You read it already?" Eric asked. "It just came out today."

"I used to run this town, kid. You think I can't get an advanced copy of the book, even all the way out in Arizona?"

The thought of his father in the desert almost made Eric laugh. Before witness protection, his father never left New York. Barely left Brooklyn. "So that's where they put you?"

"Scottsdale," his father said. "All they know about Italian food is Olive Garden. It's tragic. I tried the lasagna up front. I know my mother's lasagna. Did you do that?"

"Christine."

His face lit up. "Is she here?"

"I think you should go."

"I just got here. Let me just see her. See how she turned out."

"She turned out great, no thanks to you," Eric said. "I think we both turned out pretty damn good considering you disappeared. You gave up on this family a long time ago. I'm the one who provided for mom and Christine."

"Hey," his father said, his voice snapping. "How about a little gratitude, huh? You still found a way to profit off it."

Eric felt himself grow flush. Wondered if he should hold back, but decided he shouldn't. His greatest strength was his words, so he aimed them at his father like a barrage of bullets. "I would trade everything this book has brought me if it meant you stayed. Instead you ratted out a bunch of guys and ran and hid. Like a coward. You gave us nothing. You left us nothing. All we have is your absence. I figured out a way to make it provide for me and Christine. That's what this book is. You leaving was the only gift you ever gave us."

"Eric," his father said, stepping forward, his eyes misting. "Please. It's Christmas. And I'm trying. Doesn't that mean something?"

Eric turned and looked away, not wanting his father to see him cry. Remembering what happened the last time, when his fourth grade teacher died suddenly; a sharp, disappointed admonishment that it's not what "real men" did.

After a few moments of silence his father said, "I was not a good father. But I loved you and your sister and your mother. I want you to know that. For whatever it means to you. Even if it means nothing. The things I did . . . I did them because I was protecting you. That was always the most important thing."

A pause.

"I love you, Eric. Best of luck with the book, okay?"

Eric heard the sound of footsteps, and the door creaking open.

He turned, and found he was alone in the small space, the door swinging closed.

Officer Rebecca Bhati grasped the heavy-duty headphones and pulled them off her ears. They were digging into her head and she needed a little relief. Not that she needed to wear them. She could barely hear over the din coming from inside the bookstore. It sounded like waves crashing into a rocky shore.

But she liked to listen. It was good to be thorough. There wasn't much else to do besides try and find a comfortable position in the ancient office chair, arrived here from points unknown.

The NYPD surveillance van wasn't pleasant. And it didn't smell good. The outside was branded with the logo of the Fulton Fish Market and she idly wondered if that was a cover, or if that's where the department bought it from. The brackish smell seemed to confirm her suspicion, but that could also be years of accumulated sweat and takeout.

She turned to her right, to Detective Seth Tanner, spilling out of his own office chair, peering at the hodgepodge of monitors, his face cast blue in the flickering light. The setup looked like someone raided a Radio Shack that was going out of business.

She looked up at the mug shot of Manetto "Manny" Calabrese taped to the wall of the van.

"You sure it was him?" she asked Tanner.

"I think so," Tanner said, not looking away from the monitor. "No one's seen the guy in two decades, but I think it was him. Lost some weight, but same hair. Same gait." Tanner looked down at the keyboard like it was alien technology. "I don't even know where to start with this. Can you play it back?"

Bhati slid her chair across the cramped space to the keyboard, tapped the hotkeys that would rewind and then replay the video. She watched as a hunched figure strode past the camera and turned into the bookstore.

To her eyes, it was a blur.

But Tanner seemed convinced.

Because he was smiling. And Tanner was not a guy who smiled.

"If this is him, it's a pretty big deal, right?" Bhati asked, her breath pluming in front of her.

Tanner reached down and clicked on the space heater by his feet. Within moments, it would smell like a bundle of hair caught fire, but that would be enough to bring the temperature up to a more comfortable level.

"If it's him," Tanner said.

Bhati looked down at the space heater. "Are you sure that thing is safe to be using in here?"

"Not really, no," Tanner said.

Bhati picked up her headphones again, placing them carefully over her ears. Same sounds. Waves crashing. She thought she could pick out a word here or there, but it'd all be useless until the tech people cleaned it up. Which might not even be necessary. She took the headphones off again.

"What do we even do?" Bhati asked. "The Feds have had him in witness protection. There's no active warrant on him. He's just . . . a guy now. I don't mean to speak out of turn, sir, but why are we here?"

"First," Tanner said. "He's not just a man. He's a monster. Three confirmed kills, and two more suspected. Plus all the lives he ruined. And what, he gets to skate because he dimed somebody out? It's a miscarriage of justice."

"Right, but, we're not going after him just to go after him." Bhati looked at Tanner and raised an eyebrow. "Are we?"

The scorched smell from the heater was overwhelming. Tanner noticed, too. He reached down and clicked it off, the red glow of the coils fading.

"He killed my partner," Tanner said.

Bhati paused. That was a violation not to be taken lightly.

"If you have new evidence . . ." Bhati started.

Tanner put his hand up. "I'm the detective. You're the officer. Let's do the job and then we can go home, okay?"

Bhati nodded, put the headphones back on her head.

But she couldn't ignore the feeling that was prodding her. Because the more she thought about it, the more she had to question the circumstances that evening. As a member of the Intelligence division she'd done six stakeouts, and all six included a lot of planning, as well as a good bit of paperwork to sign out the van and the equipment.

Tonight was different.

Tanner approached her at her desk. He asked for her help on a special assignment. They van was parked around the street from the precinct, not in the depot. She went along because Tanner had been on the job since before she was born, and she had no reason to doubt him.

But something wasn't adding up.

"Sir," Bhati asked. "I don't mean to be difficult. But . . . is this official NYPD business?"

Tanner finally looked away from the screen. Held her gaze. His face was all sharp angles and deep shadows, the way the light from the monitors flickered across it.

When he spoke, he did so in a quiet rumble.

"Do the job," he said. "I can make your life in the department a lot harder. You're free to go, file a complaint about me, whatever. But then you're inviting that upon yourself. Or let's just sit here a little while longer and we can go home. Deal?"

Bhati held his gaze.

She knew that, sometimes, rules needed to be bent in the course of doing the right thing. But only as a last resort. Only as long as the rule would snap back into place, unbroken and intact.

That kind of thing, she could live with.

But this was too much. This was the kind of thing that could result in a major reprimand, if not getting kicked off the force entirely.

She was about to push again when there was a knock on the side of the van.

"Holy . . ." Tanner said.

"What?" she asked.

"It's him."

She leaned over in her seat and saw Calabrese looking into the pinhole camera next to the door, his features fish-eyed by the lens.

But it was clear that he was smiling.

Tanner ran his hand down his pant leg, to make sure his ankle holster was in place. He hated wearing his regular holster on stakeouts, since he spent most of the time hunched over, and it dug into his ribs.

After he confirmed everything was where it should be, he slid the door open.

Most days, the memory burned a small hole in his gut.

But seeing Calabrese standing there, it hit him full force.

Reggie Sacks bleeding out from a bullet to the throat on a filthy warehouse floor. Pleading with Tanner, but nothing coming out of his mouth but blood and wet gurgles.

Tanner didn't see Calabrese pull the trigger. Didn't even see him at the scene. But they'd been following him for weeks, trying to put together enough evidence for a RICO case that would cripple the Calabrese family.

Instead Tanner wandered off to take a leak and came back to find the life leaking out of Reggie, whose last word he croaked out before coughing up a river of blood and dying.

"Manny."

Manny Calabrese.

It was all Tanner needed to know.

And here was Calabrese, standing there with a smile on his face. Tanner's hand shook. He wanted more than anything to pull his gun and give Calabrese a taste of what he did to Reggie.

He gripped his knee, fingers digging into the bone until it hurt.

Calabrese was holding two Tupperware containers, flecks of snow layering on the shoulders of his tan coat. He looked over at Bhati, then above her head, at the mugshot. He nodded toward it. "You might be surprised, but that handsome fella up there is me. That photo was taken a long time ago, obviously."

Tanner tried to speak but found rage blocking his throat.

Calabrese nodded to Bhati and said, "Darling, your partner and I have some things to discuss. Why don't you head on inside, huh? Get yourself a slice of lasagna. Probably the best lasagna you'll ever have."

Bhati looked at Tanner.

Tanner could see it in her eyes. She was worried that if she left, something bad would happen. And she was right. But he still outranked her, and at this point, it didn't matter.

Best she not be around to see this.

"Go ahead," Tanner said.

"But . . ."

"Now."

Bhati exhaled, hung her headphones from the hook next to the monitors. Climbed out of the van, careful to give Calabrese a wide berth, and headed across the street to the bookshop.

Calabrese climbed into the van, pulled the door shut, and put the Tupperware containers on the makeshift desk under the monitors. He eased himself into the battered office chair that Bhati had just occupied.

Tanner's heart slammed against the inside of his chest. The last time he saw this man, he was thirty pounds lighter, still had all of his hair, could read small text without squinting. It felt like a lifetime. Calabrese, too, looked so different. Like he was slowly disappearing.

Calabrese slid the chair forward, the wheels creaking and grunting with the exertion, so he could reach past Tanner and turn on the space heater. It crackled and roared to life.

"There, that's better," Calabrese said. "So how are things?"

"Don't you dare . . ."

"I didn't kill your partner, you know," he said. "Sacks, right? He was a good cop. Believe it or not, I respect cops. You do your job, I do mine. It just so happens they run in conflict with each other. I'd never kill a good cop."

Tanner reached down to his ankle, removed the black Ruger LCR, and placed it in his lap. Not so much as a threat, but to set the tone of the proceedings.

Calabrese shook his head. "I bring you a peace offering," he said. "My mother's lasagna. Best in the world. It's four days before Christmas, no less. And this is how you respond."

"Say your piece," Tanner said. "Because you've got about two minutes before I paint the inside of this van with your brain."

Calabrese sighed. "I get it. I would be angry too. But you have to understand, what happened that day . . ."

"He said your name."

"I'm sure he did. I was there."

Tanner gripped the gun.

"Here's how it went down," Calabrese said, leaning forward. "I was at the warehouse following up on a thing. And I run into this guy. You remember Lou Rossi? The man was a thug. An animal. He was cheating on the family, you know what I mean? So I run into him doing something he shouldn't be doing, but he gets the drop on me. He's holding me at gunpoint."

Calabrese extended his index finger, thumb pointed up, imitating a gun.

"And Sacks comes wandering in."

He swung his hand in a wide arc and cocked his thumb.

"And, *bang*. Rossi shoots Sacks in the throat. I don't even think Rossi knew what he was doing. He was just startled, is all."

"And you just left Reggie there to die," Tanner said.

"I heard you coming. You're not exactly light on your feet. Not even then. What was I going to do, besides get blamed for it?"

"Then why did he say your name?" Tanner asked. "It was the last thing he said before he died."

"How should I know?" Calabrese said, shrugging. "Maybe he was saying 'Manny didn't do it, you dim-bulb.' All I know is, Rossi's gun killed your partner. Not mine."

"Right. And where's Rossi? Let's see if he can corroborate."

Calabrese shook his head. "That's not going to happen, unless you've got a medium on staff, or a Ouija board or something."

Tanner sat back in the chair. It groaned under his weight.

The thought of revenge was the only thing that sustained him. The promise of a period on the end of the sentence that had been running on for the past twenty years. All he had left was an empty apartment in Queens, a few plants, and a futon. The best he could do with the alimony payments, the child support payments. The penalties he paid for a life that became consumed by his hunt for Calabrese.

And now it had been taken from him.

No, it couldn't be true.

Calabrese was trying to save himself. That's all.

"I don't believe you," Tanner said.

"I wish you did. Not that it matters. You want to kill me right now, go ahead. You're only moving up the deadline a bit."

"What do you mean?"

Calabrese sighed. Placed a hand on his stomach.

"Pancreatic cancer," he said. "The thing about the pancreas is, it's all the way in the back of your abdomen, out of sight. Most times, when the doctors find it, it's already too late. I'm on stage four. There's no stage five. I got a few months left, maybe."

The news cast Calabrese in a different light.

His face didn't look thin, it looked sunken.

He didn't look tired, he looked weak.

"What am I supposed to do?" Tanner asked. "Feel sorry for you? Even if what you said is true, you're still a killer. You ruined lives for your own personal gain."

"No, I did it because . . ." Calabrese stopped. Thought about it. Shook his head. "I'm not here for a philosophical discussion. I was pretty sure this had been eating at you and I wanted to put it to rest. Even if not for you, for me. Now, here . . ."

Calabrese took the two Tupperware containers off the desk and held them.

"I know we're not pals," he said. "But it's Christmas. Let's put all that hate and regret behind us. Sit here and just enjoy one last meal together. Then you can do whatever the hell you want to me, okay?"

Tanner breathed deep.

Then he reached over and clicked off the transmitter that was recording everything going on in the store, along with the conversation they were having.

Calabrese seemed to get that this was not an insignificant gesture. A look of fear flashed across his face.

"I hate you wiseguys so much," Tanner said. "Stuff like *The Sopranos. The Godfather.* All these movies and television shows that take the horrible stuff you do and glorify it. I bust my hump for going on thirty years trying to make the world a better place, and kids got stars in their eyes for Michael Corleone, like he's a hero or something."

Tanner slid his chair forward until he was closer to Calabrese. Until he could smell the man's wool jacket.

His breath.

"Here's the truth," Tanner said. "Your entire family is a blight. After I'm done with you, I'm coming for your kids. The two of them were raised on the backs of dead men. Right now your son is in there profiting off your legacy. It's obscene. Pretty soon he's going to find himself in a pair of cuffs. I'll find a way. And once I do that, I am going to take the Son of Sam law and swing it at him like a bat. I will make sure he never sees one more red cent from that book."

Calabrese frowned. "I've done some bad things, but I've never threatened a man's family. Never."

"You made your bed."

Calabrese's nostrils flared.

The scorched smell of the space heater filled the small space.

"A threat like that would not have worked out well for you, back in the day," Calabrese said. "But times have changed. I'm willing to set all this aside. I will do whatever you want. Just leave my family out of it."

Calabrese's gaze softened.

He added: "Please?"

Tanner shook his head. "No. No, I can't do that." He almost said "I'm sorry," but caught himself before the words left his mouth.

This man didn't deserve his sympathy.

Calabrese looked down in his hands, at the blue Tupperware containers. He considered them for a moment before handing the one in his left hand to Tanner.

"I'll tell you what," he said. "Let's just eat. Pretend for a few seconds like we're two men whose lives haven't been ruined by the mistakes we've made. Then you can do whatever the hell you want to me. Right here, right now. Shoot me in the head, beat me to death, I don't care. My son . . ." A tear formed in the corner of his eye. "He didn't even want me there. He told me to leave. You can't hurt me by hurting him. Not anymore." His voice dropped and cracked. "I've punished him and his sister enough."

"Fine," Tanner said, snatching the Tupperware container out of Calabrese's hand. "If it'll shut you up."

He popped the cover and picked up a plastic fork sitting on the desk, speared a bite and shoved it in his mouth. Not that he wanted to accept the gift. But there was no sense in letting it go to waste, and anyway, he hadn't eaten since breakfast.

If this was the formality that'd buy them some private time together, so be it.

He could drive the van down to a quiet spot in Brooklyn. Really go to town. Work out all those years of frustration.

He was pretty sure he saw a hammer next to the driver's seat.

The lasagna was delicious. And still warm, too. It exploded in his mouth, a far cry from the cold, congealed pizza and Chinese food that filled his refrigerator lately. Calabrese nodded and opened his own container, produced a plastic fork from his coat, and began to eat.

"Merry Christmas, by the way," Calabrese said, before taking a bite.

"Hmhmmh," Tanner mumbled, his mouth full of food.

They finished at the same time, placing the blue plastic containers on the desk. Calabrese wiped his mouth as Tanner swallowed and went to pick up the gun.

It slipped from his hand and tumbled to the floor.

For a moment he thought his hands were just a little cold, but then realized he couldn't make his fingers curl.

"Well, that's enough of that," Calabrese said, climbing out of his seat and reaching for the door of the van.

Tanner tried to reach for him, but found his arms didn't want to obey him either. They hung from his sides like lumps of dead meat. He tried to speak but only managed to produce a raspy gurgle, as a crooked hand wrapped around his heart and squeezed, hard.

Calabrese opened the door and stepped down to the street.

"For the record," Calabrese said, "I gave you the slice I was going to eat. Figured you'd get your closure and I'd get mine. But then you had to go and threaten my family. That's low. So, here we find ourselves. I know I said I don't kill good cops, but you're not a good cop."

Tanner heaved himself forward and tried to stand, one last desperate attempt to get Calabrese before he died. But his feet buckled under him and he tumbled forward, his face smashing into the floor of the van.

The door slid closed with a *thump* and he watched as the flickering glow of the surveillance monitors faded into blackness.

❄

Eric exited the bathroom to find Ian standing in the back room, wearing a concerned look.

"Are you okay?" he asked. "I thought we lost you."

The truth was, Eric needed some time for the swelling around his eyes to go down, so it wouldn't be so obvious he was crying. But he didn't want to say that.

He settled on: "I'm sorry, I just needed a few minutes."

"No worries," Ian said. "But we should get going."

Eric followed Ian into the main part of the store, the space filled with people standing shoulder-to-shoulder.

"If I could have your attention, everyone," Ian yelled. Conversations were abandoned as everyone turned. "We're very excited to welcome Eric Calabrese, the author of *White Sheep*. We don't do a lot of memoir here, but it's a great book, and we're happy to have him. Eric is going to talk a little bit about it, and maybe take some questions. Without further ado . . ."

Ian gestured to Eric as the room erupted in applause.

When it died down, Eric said, "Actually, I want to read a bit."

He thumbed open the book, skipping past the sticky notes to a passage he didn't intend to read, but felt right given the circumstances.

"The truth is, my father . . ."

"We can't hear you!"

It was his sister, Christine, calling from the front of the store. He smiled, climbed on a chair so he could get a good look at everyone—including Christine, who was throwing a thumbs-up—and began to read again.

"The truth is, my father was a complicated man.

"The hands that strangled the life out of Vincent Abruzzo on October 16, 1985, are the same hands that played catch with me in the yard of our home in Gravesend. The hands that beat Michael Moretti to death on June 5,

1987, are the same hands that cradled my sister when she woke up crying in the middle of the night.

"I have spent my entire life trying to process this.

"It's left me wondering if I'm tainted. If the kind of evil that afflicted my father was genetic, if it could be passed down to us. Or if we had the freedom to make our own choices, to move past it.

"I choose to believe the latter, but live in fear of the former.

"There is one truth though, in all of this, and it's that my father did not think of himself as an evil. Not good, maybe. I think he was smart enough to know the consequences of his actions, and how they reflected on the world around him. But everything he did was to provide a good life for myself and my sister. And until he disappeared—after testimony in open court twenty years prior to the publication of this book forced him into witness protection—he did.

"We never wanted for anything. He never raised a hand to us. If we fell, he picked us up . . ."

Eric felt his throat growing thick. He paused and looked up.

Standing outside the store, his hand pressed against the glass, was his father.

The words on the page grew blurry, and Eric swallowed, did his best to recover quickly, lest anyone look back.

Because despite the gulf between them, he was afraid someone might see him, and didn't want his presence to get him in trouble.

Eric smiled and nodded and hoped his father noticed.

Manny wished he could go back into the store, but knew that wasn't an option. He met eyes with his son, who smiled and nodded before going back to reading.

That would have to be enough.

Footsteps crunched in the snow to his left. He turned and saw the pretty young police officer who had been in the van. She was holding aloft a steaming cup of bodega coffee.

"Hi," she said.

"Hi," Manny said back.

"Well, this is awkward," she said, with a half-smile.

Manny figured Tanner could use another couple of minutes to stew.

"Listen, Detective Tanner said if I saw you, to ask you to get him a cup of coffee," he said. "I see you've already got one, and I'm sorry if it's an inconvenience . . ."

A look of relief washed over her face. Like she was happy to be getting away from him. "Oh, I don't mind."

She offered another smile and turned.

"Hey," he called after her.

She looked over her shoulder.

"You seem like a bright kid," he told her. "Tanner is not a nice man. I know, I'm not one to judge. But, you should know that, all right?"

She paused like she wanted to say something, then nodded and walked off, rounding the corner.

Manny looked across the street.

There used to be a bar there, the Raccoon Lodge, that had a fireplace in a little alcove in the back. A great spot on a night like this, but the shutter was down. Probably another victim of the real estate market.

He took out his cell phone and dialed the only number programmed into it. It rang three times before a groggy voice answered, "Hello?"

"Agent Wilks?"

"Wait . . . Manny? Why are you calling? Is everything okay?"

"Not really, no. Listen, you still living in Staten Island?"

"I am, but if there's a problem I have to contact the local field office in Scottsdale . . ."

"I'm in Manhattan."

"*What?*"

"It's a long story. Any chance you can come out and meet me? Is McSorley's still open? Or did the rat developers get that one too?"

"It's still open, but we have to get you back before someone sees you."

"Doesn't matter now," he says. "Only place I'm going at this point is central booking. That still over at the Tombs?"

"Manny, what the hell are you talking about?"

"Why don't you meet me at McSorley's? I'm going to have one last drink. I'll order you one. You want light or dark?"

Silence on the other end of the phone.

"I'll be there in twenty minutes."

"Don't rush. Drive safe. I'm not going anywhere."

Manny hung up the phone and stuck it in his pocket. Gave one last look at the bookstore. Eric was still standing on the chair, reading from his book. Manny couldn't make out what he was saying.

His daughter Christine was in there somewhere, too.

The pair of them, better than he could have hoped.

Better than he deserved.

He turned and headed toward Broadway, where it would be easier to get a cab. The last day hadn't been so pleasant. He'd lost his taste for the cold, between the years living in the desert, and the thing eating him from the inside out.

But as he walked down Warren Street, he found the cold wasn't so bad. The way it is sometimes when it snows and the air is calm, like the flakes are sucking in the chill, pulling it away as they fall to the ground.

It made him think of their last Christmas together. Before he made the hardest decision of his life. The one that weighed on him so heavily he hadn't slept a good night since.

To leave.

That morning, the kids got up early. The Christmas prior to that, they'd set a rule for Eric; no presents until the sun came up. The second there was a trace of light in the sky, he had bounded into their room and jumped into their bed.

Manny went to Christine's room and found her awake, contentedly playing with her fingers, like she was waiting for him. He scooped her out of the crib and they made their way down to the tree, where Eric's face lit up like a fireworks display as he tore open the wrapping around his new bike. Christine cooed at the sparkling lights on the tree, not old enough to understand the significance of the holiday. She was so small, and so perfect.

Calabrese stopped. Reached his hand out to the brick wall of an apartment building, to steady himself. Turned and took one last look at the van.

At the last gift he would ever give his children.

And he walked on.

SNOWFLAKE TIME

Laura Lippman

I don't remember the date. Later, lawyers tried to make hay out of that fact, as if it proved my behavior was "chronic," indicating a "pattern of abuse." But it was the opposite. I couldn't remember the date precisely because nothing extraordinary happened that day. I didn't do what they said I did, it's that simple, and a man can't remember the things he didn't do. After everything that has happened to me, I think that's what I find most galling. I was an innocent man and I didn't get my day in court because I couldn't remember the exact day in which I said the thing I never said. It was cheaper to reward the women claiming offense, cheaper to punish me. Kill two birds with one stone. Follow the money. Those are clichés I wouldn't allow in my fiction, but real life trumps fiction every time.

It was August 2016, I am sure of that much. I had arrived at work, Gotham News Network, my place of employment for the last fifteen years, and was preparing for my evening show, *The Doyle Dossier*, which had been the king of its time slot for more than a decade. I was going through the New York papers, reading the *Washington Post* online, looking for a topic for my final segment, Doyle's Dos and Don'ts. It looked simple, that closing segment, but finding a timely topic that can be broken down into a series of black-and-white quick takes is actually very difficult. There was a reason that no one else across the cable news landscape had enjoyed the kind of success I had.

And no one envied me more than the people in the less desirable time slots on my own network. To the world, the GNN was a tribe, a cohesive unit. But when the camera was turned off, it was nothing but a pack of jackals, all looking for a chance to take down anyone who showed a sign of weakness.

So, August 2016. I asked my assistant to go get me lunch. That's what she was there for, right? To assist me. But she was one of those Ivy League millennials who thought she should be running the network, not running errands. She rolled her eyes as I rattled off what I wanted—turkey sub, extra hots, a cream soda, I'm not some Nobu-eating fancy pants—and then she asked if it was OK if she ran a personal errand while picking up my lunch.

"Can I go to Duane Reade and get some Advil?" she said. "I have the worst menstrual cramps. I almost called in sick today the pain is so bad."

Now, in my opinion, *that* was unprofessional and typical of this generation, which finds every moment of its existence worth documenting and broadcasting. *Here's my lunch, I just checked in at a concert, I have a headache.* If I had started talking about my prostate or asked her to go fill my Cialis prescription—I don't have a Cialis prescription or anything like that, that's just a hypothetical—I'd have been hauled on the carpet faster than you can say "trigger warning." But I was trying to write my segment, I just wanted my lunch, my blood sugar was spiking, so all I said was: "I don't need to know anything about your body unless it affects my body."

She brought me my lunch. I wrote a Dos and Don'ts about a woman who was trying to keep park police from rounding up feral cats living in Central Park. I love animals—OK, I like dogs—but this woman was one of those whack jobs who thrives on publicity. In college, she had lived in a tree for several months, or something like that. A dilettante, flitting from so-called cause to so-called cause. In my day, you would have called her a dirty hippie, I don't know what you call such a person now. The park police and animal welfare people were actually trying to rescue the cats, get them to a shelter on Long Island, where they would be spayed and neutered. There was no argument to be made for feral cats in Central Park. When Peter Minuit arrived in Manhattan in 1626, there were no feral cats on the island. (Cougars don't count.)

Do honor the natural order.

Don't forget who's at the top of this food chain, Kitty Con Artist.

It was a great bit, if I do say so myself. We got a lot of mail on both sides, which is the best feedback possible. The only thing I never wanted was a neutral response.

The thing that made people nuts about my show was that no one could stick a partisan label on me. I'm not even that interested in politics, except when it threatens our civil liberties. I'm not registered as a Republican or a Democrat. Some people try to hang the libertarian mantle on me, but that's not right, either. I'm for *common sense.* If there was a political party with an IQ test, I might join that. For example, I don't vote in presidential elections in my state, or in any election where the outcome is a foregone conclusion.

End the Electoral College and I might change my mind. But, for now, my vote and, more importantly, my time are wasted by standing in line on Election Day.

Furthermore, I believe that we should have a flat income tax rate, with no deductions whatsoever. Deductions are for fat cats and they encourage waste. Eliminate deductions and you'd eliminate more than half of the lobbyists in Washington, which would help end gridlock, although I'm not sure that's a positive. I am a First Amendment absolutist. You're free to say whatever you want to say, but—here's the catch—so is the other guy. If you want to say "Happy Holidays," say "Happy Holidays," but I'm sticking to "Merry Christmas." That was one of my most popular Dos and Don'ts segments of all time.

Do offer whatever seasonal greeting you prefer.
Don't deny other people the right to do the same.

A couple of weeks went by. As you might recall, 2016 was a busy year in news, or so we thought until 2017 came along. Then, a week before Christmas, I was summoned to a meeting with legal. My former assistant—she had chosen to go work on another show because she claimed she had Lyme disease and needed a less demanding schedule—was there. And she was telling quite a tall tale about what had happened the day she volunteered to me the state of her uterus. According to her, what I said was: "I'm not interested in your body unless it's *touching* my body." It was a subtle but shrewd distinction. I couldn't claim I hadn't said anything at all and, absent a tape recorder, I couldn't prove my version over hers. By the time it was all over, she was claiming that I had told her to pick up some condoms and said that, if she were lucky, she'd find out if the ribbing really did add to her pleasure. That never happened and I wanted my day in court to prove it.

Then other women started coming forward.

Turned out the bosses had done a little witch hunt, calling women in and asking if they had "unsettling" experiences with me. They all but *incentivized* lying about me. "Look, here's this little pot of money, underwritten by our liability insurance, would you like some? All you have to say is that John Doyle said something untoward." There were five women altogether and, believe me, not a one that I would have made a pass at. But there was blood in the water and other people began showing up to nibble on my entrails. All of a sudden there were women everywhere, claiming that this was a *pattern*, that I had been doing this for years. One lawyer said he had tapes, but I sure never heard them. In the end, it was the insurance company that pushed for the settlements, based on nothing but costs-benefits analysis of the price of taking each case to trial. To the network, a not-guilty verdict was worthless if it cost them millions to get there. To me, it meant everything. He who steals my purse, etc. etc. Yes, I can quote Shakespeare. He's not just for snobs, you know.

Years ago, I reported on a story from Baltimore, about how the public buses had to have cameras installed because when there was a minor accident, people tried to get on the bus after the fact and claim injury. (*Do get your day in court. Don't try to take someone else's.*) So I was the Baltimore bus and these "ladies" jumped on and took me for a ride. But they were supposed to stay quiet and at least one of them didn't honor that part of the settlement. Oh, they were smart enough to say "no comment" when reporters began snooping around, but how did the reporters even know to start asking questions? Someone violated the confidentiality agreement. Someone, maybe several someones, should have given that money back to the insurers but shakedown artists aren't exactly principled, are they?

There was a bigger picture. Isn't there always? Whenever anything happens, anything, ask yourself: *Who benefits financially from this?* I was making—well, let's call it a hefty sum. My program was popular, my ratings weren't affected at all after the story about the settlement was leaked. The advertisers who pulled their commercials were scared, but there was never an organized boycott. Plenty of advertisers would have increased their sales by standing by me.

Instead, I was told by the brass that I had to make a public show of penance. Apologize on camera, then go into some sort of rehab. But I couldn't apologize for things I didn't do, not even for expedience's sake, and I wasn't going to go to some bogus "rehab" for speaking my mind, the only thing of which I'm guilty. I said no. They fired me with only three months' severance. No one else wanted to hire me. I was too conservative for MSNBC and CNN, not enough of a loyalist for Fox. I had always been a maverick, a lone wolf, marching to my own tune. That's why I was expendable. I didn't belong to any of the tribes.

I knew my exile from television would end eventually; I was too good at what I do not to bounce back. I started a podcast from my house in Rye, but that didn't bring in much cash and I had a big nut. I have some savings, of course. I'm a responsible person. I'm not living the high life with a place in the Hamptons and a Florida mansion and season tickets to the Knicks and the Yankees. But between our rigged tax system and two ex-wives and child support and the Rye house and the apartment I kept in the city, my monthly expenses were high. It was only a matter of time before I got another gig, but in the meantime, I needed to be more liquid.

That was when I came up with the idea of writing a mystery series.

Do be nimble when you need to be. Don't cry in your beer.

Now over the years I had built up a nice sideline, writing about great men in history. (Only great men so far. Of course there are great women, but I hadn't found one who interested me enough to stick with her story for 300 pages.) But those books took at least three months of research, plus they were already under contract. To get an infusion of cash, I decided I needed another publishing contract. People didn't realize this, but I used to write fiction. No fake news jokes, please. Almost twenty years ago, I wrote a crime novel when I was the anchor on PM Chicago, back in the day. It was fun. I basically killed—in print—anyone who had ever irritated me. I have always lived by the Conan Code: You must crush your enemies, see them driven before you and glory in the lamentations of their women. My book had lots of murder, lots of sex and a very neat variation on a locked-room mystery if I do say so myself. Unfortunately, I didn't know much about the publishing business then and I worked with a subpar company run by my college roommate, never saw a dime after my initial advance. First editions of that book now sell for $125 a pop on the Internet, but I'll never see a dime of that.

Anyway that kind of book, fun as it is, sort of James Bond meets Walter Cronkite—it wasn't right for me in my current circumstances, although I secretly believe my hero, Savoy Taylor, could knock Jack Reacher on his ass if they were ever to meet *mano à mano*. I might have said no to rehab, but I did understand that my image could use a little burnishing. My literary agent and I made a study of what was publishing. One obvious choice was a book about a woman who's not reliable (as if any women are reliable). The way it was explained to me—do you think I've had time to read fiction while doing five shows a week, forty-nine weeks a year for fifteen years?—the woman drinks or she lies or something, so you can't be sure if she's telling the truth. Do you want to know how you can tell if a woman is lying in my experience? *She's breathing.* Anyway, my agent and I agreed that's not the right kind of book for me to write right now.

So I thought about the times we live in, how much people needed to believe in a place where good would always triumph. Those "girl" books spoke to our general paranoia, which was understandable. But these are raucous, out-of-control times. Values such as self-respect and hard work are under siege. We used to pride ourselves on being rugged individualists, now we cringe if people disagree with us. In times like this, people want comfort. They want to have their values affirmed. They want to see order restored, they want good people to prosper and bad people to suffer. So I read a little Louise Penny, a little Jan Karon and decided to combine the two into my own original series. I came up with *Murder Comes to Christmas*, the first book set in the fictional town of Christmas, Ohio, a place that embodies true American ideals.

I devised the basic outline, then we hired a guy to flesh out my ideas. A lot of the best novelists work that way now. The hero is the town sheriff, Doug Champion. He doesn't always do things by the book, but he reliably does the *right* thing, no matter how unpopular. In the first book, some unknown party is trying to disrupt the annual Christmas festival, which accounts for a big chunk of the town's annual revenue. The disturbances begin small—ugly graffiti at the Christmas bazaar, defaced signs, a cat in the microwave at the local coffee shop. (Coffee *shop*, not a coffeehouse. There is a Dairy Queen in Christmas, Ohio, but no Starbucks, a Taco Bell but no Chipotle. Real food for real people.) Christmas, Ohio, had four churches, one synagogue and no atheists.

But when someone finds a body inside one of the ice sculptures in the town park, it's clear that whoever is doing this is much more than your average teen hooligan. It's a War against Christmas on multiple levels. I wanted to call the book *The War Against Christmas,* but the publisher pointed out that would look as if I'm taking sides in the culture wars, which I've always avoided. People should say what they want to say—Merry Christmas, Happy Hanukah, Cool Kwanzaa—and—this is the part that everyone has trouble with—*let other people say what they want to say.* Free speech. What a misnomer. My free speech cost me millions. Well, not me, but Gotham News's insurance company.

The pace of publishing felt dirge-like after television; it took the ghostwriter ten weeks to finish the novel. But the book was done in time to go on sale in mid-November. Pre-orders were strong and while some early reviewers took the expected shots at me and my history, I didn't write it for reviewers. I wrote for my fans and it turned out I still had a pretty good fan base. My fans—older women, for the most part—were angry with Gotham News and they bought my book as a show of support. Even without the nightly exposure of my show, I still hit the *New York Times* bestseller list at No. 7.

My publisher was ecstatic. They were talking to me about speeding up production. Could I finish another "Christmas" book by Easter? Not that they were all going to be holiday-themed. They just wanted a new one on the shelves in six-to-eight months. The working title for the next one was: *Christmas in Summer.* There was going to be a shooting at the 4th of July regatta, at the exact moment that they fired the cannon. And the romance between Sheriff Champion and Carlotta Mandible, the young widow who owned the coffee shop, was going to start heating up. Tastefully, of course. No out-and-out sex scenes. It wasn't that kind of series. My tour was extended through December, with the last event scheduled for December 20th at The Mysterious Bookshop in New York, almost a year to the day since I was betrayed by Gotham News.

Then something weird happened: My Goodreads rankings, which had been a solid 3.8, began tanking. The online reviews, which had always been good once you controlled for personal vendettas that had nothing to do with the book, began diving, too. It had every appearance of a coordinated campaign. Turned out that the whole thing had started with a tweet from an Ohio woman who had thirty-seven followers:

Disappointed that @JDoyleDossier thinks it's OK to kill cat in such a vile manner. #CatHater #Unacceptable #BoycottChristmasOhio

It's true that @JDoyleDossier was my verified Twitter handle, but I never used it; when I was at the network, one of my assistants managed the account, mainly retweeting articles and promoting the show. I don't even have the password for it and we had set up a different Twitter account to publicize the Christmas books (@ChristmasOhioIsReal). So I hadn't seen the tweet, nor realized it was gaining some kind of stealth traction on social media, with more and more outraged women—and they were all women—posting about how much they hated this one paragraph. It wasn't even gory! We had been very careful to avoid gratuitous violence or sex in the Christmas books. But I had seen a television show where someone microwaved a hamster and I thought it was pretty cool. I was very clear with my writer, some literary novelist who's never sold more than 2,000 books, that the scene should be left to the reader's imagination, that we have to cut away right before Carlotta Mandible opens the microwave and then, jump cut, she's being comforted by Sheriff Champion. That scene is pivotal because she hates him more for seeing her weak, while he finds his feelings for her are complicated now that he's seen the vulnerable woman beneath the tough, sassy exterior.

Don't respond, my publisher said. *The whole outcry will die a natural death if you don't stoke it. The outrage machine requires oxygen in the form of attention, rebuttal. They can't make you respond.*

But the comments kept coming. On Twitter, on Facebook, on Goodreads, on Amazon. Somehow, the damn cat in the microwave got linked to what happened at the network, which wasn't relevant at all. I seemed to have done the unthinkable, unite women—and it was all women, mostly old women, best I could tell—across the political spectrum. Apparently, you can grab a pussy, you can parade in your pussy hat, but you can't kill a kitty in a novel. That thought came to me late one night, when I was sitting up with a nightcap in my study, reading the latest comments on my laptop. *You can grab a pussy in real life, but you can't kill a kitty in a crime novel.*

So I tweeted just that.

Do say what you think. Don't say it when angry or irritable. Or drunk.

Within an hour, I had deleted the tweet, but someone had a screenshot. Two days later, when I showed up at a signing in a small Ohio town that claimed it was the model for Christmas (it's not) there were more people outside the store protesting than were inside the store waiting for their "Welcome to Christmas" mugs and cookies. The signs said things like "Cat Killer!" and "Leave My Pussy Alone," which made no sense at all. Some PETA knockoff group was using the whole thing to boost its public profile. I'm pretty sure they were paying people to protest. And they were wearing those stupid, stupid, stupid hats. But it was good optics, I guess, and it was a slow news day and somehow I became the story. Image Rehab 101 was not going as planned.

I got calls to appear on television, even from my old network, which wanted me to defend my God-given right as an American to write a scene in which someone puts a cat in the microwave. Someone evil! *That was the point!* Only a bad person would put a cat in the microwave. By the end of the book—spoiler alert, the killer trying to hurt Christmas is a bitter, unattractive spinster—the killer lunges for Sheriff Champion with a knife, but Carlotta foils the attack by throwing scalding coffee on her. I thought that was a good twist, the woman saving the man.

As the protests grew, some bookstores began canceling. It was bad for business. December is a big month for bookstores and the protesters made shoppers nervous. Easier to pull the plug on my appearances in order to appease all these crazy cat ladies than to stand up for the principle of free speech. I was disappointed, but that's what our country has become, a nation of craven "I've-Got-Mine" opportunists.

The Mysterious Bookshop was one of a handful of stores that stood by me. I was told they would not be intimidated by the protestors and that my event would go on as planned. As my tour limped into its final days, I found myself looking forward to that last reading. And it exceeded all expectations. For one thing, Mysterious Bookshop alerted the police when the protests started and, sure enough, those batty dames didn't have permits to protest. Technically, you don't need a permit to picket in New York City, but you do need one for amplified sound and the pickets have to keep moving. So goodbye, bullhorn, and without the bullhorn, twenty old ladies moving in lazy circles didn't attract much attention, nor did they intimidate the people who wanted to attend my signing. Half of them had decamped to the Pain Quotidien down the street before I even arrived.

Once inside the store, I was gratified to find that I had a standing-room-only crowd of more than 100 and another

200 books to sign for mail orders. I had sprung for champagne for this final signing, along with the usual case of Coors to honor Sheriff Champion, but the store also had a nice spread. Crackers, cheese, but not Brie, just good American cheeses like cheddar and Swiss. Turned out that when the controversy first started, lazy reporters, reluctant to leave Manhattan, had asked the store's staff to comment over and over again. People who hadn't realized that this gem of a store was in Tribeca had started showing up, leaving with armfuls of books.

One of the clerks explained to me what I had failed to understand: Killing a cat in a mystery is a cardinal sin. Kill a child. Kill two dozen prostitutes. Kill a bride on her wedding night. That's all fine. But to kill a cat in a so-called cozy mystery—apparently that's what I had written, a cozy, I'm not sure why it's called that—is simply never done. They told me there are even mysteries in which cats solve the crime. So: *Do kill as many people, dogs, and children as you like. Don't kill cats or curse.*

At any rate, I drank champagne from a dark plastic cup and enjoyed myself enormously. I would have rated the night a grand success on any scale—and that was before I met Vivien.

I had noticed her earlier in the evening. She seemed a little younger than most of the crowd and didn't appear to know anyone else there. Slender yet curvy, with big brown eyes and dark hair worn in a messy bun on top of her head, little tendrils falling around her face. She looked familiar, but I thought that was because she had an Audrey Hepburn cast to her features. She couldn't stop looking at me. I thought it was my imagination, but when the crowd thinned at the end of the night, she came over to where I was signing stock for the store.

"Can I get one of those?" she asked, pointing to the stack of books.

"Is it for you, or is it a gift?"

"I consider it a gift to myself. How's that?"

"May I inscribe it?" Our eyes were locked on each other's.

"To Vivien Kocia," she said.

"That's a lovely name. Is it Italian?"

"No, Polish."

"I never realized Polish was so melodious."

I'm actually very shy around women. That's something that's easily overlooked, in all the stories about me. I'm shy. The man who went on television, speaking with confidence and certitude, he disappeared when a beautiful woman walked by. I could never have said the things they claimed I said at the network, not if I were attracted to those girls. And if I wasn't attracted to them, why would I say those things? They were young, inexperienced. They probably didn't shave under their arms, yet waxed their private parts bare, which I understand is how things are done these days. Young women are baffling.

But Vivien Kocia was my type. She was at least thirty-five, maybe forty, but a terrifically maintained forty. At first glance, her clothes were conservative—a sweater dress that hung below her knees, with a big cowl at the neck, suede boots. But the dress hugged every curve and the boots must have been over the knee because I couldn't see the tops.

I wanted to see the tops.

"Do you like mystery books?" I asked, desperate to prolong the encounter, tongue-tied as a boy at a dance.

"I just started reading them," she said. "I admit, I was always a snob, but now I feel foolish. They're so satisfying. Look at your book—a spinster, driven mad by the abortion she had as a young girl, unable to have children, wreaks havoc on a small town that opens its arms to her. When she tries to kill Sheriff Champion—"

"Spoiler alert," I said with a smile, although there was no one listening to us at this point. The store had emptied, it was going on eight o'clock, closing time.

"I know it's wrong, but it's so satisfying when Carlotta throws hot coffee on her. The woman doesn't deserve to die—well she does, I believe in capital punishment, but that's for a court to determine, a fate for a jury to mete out. And yet, in the moment, how I gloried in it."

"People think of novelists as being disproportionately liberal," I told her. "Novelists and readers. But that's not true in my experience. The mystery form recognizes what a lot of us believe, in our guts. There is a right and a wrong, and there can be no wrong if it restores right. I think that's part of the reason our genre is the most commercially robust of all."

"I thought that was romance," she said, her eyes still locked on mine.

"Do you need a ride?" I asked. "I have a car outside."

"Alas," she said, "I drove into the city tonight." She pointed outside, to a panel van parked on Warren Street. "My work vehicle."

"What do you do?" I asked. "Why do you need a van?"

"Well," she said, "I'm a licensed massage therapist who uses essential oils." She reached out and kneaded my shoulder with her fingertips. "How many books have you signed in the last month? Five hundred? A thousand? I can tell you're off-balance. I bet there's pinch right here"—she kneaded the side of my neck. "If you're not careful, you'll throw your back out before the New Year."

"Do you know anyone who can help me?" I asked.

"I'm the best I know, honestly, but I'm booked up through the holidays. Although I have the night free if you'd like to try it—"

Five minutes later we were on the FDR, her van following my town car, heading to my place.

Once in my apartment, I didn't really care about the massage. I would have been happy to open a bottle of wine, segue to more of a date night vibe, take a rain check on the massage. But she was very serious and earnest, looking for the best place to set up her table. (She chose my bedroom, which made me optimistic, I'll admit.) She excused herself while I got ready, stripping down to my underwear and a towel, lying face down on the table. She told me she needed to go back to her van and grab her supply of essential oils, but she turned on a radio channel with the kind of dreamy, nothing music you hear in spas. I'm a 57-year-old man, I've lived a full life, and I'm not embarrassed to say that. I've lived a man's life, a real man's life, shaped by my understanding that people aren't that different from animals. The way lions live makes more sense than the way people live. Polygamy is rooted in human behavior. I never advocated for it on the show because it was too loaded a topic. But if I had, I might have said:

Do understand men and women are fundamentally different.

Don't claim you can simultaneously believe in Darwin and monogamous men. Pick one.

I heard her come back into the apartment, huffing and puffing as if she was carrying something heavy. But when she entered my bedroom, she just had a small bottle of oil.

"*Nepeta cataria*," she said, passing it under my nose. "Doesn't it smell wonderful?"

It seemed pretty ordinary to me, like one of those herbs they had started adding to everything. Not cilantro, but like cilantro. I hate cilantro.

"Nice," I said, wanting to be polite.

She oiled her hands and began working on me. Her touch was surprisingly light. I wasn't sure she really knew what she was doing. I didn't feel as if I were being rubbed so much as I was being coated. Every now and then she would stop and do those little karate chops, but mainly she seemed intent on rubbing the oil into my flesh, covering every inch.

"Roll over," she said huskily.

I did, making sure to keep the towel tight. I wanted whatever we did to be her decision.

"Now drink this herbal tea to help you relax."

147

"I don't—"

"Drink it," she said. She sounded very much in charge. It was kind of exciting. She propped up my head, held the mug to my lips.

The tea was foul, a mix of grass clippings and chalk, but she was now oiling my calves and, to my amazement, my face. I was glad, as I felt the oil seeping into my pores, that I didn't have to go to a television studio the next day and film. As much as I missed my job—and my paycheck—I didn't really miss being on television. Do you know the kinds of things people say about your appearance when you're a public figure? I tried not to read the comments and the hate mail, but so much of my face, my body had been dissected in public. They said I had a double chin. (I don't, that was just an unfortunate angle in the photographs.) They made fun of my skin, my hair, my complexion, which did tend to rosacea. Apparently, men were fair game, but if you even suggested that a woman had cankles you could lose your job. That's what one of the woman at the network said, that I had criticized her calves.

Do be kind.

Don't be a patsy. If someone criticizes you, feel free to criticize them. Sauce for the goose, baby.

She was pressing on my cheeks, that spot between my eyes, grooved from years of looking very serious on television. It was heavenly. It was almost better than sex because nothing was expected of me. Women think men have it so easy. We don't. We don't. We don't.

"What did you say, John?"

I hadn't realized I was speaking out loud. My tongue felt thick in my mouth. I tried to tell her not to worry. I think I asked her how she felt about being the next ex-Mrs. John Doyle, trying to make a joke, lighten the mood. My lips couldn't make words. My eyes had been closed because it was awkward, looking at someone rubbing your face, but now I found I couldn't open them. My stomach rumbled.

"It's OK, John," she said. "It's OK."

And that was the last thing anyone said for a while.

I woke up in the bathroom, retching into my toilet. Could have been minutes, hours, days later, I was that disoriented. There was nothing really in my stomach but that awful tea, which was probably the cause. My knees were weak, my legs rubbery and I had to brace myself on the sink to stand.

There was a book on the sink. My book. Vivien's book, the one I had signed to her. It must have been a bummer to have your date get sick, but that seemed rude, leaving it behind.

There was a note inside:

> *Dear John,*
>
> *I confess I told you a little white lie. I am not Vivien Kocia. I am the woman you so elegantly called the "Kitty Con Artist, the Krazy Kat Lady of Central Park." Despite your attempts to ruin me, I am still trying to protect natural feral cat sanctuaries wherever they may be, although it is sometimes necessary to remove some cats from the public, especially if they have become dangerous to themselves and others.*
>
> *Three such cats are in your apartment right now. And that oil I applied to you is made of catnip. As for the tea, it was simply Lipton's cut with ipecac and a roofie.*
>
> *Until we meet again.*
>
> *P.S. I didn't read your book, I just read the spoiler forums on Goodreads so I could fake it.*

I tried to open the bathroom door, but she had somehow barricaded me in. I called her name. Nothing. I thought about screaming until the neighbors phoned downstairs to the doorman, who would come in and investigate, if only to quell their complaints. But he would find me nude, covered in catnip oil. He might gossip. I decided to shower first and it was only then that I realized the shower was running. Why was the shower running? Had I turned it on when I stumbled in here to throw up? I wrenched open the door and the last thing I saw was three sodden masses of fur, coming right at me. They were so desperate to escape that shower that they knocked me down and I was so slippery from the oil that I couldn't get to my feet again.

My last conscious thought, as they swarmed over me, nipping and clawing, tearing my flesh, treating me like the world's largest catnip mouse, was: *I bet I can use this in a book. This would make a great scene in the next book.*

And that's when I knew I really was a novelist.

THE CHRISTMAS PARTY

Jeffery Deaver

He sat on a small, musty couch, staring at the TV but not *watching* the TV.

The man was in his late seventies, and handsome still, though there was evidence of slipping. He'd lost considerable weight in the past few months and his gray hair, while still full, needed trimming and was presently mussed.

Carmen, his main caregiver at the Silver Hills senior care center, did what she could. She'd brushed John's hair when Martin and Emily had arrived, but he'd pushed her hand away and he now looked, well, a bit mad. And in the short time they'd been here he'd tucked and untucked his faded plaid shirt a dozen times. His gray slacks were far too big.

The window shade was up and Martin could see, through a stand of bald trees, one of the busier commercial streets in Paramus, New Jersey. He looked back.

"So, Uncle John," Martin tried again. "We were talking about Christmas. Emily and I are going to her family's. You met them? In Connecticut? But we thought you could come over to our place a few days before. Have dinner?"

Martin Niles had come from work and was dressed in a gray wool suit and spiffy green tie. A white shirt, of course. He always wore white shirts. His wife Emily, a pretty, slim woman of about forty-five, was dressed more casually than her husband: Sweats and a windbreaker. She'd come from the health club, after tennis with her girlfriends.

"Hope you can, Uncle John." Emily was trying to sound enthusiastic. But Martin could see she was troubled too at his declining condition.

"Christmas?" John said, not in confirmation of the plans but as if he'd never heard the word. "When is that?"

"Three weeks, Mr. John." From Carmen. "You go to see Mr. Martin and Mrs. Emily. Dinner."

"I might have a class."

John Niles had been a professor of English literature at a private college nearby. He'd retired twenty years before, and he had not seen the inside of a classroom since then.

"I don't think you have a class. It's the holiday."

"Oh. Stupid. What was I thinking?" He went back to TV and muttered something to himself, fiddling with the remote.

The rooms at Silver Hills were not large and four people inside gave Martin a sense of claustrophobia. This was accentuated by his uncle's behavior, which he found both sad and creepy. They'd been here for a half hour, trying to make conversation. Some of Uncle John's comments were making sense. Others, completely off the wall, so different from a few months ago, when Martin and Emily had placed him in the home.

He glanced at Carmen, a round, attractive woman, with her dark hair tied back in a tight bun. A few gray hairs streaked it. Like most of the caregivers on the B Wing—devoted to the older or more infirm residents—she was in good shape. The yellow uniform was short-sleeved and Martin could see impressive muscles, necessary to get the more disabled patients into and out of beds and wheelchairs.

At least for now, Uncle John was ambulatory and—in nicer weather—would go for walks in the yard or up the street to the Quick Mart or McDonald's, always accompanied, of course; if not, residents wandered off, and a Silver Alert, a public announcement that they were missing, had to be issued.

"You like that show?" Martin tried, pointing at the TV.
Suddenly John smiled. "Who?"

Then he returned to the screen. A commercial came on,
for a laxative. "I don't know. I don't know about it."

On the table and a bookshelf nearby were dozens of books.
Murder mysteries and thrillers mostly. He ordered them from
a famous bookstore in Manhattan: The Mysterious Bookshop. John had been there often in the past, and had fond
memories of the place, located downtown. He told stories of
attending parties at the bookstore, attended by famous crime
writers and publishers.

Martin supposed the old man couldn't remember the
storyline well enough to get through a whole book.

Martin looked toward Carmen, whose lips were tight,
brow furrowed. Martin liked Carmen. She was different
from the other caregivers here. Tougher. She looked you
in the eye. She wouldn't let Uncle John get away with
being rude or having a tantrum. Although she was short,
she'd walk right up to him—he was over six feet—and put
her hands on her hips and tell him, "No, Mr. John. You
will stop that, and now." On her wrist was a small tattoo
of a word in Spanish. She was a grandmother now, but
Martin could imagine her running with a tough crowd
in her youth.

With John, though, there was not much for her to do, other than make sure he was dressed properly and got to the entertainment common room and went for those walks. A backgammon set sat forlornly on the rickety table under the window. A deck of cards, too. Martin was sure they'd been unused for a month, maybe longer.

Suddenly John grabbed the remote and changed the channel. Another commercial was on the screen. He nodded. Dropped the remote on the floor. Carmen scowled and retrieved it.

"How's Al?" John suddenly asked.

"Good. He asked about you the other day."

A moment of clarity. Al was one of the employees in the investment firm that Martin owned. John had met him once, three months ago, and they'd had what amounted to a normal conversation.

Martin looked at his watch. He had to get back to the office soon and then home; he and Emily were hosting a big dinner tonight.

"We should go," he said. "We'll talk about Christmas later, John."

John was now staring at the ceiling as if looking at clouds passing or airplanes coursing through the sky.

"Gracias," Emily said to Carmen.

"De nada."

Carmen then stood and was peering down at John. She looked up at Martin. She gave a very subtle shake of her head and her lips tightened, as if saying, "I'm sorry."

❄

"He seems worse," Martin said.

Director Holmes was a rotund man with a kindly face. His age was mid-fifties and he always dressed like a stodgy boss on casual Friday—as if he'd be more comfortable in a suit but thought he'd play along for the troops. Today: in a yellow cardigan sweater, gray slacks, a pale blue shirt.

"Somewhat." A shrug. "But sometimes he's definitely with us. Smiling, having conversations. He lectured some of our folks about *Moby Dick* the other day. It was actually very good, the talk. But I'll tell you why I was especially encouraged. I heard him mention to his caregiver that he was really looking forward to the Christmas party. We do a pageant every December. The residents love it."

Holmes stole a subtle glance at Uncle John's file. The "Religious Affiliation" section was blank. "A little bit of the manger and the Wise Men, but mostly Santa, reindeer, carols. Cookies and hot cocoa. Great fun."

Martin clicked his tongue.

A pathetic Christmas party . . . If that was a sign he was normal, the situation was not good.

"So. I'm encouraged." The room they sat in was a large, warmly lit place—presently dolled up with Christmas decorations. The window overlooked the grounds in the rear, a small garden, benches, a lawn, now covered with brown leaves.

Holmes's desk was filled with files. Silver Hills was a busy place. There were about two hundred residents. The number, of course, fluctuated, as at least once or twice a month vacancies occurred—for obvious, and inevitable, reasons.

Martin asked, "Is it Alzheimer's? Sometimes he recognizes us, sometimes he doesn't. And when he does talk, which he sure hasn't lately, he gets things confused."

The home had a small medical staff and the residents could have checkups and schedule basic treatment and procedures.

"I'm no doctor but here"—he waved his hand, indicating the home—"I've seen a lot of residents with a lot of conditions. It's dementia, I'm sure. Slow progression. If you want to schedule an MRI, we can arrange for that. But it'll be expensive—you'd have to pay what Medicare doesn't cover. I'd recommend medication. That can slow the progress significantly. We can have the clinic look into it."

"Is this related to his cancer?" Martin asked.

"No, no relation. And his last scan came back clear."

The illness was how Martin and Emily had come to care for his uncle. Martin's father, Jacob—John's younger brother—was an investment advisor; he'd done very well in the business. John had gone into academia, teaching American literature at a college nearby. Just as he'd retired, John had been diagnosed with cancer. A widower, he had no one to help him through the treatment and recuperation, so he moved in with his younger brother. Then, tragically, Jacob died of a sudden heart attack. At first John had stayed with Martin and Emily, but that hadn't worked out. They'd decided it would be better for everyone that he live in a residence. It was expensive, but Jacob's will had set up a trust to pay for his older brother's care.

"Please," Martin said, "look into the medications."

Holmes shook Emily's hand, then Martin's. In a soft voice he said, "Whenever you feel bad about him, remember the Christmas party. How he's looking forward to it. I've heard him mention it to Carmen a couple of times. That's encouraging. You should come for a visit." He gave them a flyer, on which were very bad drawings of dancing reindeer, a plate of cookies, a mug of cocoa.

The couple walked into the hallway, where a worker was stringing red and green tinsel on one side of the hallway. The other was already decorated with blue, for Hanukah.

As they pulled on their coats, Martin glanced up the hall.

"You go ahead," he told his wife. "I'll meet you in the lobby."

The dinner party ended at eleven.

Martin and Emily were good at the host game. They'd cooked filet and Potatoes Anna and broccolini, and served a good cab—the evening an effort to woo potential clients for Niles Investment Strategies. They'd also served a vegetarian dish—lasagna—for the Pouters (a nickname they'd given to Herb and Sally Pollette, but a very, very private nickname, since he was one of Martin's only multimillionaire clients).

Afterward, they had cleaned up, which took some time—the party had been for twelve. Martin carried the dishes into the kitchen for Emily to load into the dishwasher, while he sipped his second glass of after-dinner brandy.

He leaned against the marble island in the large room, which he'd helped Emily design. He poured a bit more Remy. He was looking out the window into the backyard. This house didn't have a pool, but they'd had one in the prior place. It had been heated and open all year. Martin recalled that sometimes a mist from chill air meeting warm water would cover the surface. The fog would glow, lit by underwater bulbs. A magical place. Martin missed swimming on such nights

Emily started the dishwasher and rinsed her hands, then poured herself a white wine.

"What is it?" she asked.

He rolled up his sleeves. He wasn't sure why. "After we talked to Holmes, I went up the hall?"

"Right."

"I wanted to talk to Carmen." A large sip of brandy. The first, an hour ago, had stung. This one flowed over a dull tongue. "I wanted to know the truth. Holmes was lying."

"I never liked him," she muttered.

"She said, yes, he has clear moments but the progress is bad. Last month he'd have a half-dozen bouts when he didn't know where he was, who he was. Now, it's twice that. Holmes knows it. He just doesn't want us to move him to a facility that can take better care of him. So he plays up how well he's doing."

Emily lifted her hands, silently repeating her assessment of the director from a moment before.

Martin continued, "The problem is that physically, he's in great shape—for someone his age. You know, she takes him to that little workout room they have. You've seen it?"

"I don't remember."

"He can use the equipment fine—he's strong, coordinated. She said he could keep on going for years, but his mind's becoming blank."

"Live for years."

More brandy. She, more wine.

"She said the only way to keep him stable is to bring him home here and work with him every day. There are exercises and things you can do. They help some. Not much."

Emily, he could see in the reflection of the oven, was looking his way. "There's something else. What?" Her eyes were narrow.

Martin had met Emily not long after he had taken over the company from his father. She'd come to work as his administrative assistant. They'd gotten close soon after, sharing stories about difficult domestic situations. He'd soon learned how shrewd she could be.

"There was something about the way Carmen looked at me in John's room when we left. I don't think you saw it."

"No. What do you mean, 'Something.'"

"Just a look. It made me think I could ask her a question." Martin took another long sip. "I asked . . ."

Emily offered, "If there was any way we could help . . . ease his situation."

Shrewd. . . .

"Yes." He took a deep breath. "I put it exactly that way, like I might mean: could we buy him a new bed?"

"Or get him on those meds."

"Medication, right. Or a new TV."

"Or it might mean something else," Emily whispered. "You put it that way, innocent, so she wouldn't call the police."

"But she knew what I meant. She told me that the caregivers, they understand that sometimes it's crueler to let patients linger. The administrators don't know that. To them it's all about getting the families to pay and pay. In John's case, his mind may fail but his body will go on for years." He paused. "She said there are ways . . . Overdose. Like the patients have hoarded a big supply of painkillers or sleeping pills and take them all at once. Or maybe the caregiver gives them some extra pills, so they're sleeping really deep, and get tangled up, with the sheet or a lamp cord around their neck."

"I don't like that one." Emily gave a fake air shiver.

"No, I don't either. She said usually there's no police involved but even if so, if somebody's over seventy-five and has dementia or Alzheimer's, they don't follow up."

"It's an act of mercy."

"Act of mercy."

Emily asked, whispering as if a cop lurked nearby, "Has she done it before?"

"Three or four times. Dementia. Alzheimer's. Bad strokes."

The dishwasher hummed and Martin stared out the window at the dark pool cover, remembering the fog, remembering those nice evenings.

"Let's sleep on it."

She nodded.

He finished the brandy.

An act of mercy . . .

❄

"I want to see you both," Carmen spoke English well, though with a thick Latin accent.

They were in the living room of their house. Carmen had looked around, impressed at what would to her be opulence. He wondered what she would have thought of the house they'd moved out of last year, the one with the heated pool. It was twice as big as this one.

A Christmas tree was in the corner, a full one, bristling with lights. The time was early evening, and winter wind blew outside. More snow was promised.

Martin had hardly recognized Carmen when she'd arrived; he'd only seen her in her uniform; now she was wearing a nice white blouse and dark skirt, black stockings. The blouse was open at the collar. Around her neck was a simple cross on a chain.

"For this, I am making sure, you want it to happen. You." She turned her dark eyes from Martin to Emily. "And you."

"Want?" Martin asked, frowning. "It's the last thing I *want*. I want John to be healthy and coming over to see Em's parents with the rest of the family for Christmas." He looked at his wife. "But that's not going to happen. We want what's best for him. He can't be happy now."

An act of mercy . . .

"We both do."

Carmen's face registered contentment. "That is the answer I am glad to hear you say, Mr. Martin, Mrs. Emily. I see you really feel for Mr. John. Like I do."

So, it had been a test. Martin wasn't the least offended. It meant Carmen was careful. She'd be careful, too, with the police, if it came to that.

He said, "The one thing, the most important thing: I don't want him to feel any pain, any discomfort."

"No, no pain at all, I will promise that. What I will do is I will buy a bottle of the medicines like we have at Silver Hills. Caregivers have people we know. Black market. We can get drugs. Mr. Holmes and anyone will think that he has borrowed or . . ." She frowned. "What is the word? Kept hidden?"

"Hoarded?"

"*Sí*, hoarded them. And took them all at once. He'll go to sleep. Peace for him."

Martin said, "Is there . . . I mean, if you want money, please. I can give you some money."

"No, no, not for me. For the drugs, *sí*. Three hundred." She put her hands on her thighs and looked from one to the other. "Now, maybe I go to restroom and give you two a chance to talk to yourselves. To think of what I said. To be sure."

Emily walked her to the bathroom, and returned.

They looked at each other, then, Martin noticed, he looked down to the floor while she gazed up at the cornice at the top of the fireplace.

"Marty . . ."

He said, "We have to. We have no choice." He spoke firmly, as if, were there any less resolve in his voice, he might weaken.

"Mercy."

He nodded.

Carmen returned a moment later, and sat on the couch once more.

Emily said, "One thing. He said he wanted to go to that Christmas party? He was very excited about it."

"*Sí*. The party at Silver Hills."

"Can you wait till after that?"

"*Sí*, I do that." She smiled. "Give him one last joy."

"No pain?" Martin asked.

"No pain." She looked at them both sympathetically. "Always in life, hard choices, no? Always hard."

Martin reached into his pocket and counted out money. He only had $80. He glanced at Emily. She understood. She dug into her purse and extracted tens and twenties. They counted the bills until they had three hundred.

Carmen slipped the money into her purse. She rose and donned her coat.

Martin reached into his wife's purse and removed five more twenties. He handed them to Carmen, "In case the drugs cost more."

"No, three is enough."

"Keep it."

She shrugged and put the bills in her purse and walked to the front door.

As she left Martin realized, to his shock, that what he'd just done was give someone a tip for the service of killing his uncle.

❄

Carmen Alvarez was walking down a chilly street in Paramus, New Jersey.

She would be working the late shift at the Silver Hills home, which she preferred because it was quieter. Not as many people around. Including that pig, perverted, Director Holmes.

She was, of course, nervous about what lay ahead. She'd been truthful with the Nileses about the lives she'd taken. She hadn't enjoyed it. But she felt it had been her duty. She was a Catholic and a good one, but she believed that Jesus entered the world to end suffering, and if Carmen's taking a life did the same, then it was a righteous thing to do.

But no pain, she told herself. Never any pain.

She smelled snow in the air. Her hand was in her pocket, fingers around the purchase she'd made last night in a neighborhood downtown, a tough place, not far from where she'd grown up.

She turned into a parking lot, where the wind was swirling day-old flakes through the air.

Ahead of her she saw a door open and a man step outside, glance toward the gray sky and pull his collar up. It was Martin Niles.

She walked up to him quickly.

"Carmen. What are you doing here?"

She said nothing, but pulled from her pocket what she'd bought last night. Not drugs but a .38 revolver. She shot Martin twice in the face, whose eyes went wide but whose throat had no time to scream. He dropped onto his belly, shivered once and died. Her strong hands, in latex gloves, rolled him over and opened his coat. She took his wallet and cash and car keys and then turned and hurried back toward her car.

Carmen wasn't absolutely certain that dying that way was completely painless. But at the worst the discomfort would have lasted only a second or so, and that was good enough for her.

❄

Numb, Emily Niles stood in the small chapel, located in the center of the Hartsville, NJ, cemetery.

The other mourners were gone. The memorial service had been at a church nearby and the funeral entourage had come here, led by the hearse, for the final remarks.

At a different time of year, Martin would have been interred now but the ground was too cold to dig graves; Martin would be buried at first thaw. Or possibly another thaw, if there was such a thing. Emily hadn't really been listening.

She was staring down at the coffin.

It was nice to be away from the others and to not have to field the questions and comments. "A mugging in Hartsville? Who do they think it was? Gangs, maybe . . . No, really. They're around here too.'"

And then the inevitable: "I'm so sorry, Em . . . You know, just wondering if somebody's taking over the business. Last few statements weren't looking too great." Or: "There'll be a hand on the tiller pretty soon, right? But let's chat when you're up for it."

Emily belted her black overcoat tightly and squinted as she gazed out the window. Some distance away, a woman in a camel-hair-colored coat, boots, and a scarf stood, looking toward the chapel. Emily couldn't see her face from here, but no one with that shade coat had been among the small group who had gathered here.

Emily flashed on an alarming thought. *Was it Martin's ex-wife?*

He hadn't spoken to her in years, though. So that was unlikely.

Wait! Could it be his former lover? Emily had caught her husband having an affair a few years ago. He'd begged forgiveness and promised he'd be faithful.

Had she come to say goodbye to him? Emily bristled.

She reflected, though, that she couldn't really complain; she'd been married to another man when she'd started working for Niles Investments—as had Martin—and their torrid affair had resulted in twin divorces.

Let he who is without sin . . .

But still . . . coming to *my* husband's funeral? *Bitch.*

Then a man walked up to the woman. She took his arm and they walked out of sight. They were here for another funeral.

Relax, she told herself. Focus on the important thing.

Survival.

She left the chapel and started for her car, besieged by a jumble of thoughts about what she was going to do now. She hadn't worked at the firm for a while, but she knew damn well that the operation was in a nosedive. Martin simply wasn't the investment genius that his father was. He'd been more of a slick salesman. He'd get clients to sign up, plying them with steak and cabernet and promising the moon, but then he'd lose their money. He'd taken to running a few small Ponzi schemes—mostly with elderly clients who had no experience with finance and who wouldn't have a clue they were being scammed.

Well, at least she had the insurance money. She could live comfortably on that until she found a new husband. Emily Niles was not a woman who spent her nights in bed alone. And then, too, Uncle John would be dead soon and the trust for his care would go into Martin's estate—and then into her pocket.

She walked into the parking lot, toward her Toyota, fishing for the key fob. Reflecting that when she had the Lexus, before the goddamn downsizing last year, all she had to do was be close to the car and pull the handle; it automatically unlocked. This one you had to push a button on the fob for entry.

This pissed her off. She hadn't signed on to the Niles family to be poor.

She now climbed into the car. As she did, suddenly the passenger and the back-right door opened. Two others climbed into the car and slammed the doors. She gasped, nearly screaming. Then her alarm became confusion.

In the passenger seat was the woman in the camel-hair coat she'd seen earlier.

Carmen Alvarez.

That was shocking enough. But more stunning was seeing the passenger in the back seat.

It was Uncle John. He was the one who'd greeted Carmen across the road from the chapel.

He said, "Hello, Emily. Say, why don't you turn on that engine and get the heater going. Before we all get a chill."

❄

John Niles looked over his niece-in-law.

She looked terrified.

Good.

"You're . . . here," Emily said, breathlessly.

"Not in Silver Hills?" John chuckled. "I wasn't committed, like in an asylum. I've always been free to come and go."

"What the hell is going on?" she snapped.

Carmen said, "Shhh, lady. You be quiet. You don't talk to my man that way . . ."

"Your . . . your man?"

John put his arm on Carmen's shoulder. They shared a warm look and smile.

Carmen then turned to Emily and muttered, "You, spending all your time on your phone texting, when you visit John. You, coming to visit every three weeks. You, never taking him on vacations. What kind of family does that?"

An easy answer, John reflected: The kind of family that plots their uncle's death.

He said, "Now, here's what's going to happen, Emily. There'll be an investigation into Martin's death. An anonymous witness will call and report they saw two Latino men shoot and rob him. The bullets in the gun will match bullets in two gang killings in the past year. They'll conclude it was a mugging, and that you had nothing to do with it. The insurance company will release the money. It's two million, right? Never mind, I'm sure I remember correctly."

John had to smile at the reference to memory, which was as good as any forty-five-year-old's.

"The minute the cash comes in, and I mean the minute, you will arrange to gift it to me. A nice gesture to an uncle who cared about his brother and his nephew."

"There is no goddamn way that—"

"I tell you be quiet, you be quiet." Carmen stabbed a finger into Emily's chest.

The woman shrank back. She was quiet.

"My accountant will take care of all the forms. No tax consequence to anybody with a gift. And all aboveboard."

John said, "Now, if I don't get the money, here's what's going to happen. There's a place in a deserted lot off 18th Street, a place where gangs hang out. The gun is buried there—the gun that was used to kill Martin. It's in one of your cosmetics bags."

"*What?*"

She knew she should be quiet, John guessed, but this was, understandably, involuntary.

Carmen said, "I stole it when I went to your bathroom the other day. There are some other things in the bag too. Tissues from your wastebasket and the money you paid me for the drugs—the bills I no touch, of course. Your DNA, fingerprints . . . If you no transfer the insurance to us, police get a call where gun is buried. Saw somebody from gang bury it there. They dig it up. And don't you love all the crime scene stuff on TV? John and I watch *all* those shows. The gun that kill your husband, your bag and your money. Ah, you kill him to get insurance. Goodbye, Miss Emily."

"You goddamn—"

Carmen leaned forward, and Emily was quiet again.

Then she whimpered, "But . . . what am I going to live on?"

John cocked his head. He hadn't thought about it. "I don't know."

Carmen: "You clear on what we tell you?"

Emily nodded, her eyes bewildered as she stared at a tombstone nearby. A sculpture of a bird was perched on top.

"Now go to the reception at your house. Food, wine . . . Oh, why you no invite Mr. John?"

"I—"

Carmen laughed. "I making a joke, Mrs. Emily."

John and Carmen climbed out of the car and walked back to Carmen's. She took his arm; he patted hers with a gloved hand. The cold was bracing.

"She no have any clue."

"No clue at all."

True. The poor, gold-digging secretary, sleeping her way into the boss's life, didn't have the slightest idea how she'd come to be hit by a truck.

It went back to John's illness. And his being taken in by Jacob. Older brother and younger living together later in life might have been difficult for some, but the two men, both widowers, got along just fine, going to baseball games, enjoying dinners together, spending hours talking over after-dinner drinks. John beat the cancer; Jacob's business, Niles Investments, was doing well. The brothers even double dated, occasionally, with several charming, older ladies.

But then, that terrible day, Jacob died, a sudden heart attack.

John coped with the sorrow, but at least he didn't have to worry about necessities. Jacob had set up a trust for his older brother, not relying on Martin to take care of John; he'd always considered his son about as trustworthy as a rattlesnake. He'd been planning on making changes to the corporation to keep Martin from taking over the company but he'd died before the papers were signed.

John had lived with Martin and Emily for only a short while and then they told him it would be better if he went into a home. Better for him, they said, though, of course, their goal was to get rid of him.

John would never think they meant that literally . . . until the trustee was talking to John and happened to mention that Martin had been asking about the trust, particularly what would happen in the future, when John was gone.

This was around the time that Martin's incompetence was leading the company straight toward bankruptcy. He'd had to sell the house in Saddle River and trade in the Tesla and Lexus for Toyotas. John knew, too, that Martin would inherit the trust funds if his uncle died.

It was an absurd idea that a nephew would kill his uncle for money . . . or was it?

John had to find out.

In this, he had an ally.

John and his caregiver in Silver Hills, Carmen Alvarez, had hit it off immediately upon his moving into the place. What a contrast they were. He, from the world of academia. She, growing up in the barrio, running with a gang, doing some time for robbery and assault. She showed off her gang tat to him, the Spanish word for *Beware*. He confessed he wished he'd been a bad boy. The worst he ever did was steal a book, *Walden Pond* by Thoreau, from the library. Carmen had laughed. They'd play cards and backgammon and talk and talk. They'd take turns reading aloud from the murder mysteries he loved.

He told her about his visits to The Mysterious Bookshop in Manhattan, where he spent much of his time when he was in New York on business—and how he'd spend hundreds of dollars on books. Once he'd had to buy a second suitcase to bring home all his purchases.

Then, against the rules, they'd spend time in his room with the door closed, watching TV.

And after a time, not watching TV.

They did, however, leave the set on, and volume high, to cover up the sounds they didn't want the other residents or staff in Silver Hills to hear.

Together they came up with a plan to find out if Martin and Emily were homicidal.

Their plan was that John would act more and more infirm and Carmen would seem receptive to Martin's subtle suggestions of a mercy killing. If nephew truly cared for uncle, he'd do whatever was necessary to save him—MRI scans, medication, working with him at their home. If he wanted the trust fund, Martin would go for the overdose.

He'd been saddened, but not surprised, when Martin and Emily chose the latter.

What were the next steps?

Late one night, Carmen and John found themselves lying in bed after an exhilarating, if exhausting, hour or so. She had put her hand on his chest and he could sense her anger.

"What we going to do? They want to kill you."

"The police?"

She'd laughed. "Ah, pointless. They do nothing. And Martin and that bitch of his, they try again. They want your money. They are desperate."

Neither spoke for a minute.

"There is one thing," Carmen said coyly.

"No."

Carmen said, "You know, in old days, on the street. We hear some *chulo* going to move on someone, we move first."

"That's crazy. No."

But then another thought came into John's head. But he then remembered a book that had been recommended to John years ago by the owner of The Mysterious Bookshop. It was a slim volume, a noir mystery by James M. Cain: *Double Indemnity.*

It was about murder and an insurance scam.

The plot was different from these circumstances, but the story inspired John to come up with a plan that made the murder of his nephew a bit more palatable. Martin had a two-million-dollar life insurance policy.

Hm. John had loved teaching but he hadn't been able to travel, to see exciting places, to be pampered on a professor's salary. And, though the cancer was gone, he didn't know how much time he had left (who ever did, of course?).

He had kissed her head and said, "Well, *if* anything happened to Martin, Emily would get the insurance. And if somebody could make it look like she did it . . . well, that somebody could talk her into giving them some of the insurance, or she'd be reported to the cops."

"No."

"No?" John had asked.

"That somebody could talk her into giving them *all* the insurance."

"That's a better idea." He'd then stroked her soft shoulder. "But how would something happen to him."

"I take care of that."

"No."

"I tell Mr. Martin that I know about taking lives. He thought I mean acts of mercy. I meant acts of survival. On the street. No *chulo* gangbanger suspect a pretty, round Latina, come up behind him and, bang."

John supposed he should be shocked, but he wasn't. He said, "You're only round in the right places."

Now, she kissed him. "Somebody try to hurt my man, they go down." Her eyes shone fiercely.

"You be careful?"

"I know how do these things."

"And no pain."

"No, no pain." Then Carmen added, "But one thing."

"What?"

"*Por favor,*" she whispered. "We do one more time?" She flung the sheet away, exposing her voluptuous form.

At a certain age you were wise not to miss any opportunities for one more time.

He kissed her hard and pulled her close.

And so the plan unfolded. John had pretended to grow worse and worse. Dementia, Alzheimer's. Who knew? But a knowing look from Carmen to Martin conveyed the idea that she might be willing to put him out of his misery.

And John's nephew took the bait.

Carmen returned to her old neighborhood and bought a stolen gun from a man in the Latin Kings gang.

And she paid a visit to Martin Niles in the parking lot behind his office.

Bang . . .

She parked outside of Silver Hills Home. John would pack his things and check out of the place, and go home with Carmen tonight. They were going to decorate for Christmas.

Then tomorrow they were going to a magistrate and get married. He'd proposed to her a week ago in an appropriate way: spelling out WILL YOU MARRY ME in circled letters on the bingo cards from the entertainment room at Silver Hills.

Her response, also on a card, was *Sí, Sí, Sí.*

The next day, they would travel to New York City for their honeymoon.

As they walked to the office, John said, "And on Friday we're going downtown. Near Wall Street."

"Oh, what is there?"

"It's the Christmas Party I told you I wanted to take you to."

She frowned. "Oh, I though you meant at Silver Hills."

"No, no. This is much better. It's a wonderful bookstore. Where I buy all my murder mysteries."

"*Sí*! I know you like those stories."

"It's the one I told you about: Mysterious Bookshop."

"But is better than the party at Silver Hills?"

"It's quite a bit better."

Her face slipped into a sexy pout. "But will they have cookies and cocoa?"

"I don't know. But there's a place where we can get them afterward."

"Where is that?"

John leaned forwards and whispered, "The hotel. Room service."

"That is even better." And she kissed him hard.

HERE WE COME A-WASSAILING

Thomas Perry

It was a snowy Christmas Eve in New York, and Nat Kasper had been on a book tour for two weeks trying to persuade people to buy his new courtroom novel, *Trial Balloon*. He lived far away in California, where snow was safely confined to resorts above 6,000 feet and didn't bother people who didn't bother it. But here he was, on the 24th of December, walking up Warren Street with his leather-soled dress shoes pressing perfect prints of themselves in four-inch snow.

The publicity people at Cognoscenti Books had told him there was a sweet spot on the calendar that suited Nat

Kasper books perfectly. The spot was the two weeks before and the week after Christmas. Their reasoning was that the giant bestsellers written by the titans of popular literature dominated the period from November 1 until December 20. They were stacked by all the cash registers, and the paperback versions of the titans' past books dominated the display tables. The people who bought just the right in-fashion book for a Christmas present often bought extras for themselves and others, and they did it early.

Nat Kasper wasn't a titan. He was a midlist crime writer. That may once have been an honorable designation, but in the twenty-first century it had become a sad burden to bear. Nat toured the country when nobody else was touring. The only celebrity writers who were traveling were on their way to their houses on Maui for an old-fashioned Christmas, or to Provence for an older-fashioned Christmas with their fourth wives, their third set of children, and first set of grandchildren.

Nat had reached the two-thirds point in his book tour, and he was eager to reach The Mysterious Bookshop at number 58 Warren Street. The proprietor was his old friend Otto Penzler, and as Nat reached the door and tried to open it while his feet slipped like skates on the freezing snow, he could see Otto's trim white hair and beard glowing from across the shop. Otto was talking with a male writer and two female writers. Nat knew them by sight, and felt slightly jealous that they were better known than he was and drawing everyone's attention from his own grand arrival. This reminded him that there was no exclusivity to being a friend of Otto's. Everybody who could write a grammatical sentence about violent death was a friend of Otto's.

He saw Otto spot him and stride across the room.

"Nat!" he called. "You're right on time. I was just saying how terrific your new book is. Can you sign a couple of copies right away? John, Meg, and Lisa are all leaving for a party."

"I'd be happy to," Nat said, and then realized his face felt funny. He was smiling. He had strained his face muscles in the past two weeks smiling, and now they seized up whenever he did it. He produced a pen from his coat pocket and signed with as much of a flourish as his writer's cramp would allow. "I hope you like it," he said.

"I know we will," said Meg. "Otto wouldn't squander his reputation on a bad book."

He wondered if he should say something about their latest books, *Uncooked Prey*, *Tarnished Notions*, and *Unspeaking Accuser*, but he couldn't think of a way to compliment three writers at a time, so he simply waved as they left the store.

Otto conducted Nat to the side table where there were bottles of white wine on ice, soft drinks and water bottles for customers, and then to a table where stacks of *Trial Balloon* waited to be signed.

This was the kind of signing that almost convinced Nat that the Cognoscenti Press publicists were correct. People were standing in line to buy the books he signed. Many of them talked to him, and quite a few wanted books personalized to a gift recipient: "To Audrey, with Christmas wishes." "To Nana, from your loving granddaughter Louise." Attention was confusing to a midlist writer.

During a lull, Otto came back to chat while Nat signed. "How has the tour been going?"

"The way it always does. They start you in the Pacific zone, then fly you to the Mountain zone, then the Central zone, then Eastern. Each night the hotel kitchen is closed when you get there and doesn't open until after you leave in the morning. Each day your five a.m. cab comes an hour earlier, and pretty soon you're falling asleep in bookstores."

"Why do you do it?"

"The publicists worked it out scientifically. The temperature, humidity, and the length of daylight between December 14 and January 7 are perfectly suited to the mood of my books—a little melancholy and wistful, with the occasional spark of violence and loss. What I really think is that they figure out the most dangerous time to fly, and send out the author they can most afford to lose."

"Well, it's Christmas Eve, so stay awake long enough to celebrate. It's a fine book and we'll sell as many as we can before we close at six, and then sell out next week when we open again."

Nat Kasper hoped Otto was right, but a midlist writer had to live on decades of hope to receive moments of joy. When the strange, hectic period of touring was over, Nat would be back at the desk in his lonely house writing a couple of pages a day for another whole year. But as he signed, his mood brightened. The cheerful faces of the bookstore customers made him happy.

At just after six the bookstore staff began clearing the unsold copies away. It had been a good afternoon, so there weren't many left. Kasper wasn't sure why. Maybe his readers were the sort of people who did things at the last minute, as he was. Then Otto reappeared.

"Nat, I'm sorry, but I've got to leave now if I'm going to make it to a party on time. This one was planned months ago. I've got to put on black tie, and there's a present problem. I ordered a rare first edition that hasn't come, so I have to find another gift for the host and hostess. I'm glad you're doing so well, and I'll see you when the next book comes out."

They shook hands and Nat said, "Don't worry. I'm pretty tired, and looking forward to getting back to my hotel. Thanks for everything." He looked around him. "I'd like to use the restroom before I go. Is that okay?"

"Sure. Right in there. Merry Christmas. The staff will lock up and get you a cab."

Nat went into the restroom. As he was coming out he passed the stack of unsold books, and stopped to count them. There were only twelve left. He was pleased. He stepped out into the shop. The lights were out.

"Hello?" he called. No answer. He tried the front door, then called, "I'm still here. Can you let me out?" There was a second helping of silence. He laughed. Christmas in New York. It would make a funny story to tell when he got home. He surveyed the walls of books in the dim light with pleasure. He spotted books he'd read and admired. He was reluctant to call Otto right after he'd said he was in a hurry, but he saw no alternative. He took out his phone.

On the screen was a tweet. It said, "Mr. Kasper, I just read the announcement from the bookstore and saw your signing ends at six. I'm a huge fan, and I'm on my way, not far from The Mysterious Bookshop. Please hold the door for me. Ashley Tate."

He tweeted back, "If you're not actually in transit, don't bother to come out in the snow and cold. I'm sorry, but the signing is over."

Nat was about to send it, when he heard a loud knock on the door. He walked toward it, and as he did, a woman moved to the front window. She was small and appeared to be in her mid-thirties, with long, chestnut-colored hair. She was carrying a large shopping bag that looked heavy.

She shaded her eyes with her mittened hand against the window. "I can hardly see you. Why are you in the dark?"

"They closed up and locked me in by accident."

She threw her head back and laughed. "That's hilarious. In *The Post-Modernist Post*, Zane Anderson uses a bobby pin and the screwdriver from an eyeglass repair kit to pick the lock on a door. Why don't you?"

"That was fiction," he said. "And I don't have either of those things."

"I do." She hung her shopping bag on the door, took off her mittens, reached into her small shoulder bag, and produced a small clear plastic case with tiny tools and a magnifying glass. She touched the back of her head and pulled out a bobby pin. She pushed open the mail slot in the door.

Nat accepted the two items, touching her thin, graceful fingers accidentally. He had no expertise in locksmithing.

He wrote crime novels because he knew what heroes would do, but didn't know how to do anything useful himself. But he had read enough to know he should use the bobby pin as a tension wrench and rake the tumblers with the tiny screwdriver pick.

To his utter shock, the lock clicked. He turned the bolt and Ashley Tate charged in, smiling. "You're amazing!" She set her bag down and hugged him, then picked it up, took his arm and pulled him toward the signing table.

Nat's mind was a jumble of thoughts competing for priority. He wondered why Otto didn't have an alarm. Or maybe he did, but an employee in a hurry had left it off so he could get out. Ashley Tate flipped a light switch and he saw her clearly. Everything else dissolved.

She set the bag on the table and took out a bakery box. "I brought a few things. This is a *somloi galuska*." She opened the box to reveal the chocolate-covered dumpling cake. "But I don't have to tell you. It's what Helena bakes for Dan Crain on the night in Budapest when they consummate their love in *The Comprehenders*."

"Wow," he said, which was close to speechless as he had ever been.

"I had them use your recipe from the book, so it should be authentic."

"I got it off the Internet. I don't know how to—"

She was relentless. "You *selected* it off the Internet. You knew exactly which cake would be the right one." Next she pulled out a bottle of amber liquid. "And you can guess what this is."

"I can?"

"It's what they drink—a 1962 Bertinollet XO Cognac."

He gasped. "Oh, my gosh, Ashley. Do you have any idea what that costs?"

"Of course I do. I bought it, silly."

He looked around in a panic, but saw no help anywhere.

"Don't worry," she said. "I brought the glasses too."

"Don't open it. You can get a refund. That was just a book. I looked up the best, most expensive cognac that was for sale, and just shoved it into Helena and Dan's night. It was fiction."

"I know that, Nat. Don't worry. I can afford it." Then Ashley Tate was stalking along the floor-to-ceiling bookshelves. "I love bookstores. There are the K's. Oh, look. They have a lot of your books. *The Ingrates*, *Cordite in Corsica*, *Ambivalanche*, *The*—"

"That's Otto. If he believes in your work, he's committed."

"I have them all," she said. "You know what I'd like to do?"

"No."

"Sit together on that couch over there, serve each other some *somloi galuska*, drink some cognac, and read from *The Comprehenders* together. I'll do the girl parts."

"I should hope so," Nat said.

Ashley pulled two copies of the book from the shelf and handed him one. "It will go with the refreshments. Let's start on page 184."

He opened the book and scanned. "Uh, some of this might be a little uh, embarrassing."

"This isn't our first reading, Nat. You wrote it, revised it, and read the proofs, and I've read it seventeen times. Come on."

He looked down at the page and took a breath. "He saw Helena appear in the doorway, her long chestnut hair loose and—" There was the faint wail of sirens, and they seemed to be growing louder.

"Police!" she said.

"Damn," he whispered. "There must be a silent alarm. Otto, you devious—of course he would be devious. He reads about crime every day. We've got to get out of here before the cops arrive."

Ashley stuffed things back into her bag while Nat stepped to the wall, put the two books back on the shelf, and turned the lights off. As he went to the front door, she said, "No. Let's go out the back."

They ran to the fire door, pushed the crash bar, and stepped outside. The steel door slammed behind them, and he looked at her. "You have the cognac, right?"

"No. I got the cake and the glasses. I thought you had the bottle."

"Oh, no," he said. He tried the door, but it had locked behind them.

The sirens were loud now, and then they stopped. Car doors opened and red and blue lights flashed along the walls of nearby buildings.

A cop yelled, "Who's in there? Come out with your hands up."

Ashley tugged his arm and whispered, "Come on. Forget the cognac." She began to run and he ran with her. They went around the corner and ran four blocks before she stopped.

Nat said, "Where are we going?"

"My place." She pointed to a high-rise building with large windows and balconies. They dashed to it, pushed through a pair of glass doors, and were intercepted by a huge doorman who seemed to have inherited his uniform from Mad King Rudolph.

"Merry Christmas, Mrs. Tate."

"And Merry Christmas to you, Mr. Torvaldson."

Torvaldson hit the elevator button. "By the way, thank you for the gift, ma'am. It was extremely generous, as usual."

"Great. Enjoy." Ashley stepped into the elevator and hit the 17 button. The doors rolled shut and the car rose. She looked at Nat Kasper. "What's wrong?"

"A couple of things. I'm sick about leaving the cognac."

"There are other bottles of cognac. I have some upstairs."

"And Mrs. Tate."

"I had a husband. He was a 'Get Rich or Die' guy. And he did."

She stepped out of the elevator through the hallway into the next room and brought back a bottle of Bertinollet 1959 cognac and her copy of *The Comprehenders*. She took the glasses and the cake from her shopping bag, pulled the stopper on the bottle, and poured. Then she moved to one of the couches in her opulent living room and sat. She patted the cushion beside her. "We were on page 184."

Nat joined her and they shared her copy. Ashley read Helena's part exactly as he had imagined it.

Otto's car pulled up near the police cars parked at angles in front of his store. He got out, stared at the police officers in his brightly lighted windows, went to the door and said, "I'm Otto Penzler. I got a call that there was a break-in."

The cop with sergeant's stripes said, "Sergeant Bronsky. They haven't torn the place apart, but you should take a close look and see what's missing."

Otto stepped in and walked around his store, looking at the floor-to ceiling shelves where the collection of crime fiction resided. He knew exactly what a smart crook would take, what might tempt a novice, and all of the places a criminal would look. He said, "I don't see anything missing."

"Good," said Bronsky. "We got here in time. We've been waiting for a particular pair of burglars to hit someplace tonight. They've been busy this Christmas season. They broke into an antique store two nights ago, and when the owner turned out to still be in the back of the shop, they killed him with his own cavalry sword. There's a big reward, so if you see anything, call us."

"Are you sure we had a break-in?"

"The alarm went off and the front door was unlocked."

"I didn't lock up myself. I wonder if my staff all thought somebody else was doing it, and left it unlocked." He shrugged. "Well, thanks, guys. I'll make sure to lock it right and reset the alarm. Merry Christmas."

"Here's my business card," said Sergeant Bronsky. "Call if you find anything missing or out of place later." The four cops filed out.

Otto was upset. First the rare volume he had ordered for his host and hostess, his friends Simon Worth and Maria Cervantes Worth, had gone astray somewhere over the Atlantic. And because of the burglary or false alarm, he was going to be late.

As he headed for the door, he passed the signing table and saw the unfamiliar bottle. Was that cognac? He read the label. Bertinollet XO Cognac 1962? Where had that come from? Nat Kasper. It had to be. This was an extravagant gift. Otto woke up the computer by the register and googled the brand name. The first entry was "On Sale, only $3,999 until Christmas." When he typed in the date 1962 he saw lots of "not available," "not in stock," and "please correct your request" responses.

Otto thought for a moment. The stores were closed now, so there was no question of buying a gift. He had to have something to give his hosts at Christmas. They were dear friends he'd known since he had arrived in New York some decades ago. They were also connoisseurs of fine food and drink. He took the bottle, set the alarm, locked the door, and left.

When Otto reached the Worth apartment on Sutton Place he handed the bottle to Simon and kissed Maria. "The present I'd planned for you hasn't arrived, but this is something I thought you two might try together on Christmas day."

The Worths recognized the label. "Thank you, Otto. What a wonderful gift. Your present is under the tree with the others, and we'll give them all out in a little while."

The party was already lively, full of voices loud with seasonal cheer, and Otto joined the crowd of authors, publishers, agents, book collectors, and friends.

After a few minutes, Maria and Simon headed into the kitchen from opposite ends on the same errand—to bring out the next trays of refreshments. They met at the kitchen island, and Maria whispered, "The party is going great. Maybe they can play without supervision for a few minutes while we try that cognac that Otto brought."

They stepped into the pantry where Simon opened the bottle and poured two small snifters. They each sniffed and sipped a few times. "What a wonderful idea this was," Simon said. When they had emptied the two glasses, Simon set the bottle and snifters on the top shelf of the pantry where only he could reach them.

As they emerged from the pantry, Doris Whittaker, the very British historical mystery writer known for *Halberds at Holyhead*, *Cuirassiers at Cornwall*, and the rest of the timeless series, was walking into the kitchen. "So that's where you two are hiding," she said. She held out two narrow black velvet boxes with red ribbons. "These are for you. I'm forced to produce suspense all year long and I'm sick of it, so I'll tell you. They're watches. There's no present like the time, as they say."

They both looked in the boxes. "They're beautiful," said Simon.

"Lovely," said Maria. "Thank you so much. Your present is upstairs instead of under the tree because it's special. I'll bring it down in a few minutes. But don't show it to anyone, because it's the only one, and there would be hurt feelings."

"All right," said Doris. "I'll be out there merrymaking. You always have the best people." She walked out to the living room.

Simon said to Maria, "Please tell me you weren't making that up about the gift."

"Lying through my teeth. When she didn't reply to the invitation, I thought she wasn't coming."

"So did I." He opened the narrow box in his hand and read, "Piaget. Damn."

"We have to do something. We have the cognac."

"But we drank some."

"It's corked and sealed with wax. We can fill it up again and recork it, can't we?"

"Okay," he said. "We don't have any cognac. We'll use brandy."

"I just poured the last of the brandy for Wally Bostwick."

"Scotch, then. At least the color will be close."

They closed themselves into the pantry again and he took down the cognac. He poured in some scotch and swirled it. She tried it. "No. Too peaty. Needs a fruity undertone. What else do we have?"

"Grand Marnier?" He poured some of that in, then tasted it. "That's better. It will have to do." He pushed in the cork, carefully fitted the ring of wax onto it, and handed it to Maria.

"You're a master criminal," she said. "I'll slip it to Dora." She went out into the crowd, keeping the bottle lying sideways under a linen napkin, and pulled Dora into the hall.

When she removed the napkin Dora looked at the label. "Brilliant," she said. "Merry Christmas to me. I'll think of you two when I open it." she paused to kiss Maria's cheek. "I'm afraid I have to be off, though. I'm like Santa, flying from house to house all of Christmas Eve. I want to thank you for inviting me, but I'm expected elsewhere."

Dora Whittaker took a cab to her apartment so she could leave the gifts she'd received that were weighing down her bag and load up the next lot that she was planning to deliver at the next party. As she took out her gifts, she lingered over the cognac bottle that the Worths had given her. She was beginning to feel tired, her feet hurt, and here was the elixir that would get her through this joyous, exhausting night.

She went into her kitchen, found a juice glass, and poured herself two fingers of the Bertinollet. The bouquet was heavenly, but the taste had a bite that she wasn't used to in a fine old cognac. Still, the cognac was delicious, warming, and relaxing. She felt almost ready for the next party as soon as the glass was empty. Dora returned to her stockpile of presents and found the next batch. As she refilled her bag, her phone rang. She fished it out of her purse. "Dora here."

"Dora, this is Robert Nolan. I'm in my car downstairs. Can I just run up and give you my Christmas present?"

"Crap!" she thought. "Sure, come right up," she said aloud. But instead of buzzing him in she ran to the kitchen, hid her glass in the dishwasher, and considered what to use to refill the cognac bottle. She knew that what was missing were a few of the complex fruity notes that came from the distillation process. Who the hell knew what error a distiller had made in 1962? At the time, she had been in a trailer park in Arizona, which she always told people was a girls' school in Scotland. Dora added an ounce of apple juice, shook the bottle to mix it, re-corked it, and smoothed the wax around the cork. Her phone was ringing again, so she ran to the panel by the door and buzzed Robert in. That left her enough time to tie some red ribbon around the neck of the bottle and stick a sprig of holly under it before he arrived.

Robert Nolan was her U.S. publisher, a kind, supportive, and wonderful man who also provided about three quarters of Dora's income. When she let him in, he had in his beefy hand a small box that could only hold a piece of jewelry. She said, "Sorry, Robert. I love you but I promised my mother I wouldn't marry a safecracker or a publisher."

He said, "It's not a ring, Dora, it's a brooch. I knew you were leaving for the U.K. in two days, so this was my last chance to get this to you."

She took it and looked inside the box at a small white gold hand wearing a ruby and emerald bracelet and holding a pen. She thanked him and handed him the bottle of Bertinollet XO. He opened his mouth and forgot to close it for a few seconds. "Dora, this is so kind of you."

"You deserve it because you're the one who will appreciate it most." They hugged. A minute later they rode the elevator down together and got into their cars.

Robert Nolan recited the next address to his driver and held on while the man pressed the gas pedal and roared up the street. Nolan had hired the limo for the evening because he knew he'd be going from house to house, friend to friend, and he also knew that drinks would be served. For the first time, he noticed that there was a small console in the spacious back section of the limo. When he opened it he saw liquor bottles in a row. In the drawer below it, there were several highball glasses.

His next stop was quite far, so he felt tempted to open the cognac. He said, "Can you keep the limo steady for the next few minutes?"

"Sure," said the driver, so Nolan set a glass in the cup holder and poured a bit of the cognac. He lifted it to his nose, smelled the bouquet and then drank. It was excellent, except for an overly sweet note of apple. He poured himself another dose and tried it again, but because even a small quantity of liquor imperceptibly dulls taste, he decided he had imagined the apple flavor.

In fifteen minutes the limousine pulled up in front of the New York apartment of Pierre Masciotti, the president of the Global Overreach Group, which had recently gobbled up the old and respected publishing house where Nolan was publisher. He said to his driver, "I may not be in there very long, so don't park too far away." He took an armload of presents and climbed out.

He entered the lobby, and Pierre Masciotti's assistant, Gabriella Zandi, was there as greeter. She had a clipboard and used a Mont Blanc pen to put a checkmark by his name.

"Mr. Nolan," she said. "Nice to see you."

Nolan handed her a small gift-wrapped box and said, "Merry Christmas, Gabriella."

Her eyes widened. "You shouldn't have." As he stepped into the elevator past her, she leaned close and gave him a peck on the cheek. She whispered, "And you're the only one who did. They all think I'm the boss's spy."

He said, "The others just don't know you yet. They're shy."

He rode up to the penthouse, got out of the elevator, and stepped into a scene of chaos. A group of guests in tuxedos and long dresses milled around, and the host, Pierre Masciotti, was kneeling on the floor, where the six foot four inch frame of Bronhilde Fleindorf, the literary lioness of western Europe, was lying on a Persian rug breathing into a brown paper bag that Masciotti held over her face.

Nolan knelt too, and Masciotti looked up and saw him. "Robert! Bronhilde tripped on the edge of the rug and now she's having a panic attack."

Nolan was alarmed. Only a month ago he'd read her *Zwanzig Elstern im Baum*—*Twenty Magpies in a Tree*, as it was called in translation.

Masciotti said to one of the crowd of anxious guests, "Here, hold onto the bag for her. Keep her calm." A woman Nolan didn't know took his place, and Masciotti pulled him aside.

"Robert, we almost had her. She seemed interested in letting us handle her world publishing contracts. The woman is a Nobel Prize winner, and readers love her. We can't let this opportunity slip."

Nolan said, "I'll see what I can do." He ran to the elevator, dashed outside to his limo, and got inside. He said, "This liquor back here. Is it for sale?"

"On a 'You open it, you bought it' basis," said the driver. "Take what you want, and we'll settle later."

Nolan took a bottle of gin and poured an inch of it into the Cognac bottle, re-sealed the cognac, took a fresh glass, and hurried upstairs to the party. He knelt beside the recumbent form of Bronhilde Fleindorf, poured her a half inch of the precious liquid, looked at her again, recalibrated, and poured another couple of inches. He held the bottle with its label toward her, gently pushed aside the paper bag, and held the glass up to her lips. He spoke quietly. "This is the best medicine I know for problems like yours, Fraulein. I'm subject to panic attacks myself, and a fine cognac is the answer."

Within five minutes, the great novelist Bronhilde Flein-dorf was sitting comfortably in an armchair, and within ten she was up again, regaling a knot of favored people with her wit and charm.

Masciotti whispered, "You saved us, Robert," and in a blatant display of his European origins, hugged him.

Nolan turned to the chair where he had left his gifts and handed one to Masciotti. "Merry Christmas, Pierre." After that Nolan took the rest of the presents around and gave them to his friends and colleagues. He had a wonderful time at the party, and the fate of the bottle of cognac slipped his mind.

A part-time bar helper named Dave had noticed the bottle and slipped it into a case of wine behind the bar. When the bar stopped serving, Dave carried the case out to the van and extracted the cognac bottle. Bronhilde Fleindorf had drunk about four inches of it. Dave decided that what it needed was something alcoholic but neutral so the taste wouldn't be ruined. He poured in some Chernobyl Strength vodka, which was 177 proof and 94% alcohol, replenished the vodka with water, then carefully re-capped both bottles. When he picked up his girlfriend he gave the cognac to her father, who had never really liked him.

The father drank some of the bottle of cognac, got curious about it, looked it up online, and saw the price. He read in an article that it was supposed to taste like peach cooked over an open fire. The article also said that it was aged in oak barrels and had notes of spice, wood, and leather. He built a fire in the hibachi on his balcony using pieces of oak from an old oak desk, cooked a couple of peaches, squeezed them for their juice, strained it through the buckle holes in an old leather belt, and added it. To counteract the fruitiness, he laced it with 151 rum. Then he re-corked the bottle, heated the wax to seal it, and offered it for sale on eBay. A buyer came to pick it up a half hour later.

The cognac continued across the city. Along the way, five additional recipients who needed to pass it on looked up the proper taste for it and added vanilla, spiced liqueurs, juice of white grapes, caramel, powdered nuts, pear nectar, brandy, and cask-strength 125 proof bourbon.

Just as the Christmas Eve parties were winding down, the cognac reached the home of Whitley Grandview in East Hampton, a gift from his neighbor, Willa Radford Montrose. At approximately two a.m., the Grandview house was visited by two men named Simms and Davis, who made their living stealing things. They rewired Grandview's alarm system to bypass his front door, stepped inside, and stole his famous collection of antique gold coins. As they passed by the great room, they paused under the Christmas tree and took a few promising-looking presents, among them the old bottle of cognac. Then they drove back into New York.

Earlier in the evening they had driven down Warren Street and observed the police presence and commotion at number 58. Simms said to Davis, "The last place I want to hit tonight is that bookstore. If it drew that many cops, there's something worth stealing in there."

Davis said, "What do you think could be in there that's worth anything? A Gutenberg Bible? It's a mystery bookstore."

"The cops and the owner were pretty serious about it. If they think it's full of valuable stuff, so do I."

They stopped a block away and parked. Simms put the cognac bottle in his coat pocket. "What's that for?" said Davis.

"Because 'tis the season to be jolly."

They walked to the bookstore. Simms used a glasscutter to remove the glass from the bathroom window and climbed inside, then pulled Davis in after him. The two searched the bookstore but found no books they wanted to steal. Instead they made a pile of computer equipment, telephones, and anything else with a plug. They found some plastic cups left over from Nat Kasper's signing, sat down, and opened the cognac. They were tired, this was their final stop, and it was Christmas Eve, so they poured liberally. They praised the unusual complexity of the flavor and scent of the cognac. Then they poured again and drank again.

They drank until the cognac was gone and they were incapable of climbing back out the high window carrying their loot. And then they fell asleep.

Just before dawn on Christmas morning, as Otto Penzler was on his way out of the city to his home in Connecticut, he stopped to check his store. As he walked up to the front door, he looked in the window and saw the two burglars fast asleep inside.

He took out his telephone and called the number on Sergeant Bronsky's card. He said, "This is Otto Penzler and I'm at my store. There are two burglars asleep in there."

Bronsky said, "I'm just about to go off duty, but hauling those two in would make my Christmas. Stay out of their sight, and we'll be there in about three minutes."

The events begun on Christmas Eve ended well. Sergeant Bronsky got his Christmas wish, which was to arrest the thieves who had murdered a victim. Nobody who received, adulterated, and passed the cognac on was caught at it. All of the friendships were preserved and enhanced by the unbroken chain of gift-giving.

Otto received a large reward from the City of New York for trapping the killer swillers. He filled the empty 1962 Bertinollet bottle with cognac from a $300 bottle, re-corked and re-sealed it so he could share it with Nat Kasper the following year when Nat was back to sign his next book.

Nat Kasper and Ashley Tate were married in late March in a Paris ceremony patterned after the one in Kasper's novel *The Winnowing*.

Robert Nolan was voted onto the board of directors of Global Overreach Group Unlimited, the parent company of his small publishing house.

Simon and Maria Worth's party was featured in the February issue of *American Home*, which made them famous for knowing a lot of smart people, and inspired a reality TV show about them.

Dora Whittaker was unmasked as a native of Arizona. The resulting notoriety triggered a late resurgence of her writing career, for which she became known as "The Phoenix of Phoenix." She published an Anglo-American bestseller called *Desperados in Tweed*.

And The Mysterious Bookshop demonstrated one more time that all of its mysteries were not confined between two covers.

A CHRISTMAS PUZZLE

Ragnar Jónasson

"Young man, can you help me solve a mystery?"

It was a week before Christmas and she was standing by the counter at The Mysterious Bookshop in New York.

"I'm sorry?"

He had a gentle smile and intelligent eyes.

"I just asked if you could help me solve a bit of a mystery."

"Are you looking for a book?" The bookshop specialized in mysteries, current as well as classics. "A particular title or author?"

"No, I have a mystery that needs solving. A sort of a puzzle. Nothing too complicated. I probably don't need more than half an hour of your time."

"Half an hour?" He looked at his watch. "We are closing in about ten minutes, and unfortunately I have to run, but . . ." Now he looked at her and then finally said: "I'm here again next week if you want to come back."

"That would be wonderful, thank you. I have all the time in the world. What day would that be?"

"Actually, the 24th. Is that OK? We close at noon that day, and it tends to be a bit busy with customers buying last-minute gifts, but I can probably spare fifteen minutes right after we close up."

"I think a man of your intelligence will solve this for me in fifteen minutes, so I will see you then, young man. Thank you so much."

It had been a difficult trip from her home all the way to the store. The subway was busy and the sidewalks were covered in snow. On a day like this, beautiful as it was, she certainly felt her age. She had turned eighty years old earlier this year. She hardly ever had to say it out loud—eighty—but the word didn't really ring true; it felt strange. It felt old, while she still felt quite young at heart. But the cold and the snow had a way of making her realize that she wasn't getting any younger, at least.

Many people seemed to be doing last-minute Christmas shopping, the subway was packed, the air was festive, and the city looked quite nice in the snow. The 24th was a prelude to Christmas, but in her mind the day meant a little bit more than that. She was born and raised in Iceland, daughter of an American father and an Icelandic mother, so she had grown up celebrating Christmas the Icelandic way. In Iceland, the 24th was the most important day of the Christmas holidays, when families gathered to listen to the Christmas mass on radio or in churches at six o'clock, followed by the holiday dinner and then the unwrapping of the presents. The tradition was one of giving books for Christmas, and people would sit down on Christmas Eve, perhaps by candlelight, and read new books into the night. That is how her love for books had started, and maybe that is why she had fallen in love with a book collector.

She didn't mind spending the day at the bookstore. In fact, she had looked forward to it, but tonight she would celebrate Christmas in her own way, cooking a lovely meal and reading into the night. Not necessarily a new book, but rather some old book from her late husband's library.

Her husband had certainly loved books with all his heart, and more or less lived—and died—through his love of golden age mysteries. He had started collecting at an early age, born and raised in New York in the 1930s, literally breathing the air of the golden age as a young boy without perhaps realizing that until later.

She had moved to the United States in her twenties, when her parents had decided a change of scenery was necessary. She had finished her university studies in New York, majoring in art, and she had met her husband a few years after her graduation. This was in the early sixties. He had been ten years older than she was, but it was an immediate match. Love at first sight was too much of a cliché for her, but in a way, it had been a wonderful New York romance.

Their friends were now disappearing almost by the day, old age catching up with them, and all of a sudden she found herself all alone more than six months after her husband's passing. He had been close to ninety, but she had been certain he still had some good years to go. He had always been quite healthy and she had imagined that they would enjoy their twilight years to the fullest, despite the age, traveling, reading, enjoying culture, and relaxing in their lovely brownstone house in the city. They had been fans of the theater and the opera—no shortage of cultural opportunities in such a cosmopolitan town.

Their true love, though, had always been reading. Of course, neither of them had ever managed to read through their immense library of first edition crime fiction, but in spite of that, they had kept buying new books regularly, enjoying discovering new voices.

She had introduced to him the tradition of giving a new book for Christmas, but this year there would be no new book, no presents. She had no one to give books to, and no one gave her any presents. Well, instead she had already picked out a classic from the 1930s that she hadn't yet read, a New York-set Philo Vance mystery.

She walked the final steps towards the bookstore in the snow. She was quite far away from home, the other side of Manhattan, but in the presence of so many books, she would most certainly feel at home. There were some ornamental snowflakes in the windows, as well as stacks of the latest titles, and when she walked into the store she was greeted by a lovely looking Christmas tree. There was even a smell of cinnamon in the air, surprising at first, until she noticed the large scented candle burning on the counter. And there he was, the young man, with a smile on his face. There wasn't a single customer in the store.

"I'm sorry, I am a bit early," she said in her most apologetic voice.

"Oh, never mind. It has been a fairly quiet day. I'll be closing in five minutes. It's the weather, I guess."

"Or the fact that people just don't appreciate books the way they used to," she replied.

"Well, I certainly hope that is not the reason." He smiled again.

"I'll just browse a bit, if you don't mind, and then we can sit down once the store has been closed."

"Perfect."

"I can perhaps make us two cups of coffee, if you want. I need something warm and strong to get rid of the winter chill, to be honest," she said.

"Well, yes, why not? We have a coffee maker back there." He pointed towards a door at the far end of the store.

"Lovely," she said, and walked slowly over to the back, breathing in the scent of the old books lining the walls. Bookstores most certainly were the closest thing to heaven.

❉

"Have you just started working here?" she asked, and had a sip of her coffee.

They were sitting by the counter. He had arranged an extra chair for her and seemed ready and willing to help, although she felt that he would perhaps not want to spend too much of this festive day with a stranger. He was still quite polite, though, and she certainly didn't plan to spend more than half an hour there. He looked clever enough to be able to solve the mystery fairly quickly.

"Actually, yes, just this December. It's a temporary gig, unless things change. I love books, and I was out of work, and one of their permanent employees had to take a few months' leave."

"Are you enjoying this proximity to books, day in, day out?"

"Absolutely. It's perfect."

"I can imagine," she said, trying to keep the irony out of her tone.

"So, you said there was a mystery to solve? A puzzle?" he asked, and now she sensed he was perhaps slightly impatient.

"Yes, indeed, and I am quite out of my depth, to be honest. I found it in my late husband's documents, and I have been trying to solve it, without any success so far. It has something to do with mysteries, you see, crime fiction . . . That is all I know. And it's been preying on my mind this month because it is a festive puzzle."

"A festive puzzle?"

"Yes."

She opened her purse and brought out a folded, crumpled piece of paper.

"A Christmas Puzzle. That's what he wrote as heading on the page," she said, presenting the young man with the page. He unfolded it and laid it gently on the table.

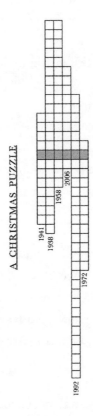

"Well, it's a crossword puzzle, of sorts, yes?"

"Yes, in a way. My husband—my late husband, that is—was a fan of crime fiction and crossword puzzles, and especially some of the old books where these two elements were combined. That has largely fallen out of fashion now, but it's a charming thought, isn't it?"

"It certainly is." He looked carefully at the paper. "You see, it's just numbers, and empty spaces. And the shaded area is presumably the clue, or a key word which we are looking for."

"Numbers, yes," he said, thoughtfully. "Years, no doubt."

"Yes. I know. But these years mean nothing to me. My only guess is that they refer to books, you know. Year of publication."

"Yes. Well, we shouldn't have too much trouble with this."

He regarded the puzzle intensely, counting the empty spaces and making notes on a side paper.

"Well. This is interesting," he said at last, drinking from his cup of coffee.

"Yes, interesting and complex," she replied. "Too complex? I really don't want to keep you for too long. It's Christmas, after all."

"Christmas is coming, that's for sure, but we'll do this in no time. It's the most fun I've had today, to be honest. A slow day at the shop, as I said."

He looked at the paper again and then said, reading from the puzzle and his notes:

"1941, twelve letters. 1938, twenty-three letters. 1958, eighteen letters. 2006—that's quite recent—eleven letters. 1992, thirty-one letters. And 1972—fourteen letters."

"Not all golden age, then," she said after a moment's silence.

"Absolutely not. I'm sure some of the regular staff here could solve this without even consulting the computer, or our shelves, for that matter."

"Anything that comes to mind, right away?"

"Well, Agatha Christie, of course. That seems obvious."

"Which one?"

"I would imagine that *Hercule Poirot's Christmas* needs to be here. I can't remember the year of publication, but it is . . ." He wrote the title down and counted the letters. "Yes, twenty-three letters. It fits the second line, so I'll bet it was published in 1938. Let me look it up."

He turned to the store computer.

"It is a bit slow, so bear with me," he said, tapping the keyboard.

She smiled. "Absolutely. I am in no hurry. I just need to get this right."

He smiled back. "I understand," he said, but the look on his face told a slightly different story, pity for the old woman perhaps, that this strange crossword puzzle was the highlight of her day.

Of course, she couldn't expect him to understand. "I'm sure it's that one, the Christmas one about Poirot," she said, to break the silence, previously filled with only the humming of the old computer. "It's a lovely book, I read it years ago but I've never forgotten it. The identity of the murderer was so cleverly concealed."

"Hard to disagree there," he replied.

"Sometimes it's like that. You never know in those old mysteries. The killer is the one you would never suspect, yes?"

"Definitely, that's . . . Oh, sorry, here it is. Yes, 1938, of course. So, one down, five to go." He looked at his watch, perhaps quietly calculating in his mind how long the rest of the puzzle would take at the same rate.

"That gives us an O," she said in her most pleasant manner.

"O? I'm sorry . . . I . . . ?"

"In the crossword puzzle, we use the first O in Poirot's name for our keyword," she said, then adding: "I do love a good game."

"Yes, that's true. All in the spirit of the holiday season, I guess."

"Anything else that springs to mind?" she asked, looking at the puzzle.

He didn't reply right away. "Well . . . Not really. And you?"

"I'm not really good with names and years, to be honest. But I've read a lot of mysteries, so I might have read everything there, who knows? I was hoping you could point me in the right direction."

"Well, let's give it a go. Maybe it's all from the golden age, how about we start there?"

"That is an excellent starting point, I must say."

"Dorothy L. Sayers," he said, more to himself than to her.

"Well, I do remember reading a Christmas story of hers," she said. "A missing pearl necklace, I think. Definitely a Christmas setting. I wonder if that's one of those?"

"*The Necklace of Pearls*, actually. But it's a short story, not a novel."

"Ah, yes, unlikely then. How many letters?"

Again, he counted.

"Nineteen."

"No, that doesn't work."

"Ngaio Marsh?"

"Another great one," she said, nodding in agreement. "Well, I actually read one of hers as well, set at Christmas. And that one *was* a full-length novel. Quite good."

"Very good, yes. Very atmospheric, lots and lots of snow," he said. "It's called *Tied Up in Tinsel*."

"Does that one fit, do you think?"

"Well, it was a late Marsh, so maybe this one, the 1972 one . . ."

Now she counted the letters out loud: "*Tied Up in Tinsel*, one, two . . . eight, nine . . . thirteen, fourteen, yes, wonderful. Fourteen!"

"Let me double check the publication date. We'll breeze through this, it seems."

This time around the computer appeared to be working better.

"1972 it is," he said.

"And that's an E."

He was still staring at the computer screen.

"I'm wondering if we can perhaps do a bit of cheating. I know, fair play is essential and all that, but we have the bookstore database at our disposal here . . ."

"Well, what do you propose, young man?"

She noticed that outside it had started snowing. Hopefully this wonderful weather would keep into the night. This reminded her of childhood Christmas celebrations in Iceland, where there was never any lack of snow in wintertime. And, even more appropriately, this reminded her of the first Christmas Eve she had spent with her late husband.

"This is lovely," she commented, pointing to the falling snow.

The man shrugged his shoulders. "I guess. I'm not really the festive type."

"I see."

"But, on the puzzle at hand, I was thinking, what if we search our database for the word 'Christmas?' "

She smiled. "I like the idea. That should get us near the finish line."

It took a while for him to deliver the results.

"*A Maigret Christmas and Other Short Stories?*"

"Simenon. Hardly, if it's a short story collection," she said.

"*The Big Book of Christmas Mysteries*, edited by Otto Penzler."

"Again, short stories, I presume." He nodded.

"*Hercule Poirot's Christmas* pops up, of course, but we have that one already. And here we have C.H.B. Kitchin. *Crime at Christmas*. We have a first edition here, from 1934, but that doesn't fit into the game."

"Nothing else?"

"A few that I don't think will fit. There is a Georgette Heyer novel, a recent reissue. It might be the 1941 one, but the title doesn't fit. Sorry."

"What is it?"

"*A Christmas Party.*"

"Aha. Too long, then."

"Yes."

He looked at the computer screen, and appeared to be scrolling further down the list. "Wait a minute, here's one. *The Christmas Crimes at Puzzle Manor*, a Simon Brett novel."

"What year?"

"We have one copy of the first edition, 1992."

She looked down at the puzzle. "That's excellent. Let me see . . . Yes, a perfect fit for the second to last title. Which gives us . . ."

"An L," he said.

"Excellent. We have an O, an L and an E. Anything come to mind?"

"Not really. But I think I've run out of Christmas books on this list, so I guess we'll have to improvise a bit. 1941, 1958 and 2006. One golden age title, one from the fifties and one a more recent one."

"Any obvious authors we are missing?" she asked. "Well, we have Christie and Marsh from the golden age. We've sort of eliminated Sayers. Van Dine or Ellery Queen, perhaps?"

"1941 would fit well, then."

"Let me check." Again, he consulted his computer. "There doesn't seem to have been an Ellery Queen novel in 1941, and Van Dine had actually passed away by that time."

"Did they write anything with a Christmas setting?" she asked.

"I've read all of the Van Dines at some point, and I don't think so. Although I may be forgetting something. But there was a late Ellery Queen, I forget which title . . . A very good one, I seem to recall."

"Do you have some in stock maybe? And speaking of books in stock—the Simon Brett one, by the way—I would very much like to buy that one, if it's not too expensive. I have never read that book, and I'd love a good mystery for Christmas."

"Of course." He sounded quite pleased at the prospect of perhaps making a sale out of this whole thing.

She followed him into the main area of the bookstore, again overwhelmed by the sheer number of books. Shelves everywhere, from floor to ceiling, and tables filled with books as well.

He had to climb a ladder further up than she would have dared go to get her the Brett book. The Ellery Queen titles were at a more reasonable height, and there were lots of them. *The Roman Hat Mystery* in various formats, and also a few copies of her favorite one, *The Dutch Shoe Mystery*. And then, at last, he picked a title and brought it from the shelf.

"*The Finishing Stroke*, that's it! Of course. Have you read it?"

"Honestly, I cannot remember, but it's a nice cover anyway."

They walked back to the front desk.

He opened the Ellery Queen book. "Yes, 1958—and it fits. *The Finishing Stroke*. We have an F for our solution."

"Well done, young man. Only two to go then."

He looked at his watch and had a sip of the coffee, which was probably getting slightly cold by now.

"I'll be leaving soon . . ." he said.

"I know," she replied without much emotion.

"Perhaps we're close enough to the solution for the time being, and you have your Simon Brett book as well for the holidays. How do you want to pay for it?"

"I don't have a lot of money, to be honest. My husband didn't leave me much, following a life of hard work and investments."

"Oh . . ." The man rolled his eyes. "I'm sorry to . . ."

"Let's finish the puzzle, shall we?" She framed it as a question but in fact it was closer to a command.

"OK, well, let's give it five more minutes, then."

"That's all I need."

"1941 and 2006."

"1941, maybe an obscure author, an obscure title?" she asked.

"Could be, but if that's the case it might take us forever to find out, if the title doesn't have Christmas in it."

"And the more recent one?"

"2006? Well, I'm sure there are lots of recent books that are set around the holidays."

"Which current authors are your best-selling ones?" He paused for a moment.

"I really don't know, as I told you I've just started here. But I'm sure our bestseller list isn't far from the national ones. Well, John Grisham, David Baldacci, Lee Child, James Patterson, Louise Penny, Michael Connelly . . . Take your pick!" He smiled.

"I read a good one by Louise Penny a few years ago, set at Christmas. But I can't really remember the title."

He frowned. "Oh, I think it's . . . Yes, it's *A Fatal Grace*."

He turned to the computer. "Well, you've got it. 2006. So there we have it."

He filled in the appropriate blank spaces in the puzzle.

"So, we have a blank, and then O, double F, L, E. It doesn't really make sense?"

"Not everything makes sense, young man."

"Maybe it's an anagram?"

"I guess we'll find out. We just need the first one."

"Yes." The look on his face was one of annoyance, but perhaps of a slight suspicion as well.

"1941," she said. "Any of the Christmas titles earlier that fit that year?"

"Well, let me have a look," he said, obviously not really wanting to.

She waited patiently. As she had told him, she truly had all the time in the world.

"He collected books, I think I mentioned that," she said. "Sorry?"

"My late husband. He collected books, lots of valuable books. And he was a shrewd investor as well, earlier in his life, that is. His faculties weren't as good in his later years. He wasn't as careful."

The man was looking at the computer.

"There is one, but we had ruled that one out," he said, as if he hadn't heard her comments. "Georgette Heyer. *A Christmas Party*. Originally 1941." He looked at the screen more carefully. "Oh. Well, it actually had a different title originally. Well . . . It was, let me see, *Envious Casca*. That *is* an original title."

"Could that be it?"

"Twelve letters . . ."

"For the twelve days of Christmas, perhaps?" She smiled.

"Well, it fits. *Envious Casca*. Interesting, we have a C then, but still this makes no sense. An anagram, I guess."

"He had his office downtown for most of his life."

"Sorry?"

"My husband. He conducted his business from there well into his eighties, and in the final months he had taken on a partner of sorts. Someone to help him with his finances, a young man who shared his love for books."

"Really? Well, who doesn't love books?" he said, his voice a bit shaky.

"Yes, I never met him, you see. My husband gave him a few rare books, which annoyed me a bit, but this guy was really helping him out, so I didn't give it much thought. But I knew which titles, quite rare, some of them."

"I see."

"And then, one day, this guy just disappeared."

"Really? Did something happen?"

"To him? No. But my husband's investments were gone. Money withdrawn in cash, investments liquidated, cash transferred into offshore accounts, I think the police said. It's not something I can explain clearly, I just know that my husband died almost penniless. In the end, all I had was our house—thankfully—plus his collection of books, except for the ones he gave away. The police were unable to track down this guy, but then, a few weeks ago, I saw one of these rare titles go up for sale online. It was inscribed, so I knew it was the exact same copy. I made an offer to buy that one in exchange for three other books plus some cash, and I knew very well that the titles I offered were much more valuable. So that's how I found him, I sent the books to his address and then went and spied on him, found out his name, where he works, you see . . . And he perfectly fit the description of the man my husband had been working with."

"Yes." There was anger in his eyes, but it was also as if he had lost his focus a bit.

"Do you want to know what happened to my husband?"

He didn't reply.

"He died. He basically gave up. This was too much for him. I lost him to this fraudster."

Again, no comment from the young man.

"I felt I had two or three options. One, of course, would be to go to the police, try to recover some of the money, but to be honest I don't need the money. I'm selling books from the library and then I live mortgage-free in a lovely house. I just need my husband, but I can't have him back. Another option would have been to tell the lovely people who run this bookstore that they had hired a criminal as a temporary employee, to get him fired—well, to get *you* fired . . . A small consolation, but not enough."

"I see." He was still sitting, but she stood up. She was about to leave.

"I felt you had to pay for what you had done, properly pay."

"Your husband was very old and, as you say, you had no use for the money," he said, seeming quite remorseless.

"I'll take this one with me," she said, holding the Simon Brett book. "And you misspelled it when trying to solve the puzzle I made for you. But then again, I thought you might."

"So, it was *your* puzzle? I should have guessed. Tricking me into solving a puzzle, was that your idea of revenge?"

"Not quite. The title of the book is *The Christmas Crimes at Puzzel Manor. Puzzel*, not Puzzle. So you got your letters mixed up in the keyword we were looking for."

"Oh?" He looked down. "E, not L."

"OK. Very clever. It reads . . ." He hesitated for a moment. "It reads COFFEE. Is that it, coffee? Is that the secret word?"

"Yes. You see, the poison is in your cup of coffee, young man."

HESTER'S GIFT

Tom Mead

T wo mystery writers walk into a bar . . .

If there's a punchline to that gag that doesn't end in bloodshed, I've yet to find it.

The bar in question was the Mermaid Room at the Park Central Hotel in Midtown Manhattan. A favored spot for musos thanks to its proximity to both Carnegie Hall and brilliant, blazing Broadway.

The mystery writers in question were both men, both middle-aged and past their prime. But there was one big difference between them: Clayton Lewis's books made money, while Manny Rhodes's did not. Manny Rhodes perched on a bar stool and ordered two whiskies. He felt no shame in letting Lewis foot the bill.

He looked up at the banner hanging limply behind the bar: mystery writers' convention, Christmas '82. The festivities were not yet underway—this evening was merely a prelude to the main event. But the convention was off to a rocky start thanks to unanticipated blizzards. Rhodes had only just arrived after a hellish journey and already he was wondering why he had bothered.

Lewis sat down beside him. They clinked glasses without a word and sipped their drinks thoughtfully. The whisky was good and warm. Rhodes instantly felt his mood begin to improve.

Lewis glanced around, taking in the towering Christmas tree that twinkled with fairy lights and the clusters of colleagues talking urbanely among themselves.

Eventually, Lewis was the one who broke the silence. "You like Hitchcock, don't you, Manny?"

Rhodes peered at him sideways. "Sure I do."

"You remember that movie . . . with the tennis player?"

"*Strangers on a Train.*"

Lewis snapped his fingers. "That's it! Couldn't recall the name of it. I like that movie. I think it might be my favorite."

Rhodes moistened his lips. "It's a good movie."

Lewis nudged him: "Just wish you'd written it, huh, Manny?"

Rhodes turned on his seat to look at Lewis. "What are you getting at? If you have something to say, you may as well say it."

Lewis smiled and swirled his whisky tumbler. "You know I think about that movie a lot. It's such a simple premise: two men meet on a train; they don't know each other. But they enter into an agreement to commit murder. Really it's a perfect crime. They swap victims—each man kills the other's enemy. And of course, there's nothing to tie the two men together. Nothing except that train journey."

Rhodes replaced his glass—now empty—on the bar. He signaled for the barman to refill it and watched as the amber fluid sloshed into the bottom of the glass. Then he spoke. "You're forgetting how the movie ends."

"Well, that's just Hollywood. They can't let the bad guys get away with anything. But you know, if that were to happen in real life, and two men who did not know or even like each other were to enter into an agreement like that, there's not a damn thing the law could do to stop them."

"You sound as though you're cooking something up, Clayton."

Lewis's smile broadened to a grin. "Maybe I am," he said.

❄

The hotel swarmed with crime-writing luminaries—really just a roster of people Manny Rhodes wanted to avoid. People who had loaned him money, or had stolen his ideas, or had their ideas stolen by him. There were to be speeches and discussions and a prize-giving at the end of the weekend. It was a lovely, civilized event and Manny Rhodes knew he was going to hate every minute of it.

So when Clayton Lewis put forward his idea for a murder-switch, let's just say Manny Rhodes's interest was piqued. You might wonder why Clayton Lewis wanted anyone dead. After all, he was a bestseller *and* a darling of the critics—which is no mean feat in the cutthroat field of literary crime.

Manny Rhodes on the other hand had no shortage of potential victims. He would have trouble narrowing it down to one. So while Lewis explained the scheme, Manny Rhodes listened patiently.

"What do you see when you look at me, Manny?" Lewis inquired rhetorically. "You think I'm a success, don't you? You think I've made my money and I'm living off the spoils. Well it's not like that, pal. God knows, I wish it was. I've got debts. Bad debts."

"*Debts*?" Rhodes could not help repeating.

"You don't need to know the details. But I've got creditors on my back and I can't pay them."

Rhodes took a moment to digest this.

Then Lewis continued: "And I happen to know you've got rather a money problem of your own."

"Don't we all? Writing is a bad business to be in. Throw a rock in this room, I bet you'll hit a writer who can't pay his heating bills."

Lewis smiled. "That's where my idea comes in. You see, my biggest creditor happens to be in town. Happens to be in this very room, in fact. And he's looking to get paid."

Rhodes whistled. "Sounds like you're in a jam."

"That's putting it mildly. I can't pay this guy. I barely have enough for a train fare home. Which is why I want to put a proposition to you." He took a deep breath. Then he plunged. "I want you to kill him for me."

"Is this a joke?"

"No joke. Kill him for me, Manny. I know you can do it—don't tell me that brain of yours isn't *teeming* with methods for a perfect murder?"

"Well, let's just say for a moment you aren't kidding, and you aren't crazy. Let's say I kill this guy for you. What's in it for me?"

"I happen to know you have a little human obstacle of your own. I know your wife keeps a tight rein on the purse strings. I know she's the one with the money. I also know that she's planning to divorce you, and take all that gorgeous money with her."

Manny Rhodes chuckled. "You want to kill my wife."

"It's not a question of *wanting* to. It's a question of a trade. Like the movie. We swap crimes."

"Okay," said Manny, "you've got my attention."

"My idea," Lewis continued, "is to create two perfect crimes, which *neither* of us could possibly have committed. You kill my creditor. And I kill your wife."

"And just who is this creditor?"

Lewis nodded toward a man in a linen suit, who was holding sway over an animated discussion in the far corner of the bar. He was a flamboyant, mustachioed fellow whose ribald laughter cut through the hum of subdued chatter and drifted over to the two schemers. Rhodes recognized him instantly. It was Gordon Grady—the self-styled court jester in the kingdom of crime.

"Grady?"

"Don't let the smile fool you. He's stone cold underneath it all."

"I can believe it. And you want me to kill him?"

Lewis smiled. "Quid pro quo."

❄

The following morning (Saturday, December 18) 7th Avenue was brilliant, toothy white beyond the wide windows of the Park Central. A shrill wind whistled round the hotel's Italianate eaves, though this was swiftly drowned out by a cheery chorus of carol singers in the lobby.

Hester Queeg traipsed over to the front desk looking flustered. She had only just arrived, and dragged a heavy case along the smooth tiled floor. It was not the snow that troubled her, nor the fact that her journey from Walnut Creek to Manhattan had been prolonged by a solid ten hours. It was not even the fact she was running so late that she would likely miss the first of the day's speeches, when she should in fact have got in the previous evening. What troubled her was the card game.

While her train progressed arduously through the snow, two men sitting across the aisle from Hester had been engrossed in a game of Texas Hold 'Em. One was a buttoned-up business type with a gold Rolex, while the other was a younger man with his sleeves rolled up and an unappealing, slightly sleazy parting in his slick, dark hair. They seemed to be evenly matched, but Hester found herself almost hypnotized by each man's decidedly idiosyncratic style of play.

To begin, the businessman dealt the cards, but the younger man ended up with the best hand. At one point, the younger man shifted in his seat, getting comfortable, and in the process flashed his hand in Hester's direction. She saw a pair of aces. And yet he folded before the ante could be upped. Next, the businessman went all in on a lousy pair of threes. It was a crazy, compelling game, and it left Hester uneasy. One of them was hustling. But which? Both seemed to know what they were doing, and the heap of coins migrated back and forth from one player to the other with unusual frequency. Whoever the con man was, he was so well-versed in his art as to be almost indistinguishable from the mark. She wouldn't know for sure, she realized, until the game was over and the coins were counted.

The young man dealt the next hand, and the businessman groaned when he looked at his cards. The young man just laughed. Hester's little laser beam eyes flicked from one man to the other, but it was no good. She simply could not tell. When the train reached its terminus there was a sudden scuffle of passengers slipping into coats and gathering luggage, jostling shoulders in the cramped aisle. Hester lost track of the game and who got away with the heap of coins.

But the game haunted her. She knew there was a con, but she could not have said who was conning whom. It was the sort of puzzle Hester might have untangled in her sleep. And yet she could not. As she made her way through snowbound NYC toward the Park Central, she had turned it over in her mind. There was only one conclusion. She was slipping.

For years now, Hester Queeg had considered herself a detective. She had never once received a paycheck for her detections, but she'd made a name for herself in the small town of Walnut Creek, California. Detective Ed Kemble of the local PD frequently called on her to assist him with his most challenging cases. They had a cordial working relationship, with his street smarts neatly complementing her steely logical eye. But if she was losing her touch . . .

She tried to push this nagging suspicion to the back of her mind as she checked in. Though not a mystery writer herself she was an avowed lover of the genre, making her attendance at this convention an absolute must. She positively devoured every cheap paperback she could lay her hands on. Now she was getting older (she turned fifty-six this year) and the kids had grown up and left home, her husband urged her to get out more. To treat herself. For decades she had been a full-time housewife and mother. So she had decided to try something different, to make the trip and meet some of her favorite authors. It was just a shame that her pilgrimage to the Mystery Writers' Convention had begun so inauspiciously.

"Have I missed Gordon Grady?" she asked the desk clerk, raising her voice over the sound of the choir.

"No, ma'am. You've got about fifteen minutes. If you'd like to leave your bag with me, I'll see that it's taken up to your room."

She sighed. "Thank goodness. And thank you for your help." She took her room key and headed off, following a signpost for "The Roosevelt Suite." This was the large conference room where several of the keynote addresses would be taking place throughout the weekend.

She made it just in time. She had paid extra to reserve a seat in the front row, and found it waiting for her in the packed conference suite. By the time Gordon Grady took to the stage, her habitual sprightly demeanor was back. She sat as upright and attentive as a kid on her first day of school.

Gordon Grady was his usual flamboyant self—his address was on the subject of comedy in crime. He read an extract from Dashiell Hammett's *The Thin Man* and talked about the crisp badinage between the married couple, Nick and Nora Charles. Then he talked of his own approach to crime fiction—that of an elaborate practical joker.

He was nearing the end of his address when someone appeared from the wings, a figure looming at the edge of the stage. The rest of the audience did not seem to notice him at first, but Hester did. It was only when Manny Rhodes strode out to the center of the stage that people began to murmur.

Gordon Grady continued speaking and seemed almost not to notice the uninvited guest joining him at the podium. With the spotlights on him and a steely glare in his ice-blue eyes, Rhodes produced from the pocket of his blazer a revolver.

"Hey, wait a minute," said Grady, rounding on him finally. "What's going on here, Manny?"

And Manny Rhodes pulled the trigger.

The shot cracked the air with the resonance of an atomic blast. The audience watched Gordon Grady drop to his knees, blood dribbling darkly from the fresh wound in his chest. Then he keeled forward onto his face.

The yells and screams of the crowd were unbearable in that confined space, but it appeared that Manny Rhodes posed no further imminent danger. He dropped the revolver to the stage and stood still with his hands in the air. He was still like that when the officers came to take him away.

"What happened, do you think?" one of the other guests was saying, "some kind of a psychotic break or something?"

"He sure looked crazy to me. And he didn't even try to run. Just shot Grady down in cold blood and stood there like a statue. Now what do you make of *that*?"

But Hester's attention lay elsewhere. She was looking at the stage, where Gordon Grady still lay. He had been covered with a tablecloth embroidered with the Grosvenor Hotel crest.

Hester was looking at the smoking gun, and she began to realize why Manny Rhodes had not run. The gun had the look of a common or garden revolver, the sort you might see in any old gangster picture. White smoke trailed thinly upward from the bullet-wheel, but not from the barrel. Leaning in for a closer look, Hester soon saw why. The barrel of the pistol was solid metal. It was not even hollow. The gun she was looking at could not possibly have been used to shoot down Gordon Grady. It was a cap pistol. A harmless child's toy.

An hour later, Detective Ralph Rubik arrived on the scene. Rubik like the cube, he sometimes said. And this crime was a puzzle all right. He breathed a heavy sigh as he stepped across the threshold of the Roosevelt Suite.

When he had given the scene—and the corpse—a full going-over, he oversaw the questioning of the witnesses, which was to be conducted by a squadron of uniformed officers. A woman from the front row sidled up to him.

"Could I speak with you, Detective Rubik?"

"One of the officers will be with you in a moment, ma'am," Rubik said, still focused on his notebook.

"I'd like to speak with *you*, Detective."

At last he looked up at her. She was a matronly type, the kind who like to make nuisances of themselves. "What is your name, ma'am?"

"Mrs. Hester Queeg," she announced, "of Walnut Creek, California. And I think I may be able to help you."

Rubik cocked his head ironically. "Is that so? You think you can make something of this mess, Mrs. Queeg?"

"Possibly."

"Well, the situation is this," said Rubik, "Manny Rhodes shot Gordon Grady down in front of a room full of hundreds of people, with a *cap pistol*."

"That *does* seem to be the situation, yes," said Hester.

"Well, all right. Now we know that can't possibly be, because the gun has been examined by our ballistics experts. It's a toy, designed to make a loud noise but incapable of firing so much as a wad of paper. So what other options are there?"

"Well, the only idea I can come up with is of some sort of sleight of hand trick. Maybe Manny Rhodes was able to get rid of the real weapon and replace it with the toy."

Rubik shook his head. "Manny Rhodes was observed by everyone the whole time. The slightest twitch would have been noticed by anybody in that room. And everybody—yourself included, Mrs. Queeg—has confirmed he didn't budge an inch."

"Could he have hidden it somewhere about his person?"

"No. The first thing we did when we got him under arrest was give him a full search. No smoking gun."

"What about an accomplice?"

Rubik was stony-faced. "You were in the front row, Mrs. Queeg. Does that seem likely to you?"

Hester had to concede that it did not. The front row of the audience was at least six feet from Rhodes up on the stage. If anybody had tried to approach, all eyes would have been on them. But nobody went up onto that stage until the two uniformed officers arrived to make the arrest and restore order.

The stage could not be gimmicked. It had no trapdoors. The "wings" from which Manny Rhodes had emerged were equally deserted. A perimeter was established and a thorough search of the environs conducted, but no pistol was found. So how did Gordon Grady die? Here was the puzzle: it seemed as though the murderer was the *only* person who could not possibly have committed the crime.

Not long after Manny Rhodes was escorted from the scene, Hester Queeg sat in the lobby when a man in a thickly pinstriped three-piece suit entered the foyer, accompanied by a gust of chilly air and a flurry of snowflakes. Hester recognized him instantly. He looked to be just arriving and seemed nonplussed at all the police activity. Hester approached.

"It's Mr. Lewis, isn't it? Mr. Clayton Lewis?"

"At your service," said the man, peering around her to see what was going on.

"My name's Hester Queeg, I'm a big fan of yours. But I'm afraid something terrible's happened here."

"Oh? And what's that?"

"Gordon Grady, sir. He's dead."

"Grady? No! His heart, was it?"

"I'm afraid not. I'm afraid he was murdered."

Lewis narrowed his eyes at her. "You can't be serious."

"Oh, I am. He was shot down in cold blood by Manny Rhodes."

Clayton Lewis, it transpired, had been enjoying brunch in a nearby bistro when the fatal shot was fired. He had a crew of fans who could attest to the fact.

"Old Manny Rhodes. I don't know what to say. Except that there always was something a little strange about that fella."

"The strangest is yet to come," said Hester. "A room full of people watched Manny Rhodes shoot Gordon Grady. And yet he couldn't possibly have killed him."

Lewis, who had always fancied himself as an actor, listened with a look of disbelief and mounting horror.

❄

The following morning, Detective Rubik sat in his office with his feet crossed on the desk and his eyes closed. He had not slept a wink—not even in the knowledge that Manny Rhodes was safe and snug in the holding cell belowstairs. Propped open on Rubik's chest was the forensics report on the shooting.

The report concluded that Gordon Grady's wound was consistent with a shot fired at close range. The blackened fringes of the bullet hole were peppered with gunpowder residue, as was the exit wound in his back. The bullet itself was found embedded in the wall to the side of the stage—a 9mm. Just the kind of bullet that a real revolver would have fired.

All the ingredients were there, except one: the weapon.

Rubik was also curious about something else. The woman he had met at the crime scene—Hester Queeg. There was something about her that was almost familiar, as though their paths had crossed already. Was it the name?

Hester Queeg. Not an easy moniker to forget. Eventually, he relented and put in a long-distance call to the Walnut Creek PD. The operator patched him through directly to one Ed Kemble, who swiftly filled him in on Mrs. Queeg's credentials.

At once, it all fell into place. Hester Queeg! She was one of those "amateur sleuths" you sometimes read about in bad fiction. A housewife who fancied herself a detective. A while ago—a *long* while ago—one of her cases had made national headlines. Something about "The Walnut Creek Vampire." *That* must be where Rubik had heard about her. And now she was here, in *his* city, under *his* feet instead of Kemble's. He lit a cigarette and closed his eyes.

Rubik met with Hester Queeg in the Mermaid Room at lunchtime. Hester had a plate of sandwiches in front of her, at which she picked while they chatted.

"How's Rhodes holding up under questioning?"

Rubik sighed. "He isn't. We let him go an hour ago."

"Why?"

"Fans in high places," said Rubik with a shrug.

"But surely with all the evidence . . ."

"Eyewitness evidence," said Rubik disdainfully. "When it comes down to eyewitness evidence versus ballistics, ballistics will win every time. Eyewitness testimony is less than worthless in a court of law."

"But all those people *saw* him commit murder. *I* saw him commit the murder . . ."

"And a good lawyer will pick holes in each and every story. Even yours, Mrs. Queeg. It all comes down to the gun. Because that cap gun was the only gun found at the scene, it looks as though Manny Rhodes could not possibly have been the triggerman. The fact that you witnessed the murder is merely circumstantial."

"But that's ridiculous!"

"What's ridiculous is that none of my men have managed to turn up the real murder weapon. Because it sure as hell isn't that kiddie's toy."

"Are you sure about that? You're positive it couldn't have been rigged in some way to fire a bullet?"

"Absolutely not. The ballistics boys took it apart. Just like a defense lawyer will take apart our case."

"Well," said Hester, "then we're back to square one, aren't we?"

❄

Against all odds, the convention continued. Sunday was to be the last full day anyway, so it was tacitly agreed to devote the day to a solemn celebration of Gordon Grady's dedication to the genre by persevering with the program as advertised.

Hester and Rubik were there throughout, and mildly disappointed by the dip in the atmosphere. There was, however, a brief spike in the communal enthusiasm on the Sunday afternoon, when it came time for the award ceremony. The guest of honor was of course Clayton Lewis. He stood resplendent at the podium in black-tie, beaming. Both Hester and Rubik were in the front row, and joined in the applause—Rubik a little half-heartedly.

The MC gave a brief address outlining a few of Lewis's greatest literary achievements, during which Lewis himself stood gazing down at his gleaming shoes in faux humility. Then came the actual prize-giving and the speech.

"My friends and honored guests," said Lewis, "this is one of the greatest moments of my life . . ."

And that was when she came into the room. The door to the rear of the hall swung open with a messy clatter and a woman of about forty years' age exploded across the threshold in a burst of indignant energy. For a brief moment, she and Lewis locked eyes. Hester recognized her from the nationwide tabloids that had covered the shooting of Gordon Grady. Her name was Elizabeth Rhodes—Manny's wife. Maybe she was looking for Manny.

"I . . ." Lewis trailed off mid-speech. His eyes grew dark and heavy-lidded. The audience began to murmur. Some unspoken conversation was going on across the room between these two people.

And then Lewis drew a pistol from inside his dinner jacket. He fired three times—great explosions that punctured the humid air and sent the crowd scattering and screaming. Elizabeth Rhodes dropped to the ground, bleeding and dead.

In an instant Hester was on her feet. She did not take her eyes off Lewis as he stood stock still at the podium.

His fingers loosened their grip on the revolver. With a clatter, the gun hit the floor.

"What are you waiting for?" Rubik bellowed at the uniformed officers who had flooded into the room. One officer took the initiative and bounded up onstage, where he began frisking Lewis for any weapons—real ones, that is. But of course, there were none to be found.

Clayton Lewis was handcuffed and led away from the scene of his cold-blooded murder. But for all intents and purposes, this was another impossible crime.

Rubik was even more fervid in his disassembly of the stage. The rostrum was unscrewed from its moorings, and even the trophy Lewis had been presented with was cracked open and examined. But there was no weapon in sight.

The grim ritual was conducted as before. Clayton Lewis was arrested and processed, as Manny Rhodes had been. He was questioned—throughout which he remained stoically silent. And the following morning, with no sign of a weapon forthcoming, he was released.

Ralph Rubik stood out front of the station, shards of snow biting at his face. He watched as Clayton Lewis walked away a free man. Rubik's fury blazed like a blue flame, and he clenched his teeth around the filter of his cigarette as Lewis clambered into a cab and was swiftly driven away.

Hester Queeg sat alone in the Mermaid Room, nursing a Shirley Temple. She had initially ordered scotch, but decided she would need a clear head if she was going to solve this thing. That was when she spotted the two men at the other end of the bar.

At first, she could not quite believe what she was seeing. But after a moment's scrutiny, she realized it was no hallucination. The two men from the train, the younger man and the businessman, were here at the Park Central. The businessman now wore a neatly pinstriped three-piece, while the younger man wore a t-shirt that said I ♥ NY. They were in quiet conference over drinks, and Hester watched from behind a menu as the younger man got up and headed for an armchair in the far corner. The businessman remained on his barstool, and was soon joined by a third man, a man Hester had never seen before, also wearing a suit and looking considerably more anxious about the whole thing than the smiling businessman. Meanwhile, the younger man sat in his armchair and pretended to doze.

Watching the scene unfold, Hester broke into a grin. She realized what she had witnessed on the train. The card game made sense at last. There was not one con man in that game; in fact, there were two. Partners in crime, traveling to Manhattan on the hunt for fresh meat. And here at the Park Central, they had found it.

It answered the question of who was hustling in that game of Texas Hold 'Em: they both were. Hester thought back to their eccentric playing styles, and was delighted to realize they finally made sense. The businessman dealt a loaded deck, while the younger man palmed aces as and when required. Two different cons in the same game. But of course each man knew he was being conned, so really it was not a con at all.

Hester Queeg downed her Shirley Temple feeling like a new woman. This little mystery had been a Christmas gift—the answer to an altogether different riddle, wrapped up in a splendid bow. She went out into the lobby and headed for the bank of payphones. She put in a call to Detective Rubik.

"It makes sense now," she gushed, "I know how they did it. Rhodes and Lewis. We were looking for *one* solution to the murders when we should have been looking for two."

"Slow down, Mrs. Queeg," said Rubik. "What do you mean?"

"I mean that there were two different cons in the same game. Two *different* cons in the *same game!*" she repeated triumphantly.

❋

It was Tuesday, December 21, when Manny Rhodes and Clayton Lewis had their final rendezvous. Neither man particularly liked the idea of returning to the Park Central, so they opted for a nearby bookstore along West 56th Street.

Manny Rhodes smiled when he saw the name of the place.

"Mysterious indeed," Lewis observed, "and some mysteries are best left unsolved, don't you agree?"

"I'll drink to that," said Rhodes.

The place was of course crammed with books from floor to ceiling: exquisite arrays of multicolored spines emblazoned with names. Delano Ames, Charlotte Armstrong, Lawrence

Block, Fredric Brown, Agatha Christie, John Dickson Carr. Manny Rhodes spent a moment searching for his own name among these luminaries. He eventually found one of his titles sandwiched between Bill Pronzini and Ellery Queen. Auspicious company.

Clayton Lewis was obviously doing the same thing. He smiled when he glimpsed one of his books alongside a number of slim Ed McBains.

Tables in the center of the store bore elaborate, origami-like displays. These were classics and first editions; books that Manny Rhodes would have killed to own. Erle Stanley Gardner, Rex Stout, Clayton Rawson; the two Helens, Reilly and McCloy . . .

"They'd be proud of us, you know," said Lewis. He was still gazing dreamily at the titles. "We did what none of them ever managed to do. They wrote about perfect crimes. We actually *pulled off* a perfect crime."

"Not once but twice," said Manny Rhodes.

Outside, it had started snowing again, chunky clumps of white pounding the pavement and sluicing down the storefront windows.

"What are you going to do next?" Lewis asked.

"Get the hell out of Dodge. I'm thinking maybe the Caribbean. You?"

Lewis cocked his head thoughtfully. "Something similar, perhaps. I haven't fully decided."

"Oh, Mr. Lewis," said a voice, making both men jump. "Mr. Rhodes. This pains me."

They whirled round and came face to face with a nondescript, middle-aged woman. Had she been in the store the entire time? Lurking in a side room, perhaps? Or seated in one of the leather armchairs? She was holding a first-edition Patricia Highsmith. Rhodes and Lewis gave each other a bemused sideways glance.

"Help you with something?" said Manny Rhodes.

"Wait a moment," said Clayton Lewis, "I remember you. From the convention. It's . . . Mrs. Queeg, isn't it?"

She gazed solemnly at the book in her hands. "It truly pains me. You see, I was *such* an admirer of you both."

"Afternoon, gentlemen," said another voice, and the two murderers whirled back again, like spectators at an especially frenzied tennis match. Detective Rubik was grinning.

"Is there something I can help you with?" said Lewis.

"No thanks," answered Rubik. "I had all the help I needed. Gentlemen, you're under arrest for murder."

"Rubik, what the hell is this?" Manny Rhodes demanded.

"Come now, Manny," Rubik chided him, "you can't have thought you could get away with it forever."

"Keep your mouth shut, Manny," Lewis hissed. "They can't prove a thing."

"You thought you were so clever, committing two murders in plain sight," Rubik announced with disdain.

Hester put in: "Oh they *were* clever all right, there's no getting away from it. Imagine trying to argue against them in a court of law. Inevitably it would have been impossible to prove who pulled the trigger in each case. All the evidence—including the eyewitness reports—would be circumstantial. All they had to do was grit their teeth and they would have walked away scot-free at the end of it all."

"Well," Rubik said benignly, "not anymore."

And Hester began her little soliloquy. "Their mastery of misdirection is what led us to believe they had devised a method for impossible murder—shooting someone dead with a child's toy. In both cases that appeared to be exactly what they had done. But where they were cleverest was in setting up two very different crimes to *look* identical. They led us willingly by the nose, and made us think the same trick had been used in both murders. Of course that wasn't the case.

"First, let's look at the Gordon Grady killing. In front of an audience, Manny Rhodes walked up onstage and shot him straight through the heart. Then he dropped the gun to the floor, and it was discovered to be a child's toy. Which is exactly what it was. When Manny Rhodes pulled the trigger, he fired a cap pistol. I thought it was a little unlikely that a single shot could have been aimed so perfectly at the dead center of Gordon Grady's heart. That's because it wasn't.

"We all know Gordon Grady was a showman with a taste for practical jokes. What are the odds that the whole thing was a macabre suggestion from Manny Rhodes, in which Mr. Grady was entirely complicit? You have to admit it sounds like his sense of humor—a writer shot dead by a rival writer. All it would take was a couple of squibs and blood packs—which you can get from any magic store. One is attached to his chest, just above the heart. The other is attached to the back, to signify the exit wound. The plan is for Mister Grady to keel over dead, covered in blood, and then amid the ensuing chaos to miraculously resurrect and ghoulishly delight in the horror he had inflicted. But what he didn't know was that the squibs had been doctored—loaded with real gunpowder. So that when he triggered them, he effectively blasted a bullet hole through his own chest and out through his back.

"The burns around the bullet wound were the first clue—the shot was close range, but it wasn't *that* close range. So you could say Mister Grady was an accomplice in his own murder."

"What about the bullet hole in the wall?" Lewis put in. He was desperate.

"Just set dressing. It was probably fired earlier in the day, when there was no one around, so that after the fact we would assume it was the same bullet that had passed through Gordon Grady. When in fact no bullet went through his body at all."

"This whole thing is ridiculous," Rhodes put in, "but even if it were true, are you trying to tell me that my wife also had a bunch of squibs strapped to her?"

Hester gave a demure little laugh. "Oh, far from it. I'm sure Mrs. Rhodes wasn't the sort of lady to agree to any shenanigans like that. No, Mister Lewis shot her dead just as sure as I'm standing here."

"Then how did the cap pistol trick work?"

"A little sleight of hand. I thought about this for a long while; it's given me a few sleepless nights. But I think I've cracked it. When my son was a boy, he had a book called *Elementary Magic 101* that tells you how to make a handkerchief disappear up your sleeve by attaching it to a length of elastic which runs up the sleeve and across the shoulders. When you are holding the handkerchief, the elastic is stretched tight.

When you let go the handkerchief, the elastic will pull it up the sleeve. With a clever little manipulation of your hands, you can make it look as though the handkerchief has vanished into thin air.

"That's how Clayton Lewis was able to switch the *real* revolver he used to shoot Mrs. Rhodes for the cap pistol we found on the stage. With a length of elastic looped around the butt of the gun—the kind of elastic you get in an ordinary pair of suspenders—then stretched up his sleeve, across his shoulders and down his other sleeve, where it was tied around his left thumb. So when he appeared to be removing the revolver from his pocket, in fact he was drawing it from his sleeve. In his other hand he had the cap pistol. Maybe he even fired the cap pistol at the same time as the revolver, so it would be found smoking. And this is where the elementary magic comes in.

"It's basic misdirection—we saw him let go a revolver, then we heard a revolver clatter to the floor. So our primitive brains convinced us that they were one and the same. But they weren't. The real revolver disappeared up his sleeve, leaving the *toy* for us to find."

"So just how did he get rid of the revolver before he was searched?" Rubik queried.

"Again, it's pretty elementary. All he had to do was loosen the looped elastic from round his left thumb. Then the weight of the revolver would pull both it and the elastic out of his right sleeve. And I'm sure you remember how the room was suddenly flooded with uniformed officers—how were we to know there was one officer too many? Manny Rhodes was of course the officer who so eagerly bounded up onstage and began frisking Mr. Lewis. He was able to pocket the real revolver and then melt away in the crowd during all the fuss that followed."

"I've got to hand it to you gents," said Rubik, "to come up with not one but *two* perfect crimes."

"Listen, all this is pure slander. I defy you to prove any of it." Clayton Lewis had regained his former defiance. He stood tall, chin upraised.

"Well, you're right there," Rubik answered. "We certainly would struggle to prove any of that stuff is what happened. And that's why the two of you were so clever. A jury would have a heck of a time trying to work out who did what and when. But there's one thing you haven't thought of."

"And what's that?"

"There are two of you. And when there's two of you, you find yourselves in what's known as 'The Prisoner's Dilemma.' It's just a waiting game, really. Because I *know* that sooner or later one of you will crack and throw the other under the bus. Because that's just the way humans are made."

Lewis and Rhodes exchanged a steely glance. Neither spoke as the two men were handcuffed. Nor did they breathe a word as they were herded into two separate police cars and driven away into gathering dusk. But the mind games were in play.

"It all comes down to trust," said Rubik, lighting up a fresh cigarette. "They kill for each other—sure, that's the easy part. But will they *lie* for each other?"

"Something tells me they won't," said Hester Queeg, before adding with a satisfied smile, "and I'm rarely wrong in these matters."

SERGEANT SANTA

David Gordon

I t was the afternoon before Christmas Eve and Joe was at The Mysterious Bookshop. He still needed presents for most of the people on his list, and books were the only thing Joe really enjoyed shopping for, the one area where he trusted his taste in gifts. No one wanted Joe to pick out their clothes. Weapons, perhaps—but that wasn't quite in the proper spirit. The holiday was about sharing love, and Joe loved books, the one thing he'd never steal.

Joe had dropped his grandmother, Gladys, in the shopping war zone of Soho and walked down to Warren Street. A flat gray sky lay like a lid over the city and a steady sleet splattered like post-nasal drip over streets, cars, sidewalks and down the back of Joe's collar as he ducked into the red brick building with the familiar wooden sign. The warmth engulfed him as he wiped his feet, and the light seemed to linger, as if browsing, along the floor-to-ceiling shelves, the old leather couch and library ladders. The colored spines of all those thousands of books seemed to beam benignly down on him like stained glass. He was at home.

Gladys was first and simplest to shop for. He got her a Nero Wolfe. A long-time member of the Wolfe Pack, Gladys had first introduced Joe to the series. Now he bought her a first edition every year. For Gio, Joe's childhood friend who had grown up to run a Mafia family, he picked up an Elmore Leonard. For Carol, Gio's wife, a P.D. James. Sherlock Holmes for their kids. On impulse, he grabbed a book for Yelena too. An expert thief and a deadly killer, she was hardly the sentimental type, but she and Joe had once been lovers. Russians made a big deal out of Christmas, so he decided on something sure to make her smile: a Richard Stark. He was dithering about which title to choose when his phone rang. It was Gladys, asking where he was and could he come meet her.

"I'm still at the bookshop. Aren't you busy shopping?"

"I was," Gladys said, sounding edgy but vague, careful on the phone. "But I had to cut it short."

"I see," Joe said, calmly. "Where are you now?"

"At the noodle place on Baxter. In the back."

"I'm on my way." Joe shut his flip phone and went to the front desk. "Can you hold these for me?" he asked, handing his stack to the charming bearded fellow who was presiding.

"Sure. If you want to give us your name and a credit card . . ."

Joe pulled a roll of bills from his pocket and peeled off five hundreds. "This should cover it," he said, rushing out. "The name is Joe."

Collar up, head down, Joe moved swiftly through the crowded streets, wondering just what kind of trouble would cause Gladys to go to ground during her favorite holiday ritual. Every year, around this time, the streets and shops of the city are packed. Some folks come to buy clothes and toys and electronics. Some to wait on line for deals and new releases. Some just want to browse, checking out the window displays and posing for photos with the Santas. And for as long as Joe could remember, Gladys would be out there too, picking their pockets.

Joe's grandma had magic fingers. An old school grifter from a criminal clan, there was nothing that she loved

more than a bunch of distracted shoppers in tight prem-
ises, carrying bulky bags, holding stuffed wallets and
dressed in thick, padded clothing that made it tough to
feel a wandering hand. He remembered her coming home
after a busy day and gleefully emptying her shopping bag.
Out tumbled watches, bracelets, phones, expensive wallets
packed with credit cards, even the occasional passport, all
with a wondrous flurry of cash.

But she wasn't smiling now. Sipping tea, with an untouched
bowl of soup before her, she was sitting in the far back corner, a
white-haired, bright-eyed, rosy-cheeked little old lady, bundled
in a quilted coat.

"What's wrong?" Joe asked, sliding into the chair across
from her.

She shook her head. "I should have known, Joey; everything
was going too good. Or maybe I'm just getting old. The Apple
Store was full of tourists. In Bloomie's changing room, people
were just leaving their coats and purses hanging around open.
Victoria's Secret was like a help-yourself buffet. I was having
the best season in ages. And then, on the corner of Canal, I
take off this big guy in a cashmere overcoat, lots of bundles."

"And he caught you?" Joe asked.

"Of course not." Shaken or not, Gladys still took umbrage.
"I picked him clean."

"Then what's the problem?"

Gladys looked around, then sighed and handed him something under the table. It was a fat leather fold, worn smooth. Joe flipped it open. And saw a badge.

"What"—Joe lowered his voice to a whisper, flipping the wallet closed and stuffing it in a pocket—"were you thinking?"

"I wasn't thinking he was a cop, that's for sure. That coat alone was a grand. Italian shoes. A big watch. I mean, they call them plainclothes, not designer-clothes." She shrugged. "I thought he was a rich businessman on a shopping spree."

Joe tried to think. "The bags he had, were they local?"

Gladys nodded. "Yeah. High-end stuff, too."

"OK so, he was in the area. We drop it in a mailbox. He'll think he lost it."

"Well, there's a bit more to the story."

"Of course there is."

"Like I said, I made my move and took his wallet clean. But then I felt the gun holster on his hip. What can I say? It startled me. Anyway, I must have jerked because he looked up."

"Then what?"

"He yelled and came after me, but I bonked him good with my cane, right on the bean, and took off. He slid on the ice in those fancy shoes. I lost him in the crowd after that, but . . ." She trailed off, looking worried.

Of course, she always knew when working there was a chance of arrest. Still, the stakes were low. At her age, a pinch for petty thieving wouldn't amount to much more than time served. But a vindictive cop who'd had his badge stolen? That was bad.

"He was pissed," she said now, remembering. "Used a lot of foul language that I won't repeat."

Now Joe sighed. "Let me figure this out." He waved for the check while she put on her hat and gloves. "And in the meantime, do me a favor, please?"

"Anything, Joey."

"Just keep your hands in your own pockets."

Joe called around, trying to see if anyone he knew knew anything about this cop, whose ID read "Sergeant Darryl Bradshaw." He was a plainclothes detective assigned to Grand Larceny and the sense Joe got was that he was shady but, unfortunately, not under the shadow cast by any of the bosses he knew, who could reach out and settle things with a call. Joe was on his own; he had to find a way to return the badge he felt burning a hole in his pocket without Bradshaw knowing how or who. Or if he did find out, return it in a way that made retribution impossible.

And so Joe walked around, visiting the fateful corner where Gladys lifted his wallet, a busy shopping strip on Canal and Broadway, then moving slowly around the neighborhood, chatting with locals—shopkeepers, waiters, cooks—loosening tongues by dropping twenties and fifties as well as the names of his powerful friends.

A loquacious young bartender, tattooed with her long braids up, was happy to kill the slow pre-happy hour venting about Bradshaw. He was rude, called her sweetheart, never paid for drinks or tipped, and she'd seen the owner slip him an envelope.

The old fellow at the souvenir shop refused to even admit he spoke English till Joe made a call to his friend Cash, who worked for the boss of Flushing, and Cash called the shop owner and explained things in Chinese. Then he let fly, in impeccable New Yorkese. Bradshaw was a scoundrel who squeezed protection money from all the businesses in the area. And it was more than money: he knocked people around, took things, disrespected women and the elders. Why didn't they report it? Well, the shop owner allowed, some of the designer bags and shoes he carried might be knock-offs, purchased in good faith, of course.

The bartender admitted she served after hours and didn't always check IDs when NYU kids came in. The bakery down the block had a dice game going in the basement and the corner deli moved a little weed. It was easier and safer to pay and put up with the harassment.

All of which was interesting, but not necessarily useful. He'd actually been thinking of leaving the badge with one of these folks, and paying them to say they found it, but they were way too leery of Bradshaw. Joe was standing in the mouth of an alley just south of Canal, watching the people shuffle by and mulling this over when he heard a yelp.

Down the alley, a Chinese woman was fending off two white men, both twice her size, trying to squirm past them as they pushed her back against the wall. Joe drew closer, unzipping his jacket so he could move freely, and shuffling his boot-soles on the salted sidewalk to try to build up some extra traction, but still with an easy smile.

"Excuse me fellas, there a problem here?"

The men turned to him as the woman frantically nodded.

"Maybe, but it ain't yours," the first guy, who had a shaved head and mustache, told Joe. "We're just telling her to go back home."

"Yeah," his buddy, who was taller and jacked, a gym rat, put in. "Let her go back where she comes from."

"This is Chinatown," Joe pointed out. "She is home. Why don't you go back where you came from?"

"So you want to be smart, huh?" The bald guy said, puffing up. "Maybe you do have a problem." He pushed at Joe, palms out, thrusting hard, planning to shove Joe's chest in classic bar-brawl style, the buildup to the fistfight.

But Joe had a better idea. He sidestepped quickly, letting the guy's momentum carry him forward, and put a foot out to trip him, then swung hard and clouted him on the back of the head as he went down, face first into the slush. His pal and their victim both watched from the sidelines, stunned by the sudden turn of events. This left the gym rat wide open. Joe pivoted toward him, taking advantage of the pause to aim carefully and deliver a beautiful punch right to the kidney. No doubt he could bench press twice Joe's weight, but that doesn't help the kidneys much. He gasped, face going pale with pain, and crumpled to the ground, clutching his side.

"Oh my God, thank you so much," the terrified woman cried, heading down the alley. "I'll call the police!"

At that, Joe reacted. "No," he shouted. "Hold on." He dug in his coat pocket for the wallet, flipping it open at her. She stared, confused. It was upside down. "Sorry, hang on . . ." He showed her the badge and ID, a thumb over the photo, and put some extra gravel in his voice. "I am the police, ma'am. Detective Sergeant Bradshaw at your service."

Detective Sergeant Bradshaw was on the case. He was stung and humiliated to have his badge lifted, and by an old lady, no less, who then bonked him with her cane and skedaddled. Although he was, frankly, shaking down store clerks for free Christmas swag at the time of the incident, he was still a sworn police officer, a trained detective, and he knew how to investigate a crime. So he carefully preserved the forensic evidence, shielding the cane she'd thrown at him in his coat to keep it from the sleet, then got his old kit out and took prints, then ran them and got a hit.

Boy, did he get a hit! Gladys Brody was a one-woman crime wave, with a record going back before he was born, too far to even be digitized yet. She'd been clean for years, but Bradshaw was certain her longtime address would still be good. No one gave up a rent-controlled apartment.

He headed out, telling a colleague he was following up a lead. She grunted without looking away from her computer, suspecting he was up to no good, but choosing to ignore him.

A bully is a bully and, though he had some cronies he drank with, for the most part no one really liked him on the job, either.

He took the train to Queens, trooped the cold, wet streets, and found the building. He buzzed the super.

"Who's there?" a suspicious female voice demanded.

"Police, open up."

"What for?" she asked, which took him aback. He was the law, and not used to being questioned.

"Is this the super? I just need to speak to one of your tenants, a Mrs. Brody, about . . . a routine matter. There's no cause for alarm."

There was a long pause, which annoyed him, and then finally it buzzed. He pushed through into the lobby, only to find an apartment door ajar and a small, round, dark-haired lady in a housedress waiting, with two kids peeking out from behind her.

"I'm the super's wife," she announced. "Who are you?"

"Detective Sergeant Bradshaw, ma'am, just a routine check," he said as he headed toward the elevator.

But she put out a hand, like a traffic cop. "Let's see some ID."

❋

When Joe pulled the badge, he'd been acting on instinct. He knew if that woman called 911 to report an assault in progress, then his day would get way more complicated than it already was. For starters, he couldn't hang around with a stolen badge in his pocket, which would mean fleeing the very neighborhood that provided his only hope of resolution. So he'd flashed the badge, told her he'd handle it, and sent her on her way, with a shower of Thank Yous and God Bless Yous that actually felt pretty good, if a bit awkward under the circumstances.

By then the bald guy was on his feet, pants torn at the knees, helping up his friend, who was still groaning but breathing alright. He let them off with a warning and, as they scurried away, also gratefully thanking him, an idea began to form in his mind.

He went back to walking, searching the same blocks, but with a different intent. Then, on a corner, something caught his eye. It was a guy in shorts and sneakers, with his down coat over them, smoking a cigar and watching his bulldog squat to relieve himself on the sidewalk, right in front of a counter that sold juices and teas. When the dog finished, he started walking, puffing away.

"Excuse me sir," Joe called, stepping into his path and flashing the badge, doing it way more suavely this time, with a flip of the wrist, a couple of fingers casually hiding the photo. "Sergeant Bradshaw. I notice you forgot to pick up after your dog."

"Um . . ." The guy stopped, cigar in his mouth. He looked over, as if noticing the impressively large pile for the first time. It steamed in the cold. "Oh, yeah."

"Take care of it please, sir."

The guy looked at again, still a bit confused. "The thing is, officer, I forgot to bring a bag."

Joe nodded. "Well then, either I can charge you with unlawful defecation on public property, as well as a health code violation for proximity to food service," he said, improvising, "or you can pick it up." He stepped closer, eyeballing the guy. "With your hand."

With a deep sigh, the guy nodded and then bent over, while his dog watched, happily wagging his tail. Joe heard applause and cheering burst out from over his shoulder. Three teenagers in aprons were watching from behind the counter, clapping.

"He does that every day," one shouted.

"Thank you, officer!"

Smiling, Joe waved his badge at them. "I'm Sergeant Bradshaw, guys. Happy to be of service."

Drawn by the excitement, a few passersby had paused, and more heads popped out of doorways. The applause rippled down the block.

"Thanks, Sarge!"

"God bless you!"

Joe waved as he walked along, till he felt a hand tugging his sleeve. He looked down.

It was a boy, about ten, in a hooded sweatshirt over track pants and sneakers. "Excuse me, sir? Can you help me?"

"Oh . . . sure, kid. What's up? Are you lost?"

He scoffed. "No. I live on Hester Street. But there's these guys on the handball court, they'll never let anyone else play."

"Oh, really?" Joe said. "Is that so?"

The kid nodded. Joe patted his back.

"Come on. This sounds like a case for Sergeant Bradshaw."

❄

When the super's wife buzzed Gladys over the building intercom to warn her that a cop was looking for her, Gladys had acted fast. She slid into her slippers, grabbed keys, glasses, and half a chocolate babka she'd been saving, and dashed across the hall to Mrs. Weintraub's place. Mrs. Weintraub let her in, then locked up and put the chain on, checking through the peephole for the law. Then they joined Mrs. Wong and Mrs. Altierri around the table, and the four women began playing their usual game of mah-jongg.

But she needn't have hurried. Sergeant Bradshaw was still arguing with the super's wife, explaining why, given the nature of the mission, he had purposely not carried his badge that day.

"I'm undercover," he told her. "A badge would defeat the whole purpose. That's why they call it plainclothes. What if a dangerous criminal searched me?"

"But you said it was just a routine check," she pointed out.

He paused, trying to think, distracted by the fact that one kid, a boy, had started picking his nose and the other, a little girl, had started making faces at him behind her mother's back, crossing her eyes and sticking her tongue out. "That's part of my cover?" he was suggesting, when his phone rang. It was his commanding officer, Lieutenant Gormby. He had to take the call.

"Yes, sir?"

"Bradshaw, where are you?"

"Just following up a lead, sir," he said, while the super's wife listened. "Talking to a witness on that um, thing . . ."

"Well, you better get back here, pronto."

"Why?" he asked, his stomach pulling into a knot. "I mean, what's wrong?"

"I don't know. You tell me. Some lady dropped off a huge bouquet of flowers. She said you saved her life and fought off two rapists in an alley. And then some kids brought free bubble teas for the whole squad. Something about unlawful defecation?"

Bradshaw listened, stunned into silence as the super's wife stared curiously. He frowned and turned away. "Oh, that!" he told his boss. "I can explain that. Don't worry about anything."

"I'm not worried," Gormby said, audibly sucking through a straw. "But I did think they must have the wrong Sergeant Bradshaw." He laughed at his own joke and Bradshaw chuckled along miserably. "Are you sure you're feeling all right?"

"Yes sir," he said. "I'm feeling fine. I'll be right in." He cut the call and faced the super's wife. "I've got to go. There's been a big break in the case."

"Sounds like it," she said, and watched, along with her kids, as he fled.

❄

Meanwhile, Joe was having a ball, doing good deeds. He'd grown up in a world where, when playing cops and robbers, the kid who drew the short straw had to be the police. But now he had to admit, being a lawman was fun. He scolded the handball court hoggers. They turned out to be a group of thirty-something professionals in fancy gloves and headbands who sheepishly agreed to share. He shamed some construction workers for catcalling. He knocked on the door of a loft rented by rich out-of-town students and told them that, in future, quiet hours began at 10:00 P.M. and next time he'd toss their stereo out the window.

He used the cold as an excuse to keep his hood and scarf up as much as possible, refused all selfies and diverted cameras with some gibberish about official business and privacy laws, but word was spreading, and folks began posting things online like, "We love Sergeant Bradshaw," and "Sergeant Bradshaw for cop of the year!" Figuring it was time to split, he was actually trying to slip away when an old guy in a tiny shoe repair shop, one of those who'd insisted they didn't speak English, waved him over.

"Sorry about earlier," he said, in a clipped South Asian accent. "But that other detective, the big one in the cashmere coat? I don't trust him. He makes me polish his shoes for free. But I thought that you should know . . ."

Joe knew his next move now, but he needed help, and a different kind of disguise for a different undercover operation. He called Cash again, and Juno, his young protégé from Bed-Stuy, who was home trimming the tree with his mom. He called Josh, an Israeli ex-commando who worked for Rebbe Stone, the ultra-orthodox crime boss. Josh didn't celebrate Christmas personally, but his boyfriend Liam, an Irish gangster whose brothers still held power in Hell's Kitchen, certainly did, though when they heard Joe's plan, they were happy to oblige.

Joe called Gio, who was home on Long Island, but sent a couple of his guys, Nero and Little Eddie, instructing them to stop by the strip club first and pick up a list of items from backstage. Joe told everyone where to meet, then, noticing the time, he rushed back to The Mysterious Bookshop and collected the waiting bag marked "Joe," just before they locked the door and left for Christmas Eve.

❄

"Freeze! Police! Nobody move!"

As soon as the metal door to the warehouse lifted and the truck began rolling out, Joe and his team sprang from hiding. The shoemaker had explained about the dangerous crew of hoods who knocked off shipments to local merchants, stored the spoils in the nearby warehouse, and moved it out at night. There was no point in telling the other cop, he'd explained, since he was probably in on it, or would be if he knew.

But now, Joe was on the case, blocking the truck, badge prominently displayed. Nero and Little Eddie, who was over six feet and two hundred pounds, were pointing guns and dressed in suits, while the rest of the crew moved in quickly. The driver froze, hands up, along with his partner in the cab. Another guy in coveralls was operating the door.

"Get out slowly," ordered Nero, who knew from personal experience what to say. Eddie gave the guy in the coveralls a shove.

"On your knees! Hands on your head."

They complied. Liam and Josh took control of the truck, while Juno and Cash handcuffed the three thieves together and then locked them in the janitor's closet.

"Wait here for prisoner transport," they told them. Of course, no one was coming, and in fact they were toy handcuffs used for routines at the club, but by the time they figured that out, Joe and his crew would be long gone.

After backing the truck up, Josh tossed the keys to Joe, who opened the rear doors, grinning as his friends gathered around.

"Now that," he said, "is starting to look a lot like Christmas."

The truck was stuffed to the brim with toys, down jackets, flatscreen TVs, winter boots and new sneakers, gaming consoles, cell phones and appliances.

"Man," Juno said. "Who knew being a cop was so awesome?"

"I'd consider enlisting," Cash said, "if it weren't for my record."

"Any other night," Liam said, "this would be a proper haul."

"But it's not like any other night," Josh reminded him. "It's the night when the goyim give stuff away."

One by one, Joe had the guys pull around the vehicles they'd come in and pack the trunks and backseats with goodies. Nero and Eddie distributed costumes from backstage at the club, used for holiday-themed performances and for the big party they threw each year. Then they split up, headed for their own neighborhoods.

Dressed as elves, Cash drove to a children's hospital in Flushing, and Juno visited a shelter in Bed-Stuy for women and their kids. Liam parked on 42nd Street, outside Port Authority, wearing a Santa hat and false beard, and gave out gifts to the homeless. Then they drove to East Williamsburg, where Josh put on the beard but wore a black hat instead, and visited a home for the indigent aged. Nero and Eddie went to Staten Island, wearing elf ears and a Rudolph nose and antlers, their Caddy weighed down like Santa's sleigh.

Joe stayed in the neighborhood, as close to the precinct house as he dared, identity hidden by a full Santa costume, complete with fake beard and belly. And as he handed out gifts from a big sack on his shoulder, he shouted what he'd told the other guys to shout as they, too, spread joy all over the city, "Ho, ho, ho! Merry Christmas to one and all! With love from Sergeant Bradshaw!"

It was Christmas morning. Normally, this was a slow news day, as everybody—cops, criminals, reporters—all wanted to be at home or on vacation, anywhere but the freezing steps of a police station. But as word of the miracle spread through the city, the precinct desk was deluged, first with calls, and then with media showing up in person, until finally a hasty press conference was called.

"They call him Sergeant Santa," a reporter said, her shiny black hair tumbling from under a red hat with a big pom-pom. "And on a cold, dark New York Christmas Eve, he proved that this city does indeed have a heart. A great big one full of love."

And then, as the cameras rolled and the crowd cheered, a very confused Sergeant Bradshaw was led out like a lamb to the slaughter, escorted by Lieutenant Gormby.

"Good morning, everyone, and Merry Christmas," the lieutenant began. "This is an unofficial statement, and as some of you have noted, the events of last night are highly irregular, but then again, there's nothing regular about this great city, or this special day. And, as I can say from personal experience, there's definitely nothing regular about Sergeant Bradshaw."

He clapped Bradshaw on the back and, as the crowd roared, the sergeant blinked blankly, frozen in panic, like a reindeer in the headlights. He shivered in the cold, wishing he could just run, and slid his frozen hands into his pockets. And then a miracle happened. He smiled, wider and wider. And as the warm spirit filled him, he began to wave at the cameras.

Even if he went back later and watched the news footage, she would be hard to see, and impossible to identify—the angelic little old lady in the hat, scarf, muffler, and brand-new down jacket, who'd brushed against Bradshaw in the crowd and slipped his badge back into his pocket.

❄

Joe escorted his grandma carefully down the street, watching out for ice and puddles.

"We'll have to get you a new cane," he told her.

She waved it off. "It can wait. You know it's just for show." Instead, she steered him around a corner. "Anyway, it's

Christmas Day. And we're downtown. Let's be traditional for once and get Chinese food."

So they went back to the noodle place, where glazed ducks hung in the steamed-over window and dumplings sizzled in a pan, and ordered up a feast. And as they opened their fortune cookies, Joe presented Gladys with a lovely hardcover copy of *Black Orchids* while she reached into her own pocket and then pressed something into his hand.

"What's this?" he asked. "I though you promised you'd lay off picking pockets?"

She grinned. "It wasn't in a pocket, was it? It was on a wrist. And anyway, it's Christmas."

Joe examined the heavy gold watch. It was beautiful, he had to admit. And maybe she was right—the day did call for a special gesture. He kissed her cheek. "Thank you," he said, as he turned it over and read the inscription:

> *In honor of twenty years on the force,*
> *Congrats Lieutenant Gormby.*

END GAME

Martin Edwards

"A ghost story for Christmas!" Katie clapped her hands, and I knew she'd been hoping I'd make the suggestion. For a moment I was reminded of the excitable young woman who had swept me off my feet. "Just like old times!"

"Old times?" Gray said languidly as I moved to the inglenook and stirred the fire with a red hot poker.

"Surely Joss told you?" Katie said. "Each time she came to stay with us on Christmas Eve, Phil always told us a ghost story. He made them up specially. They were marvelous, incredible. Those stories were an absolute tradition."

For all of six years, I thought. Exaggeration is in Katie's DNA. Before we were married, she was my publicist. In her world, everything is awesome, fantastic, a thousand percent, the best ever. No wonder I was smitten. Nothing is as fragile as an author's self-esteem, and no one is better than Katie at massaging their egos.

Gray was amused, in his stylishly self-deprecating way. "Sorry. Did I put the mockers on things when I showed up in Ma's place last year?"

"Not in the least." I smiled, very much the genial host. "It was simply time for a change."

"Twelve months ago, Phil was on his best behavior with you," Katie said. "Desperate to impress his new agent."

"Quite unnecessary," Gray said with a lazy grin. "Ma always had a soft spot for Phil."

"Yes, but now Joss is on the other side of the world. Times change. Phil would never admit it, but he was afraid you'd devote your energies to the rising stars on your list. The likes of Bartley Innes. Young, thrusting crime writers with glittering careers ahead of them."

Gray shrugged. "Stories are my lifeblood. They are what I sell, whoever writes them."

I was tempted to ask why he'd failed to find a publisher for my latest mystery. Instead, I gave the fire a savage poke.

Gray warmed his hands in front of the blaze before sinking back into the rapturous embrace of his wingback armchair.

He was adored, I thought sourly, even by my furniture. Most of all by himself.

"This is the life, eh? Joss used to tell me all about your cozy Christmases together. While I was working in Canada, I felt quite envious."

He cast a quick glance at Katie. I knew exactly why he envied me.

"I mean it," he said, as though I'd contradicted him. "What could be more perfect than spending a few days together in a spooky old house in the middle of nowhere? Getting away from it all, knocking back the mulled wine and scoffing mince pies."

I lit a small cigar. No point in offering a Havana to Katie or Gray. Neither of them smoke, it's the modern way. I'm only ten years their senior, but the age gap feels like an unbridgeable gulf. Truth is, I'm as old-fashioned as Lane End House. It's been in the family for a hundred years and I've never regarded it as spooky. Even as a timid and impressionable child, I had no trouble sleeping in my room on the top floor. No nightmares for me—at least, not until recently.

Gray sipped his mulled wine. "Every Christmas when I was growing up, Joss insisted on watching one of those old BBC ghost stories on the telly."

"*A Warning to the Curious*," I murmured. "*Lost Hearts. Casting the Runes.*"

"That's right. And it wasn't all M.R. James, was it?"

"Not at all. Le Fanu's *Schalken the Painter* . . ."

"You have quite a memory for out-of-the-way facts," he said benevolently. "That's why you should try nonfiction."

My smile was polite, but only just. I'm a storyteller, not a journalist.

"Then there was *The Signalman* . . ."

"One of Dickens's finest tales."

Gray never missed a chance to remind people that he wasn't just a pretty face. Hallucinatory visions in Dickens's fiction were the subject of his PhD. He'd taught English in Toronto before coming back to Britain.

"Joss brought you up well." I sighed. "She was a good agent."

"She liked you," Gray said. "Thought you had great promise."

His words hung in the air, like wisps of smoke from my cigar. Like my whole career, really. Here one moment, gone the next.

Katie said, "We had a card from Joss. She's having a whale of a time in Sydney. All that sun. It could hardly be more different than chilly England."

Gray turned to me. "Ma still feels pangs of guilt about leaving you in the lurch. But that Aussie businessman swept her off her feet and I fancied taking over the agency. So it all worked out."

"Happy ever after," I murmured.

"This ghost story." Katie glanced at the clock. "It's close to midnight."

I test her patience, I'm acutely aware of that. Sometimes I do it deliberately. Is this what marriage does to people, slowly turning us from lovers into rivals in a game of emotional chess?

"Sorry. I keep digressing." I paused. "Funny you should mention Dickens, Gray. His spirit is at the heart of my Christmas tale."

"I'm agog," Gray said. "Is this a story of the supernatural?"

"You might think so, but it's perfectly true. It all began in New York City, last January. Each year there's a shindig there, to celebrate Sherlock Holmes's birthday on the sixth of the month. Organized by the Baker Street Irregulars."

"Who are they?"

"The first Sherlockian literary society and still the most prestigious, with members from around the world. Robbie Richardson, a chap I went to school with, is a member of the group. He's a passionate bibliophile and he made enough money in banking to indulge his taste for rare books to his heart's content. He also self-publishes mysteries—Sherlockian pastiches and so on—for his own amusement. For years he urged me to join him at the celebrations."

MARTIN EDWARDS

"I remember," Katie said. "You asked me if I wanted to come too."

"And you said you'd rather stick pins in your eyes," I said. "So you booked a week at a spa instead."

She smiled. "How fantastic it was. Incredible to have time to practice meditation and rejuvenate."

"Yes, I remember how bright you were when I got home. The treatment obviously did you good."

There was a touch, just the faintest touch, of suspicion in her smile. "You're so right, darling. Anyway, you had a good time, too?"

"It was great to catch up with Robbie and meet his friends. I even had a coffee with my American publisher."

Gray was about to speak, but stopped himself just in time. I could read his mind. *Former* American publisher, as of this summer. Poor old Phil. My pathetic attempt at schmoozing was too little, too late to rescue my career in the States.

"While I was there, Robbie invited me to join him in a pilgrimage to Tribeca, to browse the shelves at The Mysterious Bookshop. The place is an Aladdin's cave, crammed with everything from today's million-sellers to long-forgotten rarities."

Katie looked up to the heavens. "As if we don't have a houseful of books already."

"The store is legendary, how could I resist?"

"I daren't ask how much you spent," she said. "Let alone how we can afford it, when you're not . . ."

She didn't need to finish the sentence. All three of us knew my earnings were a fraction of what they once were, but she was forgetting that this house has been in my family for a century. It's my inheritance that keeps us afloat. How else could she lead the life of a lady of leisure? Lately I'd said we must cut our expenses. Things have changed since those heady days when, on the strength of my debut novel, Joss said I was her most talented client, and Katie believed I was destined for the bestseller lists.

"I swear that I didn't buy a single book. Though I was tempted by half of one."

She stared. "Half a book?"

"A beautifully bound copy of Gray's favorite Dickens novel."

He leaned forward. "You mean *The Mystery of Edwin Drood*?"

"What else?" I smiled.

Gray drained his glass and cleared his throat, a prelude to demonstrating his expertise. He has a fierce ego and a competitive streak. Six months ago I made the mistake of playing him at squash and he made me pound around the court so fast, I thought I was going to have heart failure. Come to think of it, my demise might have solved a problem or two for him.

"Because Dickens died after writing just six of the twelve installments he'd planned, people fail to appreciate their quality. As well as the potential of the episodes to come."

I shrugged. "Surely with a book that's only half-written, it's hard to be sure that the complete novel wouldn't be a damp squib?"

Gray wagged his finger at me, like a policeman reprimanding a cheeky schoolboy.

"This is Dickens we're talking about. A storytelling genius. He wrote enough of the story for any fair-minded judge to recognize its excellence. How many famous crime novels would we regard as masterpieces if the story ended midway through? Think about it, Phil. *The Medium-Sized Nap*? *And Then There Were Five*? I don't think so."

As he sniggered at his own wit, I glanced at Katie. She didn't quite manage to stifle a yawn.

"Believe me," Gray said, "a fragment from Dickens is worth a dozen books by ordinary mortals. Atmosphere, characterization, mysterious situations, *Drood* has everything. If he'd finished the book prior to his death, it would have been a game-changer. If you want my opinion, the completed novel would have transformed the mystery genre."

"His contemporaries weren't so impressed," I said mischievously. "Even Dickens's old pal Wilkie Collins had his doubts. And he was the leading thriller writer of the age."

Gray gave a know-all's smile. "You're right, for what it's worth. When Dickens died, Collins was the obvious choice to finish the book. Instead, he heaped scorn on the story. Described it as 'Dickens's last labored effort, the melancholy work of a worn-out brain.'"

Katie laughed. "Bitchy Wilkie!"

"Frankly, he produced plenty of melancholy work of his own in later life. And his relationship with Dickens was complicated. The two men were rivals as well as friends. As for his criticism of *Drood*, he was utterly mistaken."

Time to play my trump card. "I happen to know that Collins had second thoughts."

Gray frowned. "Really?"

"Sorry, I'm getting ahead of myself. As well as neglecting my hostly duties." I topped up our glasses, but Katie shook her head and said she'd had more than enough. "Whilst I was browsing, Otto Penzler came over to talk to us. He owns the bookstore and Robbie is obviously a valued customer. They talked about Robbie's collection of crime fiction. He lives alone in a swish house in Chelsea and the walls are lined with first editions. As he peered at the bookshelves, it was like watching a kid in a sweetshop."

Katie drummed her fingers on the top of an occasional table. "And the ghost story?"

"I'm coming to that. After Robbie and I flew back to England, we spent the evening together at his penthouse before I headed back here. That night, I asked him about a passing remark from the store owner. I'd found it intriguing, but Robbie had quickly changed the subject. 'About *The Mystery of Edwin Drood*,' I said. 'Did I understand correctly? Otto seemed to suggest that you were inspired to write your own ending to the story?' Robbie looked sheepish and admitted he'd mentioned the idea."

"Other people have done the same, haven't they?" Katie asked.

"Hundreds of them," Gray said in his most authoritative tone. "The question people keep asking is this: was Edwin Drood a victim of murder, or did Dickens have another explanation in mind? Unfortunately, most authors haven't done their homework, and aren't even aware that Dickens himself explained how the story was meant to end."

"He did?" Katie asked.

"Absolutely. He described the solution to a man called Forster, his first biographer."

"So what was the solution?"

"An uncle was to murder his nephew—John Jasper killed Drood, in other words—only to discover almost at once that the situation motivating his crime had ceased to exist before he had committed it."

"Ah." This seemed to amuse her. "The irony."

"Exactly. A wonderfully sophisticated idea, combining a twist of fate with a neat flavoring of poetic justice."

"Even if Dickens did say that," I said, "he might have changed his mind during the course of writing and come up with a different solution. Crime writers do it all the time. Ruth Rendell sometimes changed her murderer when working on the very last chapter."

Gray's smile was bland. I knew what was going through his mind. He didn't need to utter a word. *But you're no Ruth Rendell, Phil. You never even met her, so don't try to pretend the two of you swapped tips on writing techniques. Fact is, you're a midlist author who got lucky with his debut and since then has written a handful of potboilers. Now your sales are in freefall, and you've no one to blame but yourself. And if you're starting to wonder whether the supernatural genre offers you more than crime, think again. Face up to reality and forget about fiction. When it comes to specters, your best hope is teaming up with a celebrity. Becoming* that *kind of ghostwriter.*

"Are you going to get a move on?" Katie demanded. "It's way past my bedtime."

"Sorry," I said gently. "I wormed the truth out of Robbie. A year earlier, he'd bought a couple of letters from The Mysterious Bookshop, together with two pages of manuscript. All in Wilkie Collins's hand. The letters were addressed to a publisher called James Arrowsmith and dated six months apart. In the first, Collins relented."

"How do you mean?" Gray asked.

"He agreed to write a conclusion to *Edwin Drood*."

A snort of derision. "You're kidding."

"Trust me, Robbie showed me the letter in question. What Collins said was clear and to the point."

A decisive shake of the head. "How can you be confident the letter was genuine?"

"Robbie is no fool. He'd done his due diligence, and so had Otto when he acquired the material. You can be sure the provenance was beyond question."

"So why have we never heard about this?"

"Arrowsmith's offer was handsome, far more than he was accustomed to pay to his authors. Although Collins was no longer at the top of his game, he was still popular with readers. He had a wife and a mistress to take care of and was short of money. Whatever his scruples, he simply couldn't say no. But he insisted that nobody should know about their agreement. Given his previous denunciation of *Drood*, he was afraid of being pilloried for hypocrisy. Only when he'd completed the novel to his satisfaction could anything be said. Secrecy suited Arrowsmith. He was a smart man of business, and he wanted to make a big splash when announcing that Dickens's last novel had been completed by the man who wrote *The Moonstone*."

Gray shook his head. "I don't believe a word of it."

"Collins said he would adopt Dickens's proposed ending. There are Christmas scenes in *Drood* and he wanted to set the climax at Christmas, twelve months later. Perfect from the perspective of commercial publishing. Christmas settings sold books then, just as they do now."

"But?" Katie asked.

"But in the second letter, Collins confessed that the task had defeated him."

She frowned. "I don't get it. You promised to tell us a ghost story. Where does the ghost come in?"

"Patience, Katie."

She rolled her eyes. Patience isn't among her virtues. Once she makes up her mind about something, she never lets anything get in her way.

"There was something odd about that second letter. Even the handwriting was erratic, compared to the earlier document. Collins evidently wrote to Arrowsmith in a nervous frenzy."

"The man was a drug addict," Gray said. "Like John Jasper in *Drood*."

"Robbie didn't believe that Collins's inability to finish *Drood* was due to his taste for laudanum. One thing Collins did make very clear. Ever since he'd started work on the story, he'd suffered from terrible nightmares, the most frightening he'd ever experienced. He'd woken up convinced that he was about to be savagely murdered. The only remedy, he insisted, was to abandon the project. He even went so far as to return his advance, with interest."

Gray shook his head and muttered, "Authors, eh? He can't have been properly represented. Tell me about the manuscript."

"It's a rough draft, with several crossings-out. In an opium stupor, John Jasper, convinced that he's murdered Edwin, contemplates suicide."

"There you are then. Collins scared himself with his own melodrama."

"Why react so violently? It didn't make sense to me, but Robbie said he had a glimmering of the answer. Six months after buying the Collins material from Otto, he'd picked up a heap of stuff connected with Dorothy L. Sayers at an auction."

"Oh yes?"

"Sayers was a fervent admirer of Wilkie Collins. She spent years trying her hand at a biography, but only ever wrote part of it."

"Yet another unfinished book," Katie said wearily. "What sort of author leaves a job incomplete?"

Gray made a skeptical noise. "Some of the manuscripts I read should have been abandoned after chapter one."

Was that dig aimed at me? Gray had already made it clear that he didn't regard my latest synopsis as salable. To my surprise, I'd discovered that I no longer cared.

"Robbie told me that Sayers had seen Collins's manuscript, his abortive conclusion to *Edwin Drood*."

"How?" Gray asked.

"At that point—in the late thirties—the manuscript and Collins's letters about it came into the possession of a collector in London. The man was a huge admirer of Sayers's fiction, and knowing of her interest in Collins, he invited her to take a look at the material he'd acquired, under conditions of strict secrecy. He asked if she could be tempted to complete *Drood* herself, using Collins's fragment as a starting point, and his idea about a climax taking place at Christmas. Sayers was nothing if not ambitious, and the chance to follow in the footsteps of two favorite writers was impossible to resist. So she said yes."

Gray stared. "I've never heard anything about this."

"There's nothing in the published sources. People like Robbie Richardson don't go around bragging to all and sundry about the contents of their collections. Or write about them in scholarly journals."

"Even so. Sayers was famous in her day, a household name. Word gets about."

"Robbie showed me the proof. A long, chatty letter she wrote to the collector confirming her intention to rise to the challenge."

"Seriously? You're saying there's a long-lost Sayers manuscript completing *The Mystery of Edwin Drood*?"

I sighed. "I'm afraid not. Robbie also owns a second letter from her, dated three weeks later, and very different from the first."

"Saying what?"

"She's changed her mind and has abandoned the project."

He frowned. "Like Collins?"

"Yes, no money had changed hands, but otherwise there are strong echoes of what happened more than half a century earlier. Sayers was a devout Christian, but her tone in the letter is agitated and she gives the impression of going through some kind of extreme crisis of faith."

Gray's shrug was dismissive. "Mental health issue. Writers have them all the time."

I was tempted to ask him why that was, but I bit my tongue. "Actually, Sayers was famously robust. I once read a book of her published correspondence. This second letter bore no resemblance to anything else she wrote. Robbie and I agreed that she sounded panic-stricken. Not that he was deterred from trying to follow in her footsteps."

"What do you mean?"

"He loves mimicking Dr. Watson's voice when writing stories about Sherlock, and he thought it would be fun to try his hand at finishing *Drood*."

"An amateur attempting to step into Dickens's shoes?" Gray was scornful. "I daren't imagine what a mess he'd make of it."

I finished my cigar. "Time for a nightcap."

Katie yawned and said, "I've had enough, but don't let me stop you two."

I opened the drinks cabinet, lifting out bottles of cognac and Glenfiddich, and pouring generous measures. I've always been a brandy drinker, while Gray likes his whisky.

The two of us clinked glasses. "Unfortunately, Robbie didn't make anything of *The Mystery of Edwin Drood*. Each time he tried to write, he was plagued by the most appalling headaches. When he went to bed, his nightmares scared him so much, he kept waking up in the small hours."

"What sort of nightmares?"

"Robbie refused to discuss them. He simply said he'd never been so terrified in his entire life."

"So he gave up on the project? Just as well. We don't need any more ham-fisted attempts to emulate the great man's writing."

"Robbie never struck me as having a wild imagination. I must admit, I was intrigued. I started to wonder what might happen if I had a go myself."

Gray winced. "Please tell me you haven't frittered away your time trying to come up with an ending to a peerless Victorian classic?"

"Some time later, I met Robbie for a drink. When I said I might try to finish the book, he was appalled. Begged me to forget the whole idea. Said he wished he'd never shown me the letters from Collins and Sayers."

"Thank God for that. You need to focus, Phil. If you . . ."

"Remember when you and I had lunch in the summer?" I interrupted. "You said my writing had become stale. Lacking in energy. A change of approach would do me good."

He put his head in his hands. "No, no, trying to reinvent yourself as a poor man's Dickens is the last thing I'd want you to do."

"The more I thought about it, the more I realized you're right about the quality of *The Mystery of Edwin Drood*," I said. "And the cynical finale Dickens contemplated seemed perfect. My own fiction was going nowhere. I'd suffered from a severe case of writer's block."

"No such thing," Gray snapped. "It's simply an author's excuse for laziness or declining powers."

"I thought this might kick-start my career again," I said dreamily. "Robbie and I argued long and hard, but my mind was made up. I pleaded with him to lend me Wilkie Collins's manuscript. Against his better judgment, he agreed. And so I set to work."

Gray finished his whisky. "How far did you get?"

"Robbie was proved right. Like him, like Sayers, like Collins, I found the task beyond me. It was almost impossible to write and later, when I finally managed to get to sleep, I had the vilest nightmare. I was in a dark, smoky opium den, doped up to the eyeballs. My head was spinning and I was surrounded by menacing strangers."

He frowned. "Sounds like the opening pages of *Edwin Drood.*"

"Except that the men were brandishing knuckledusters and the women flourishing knives. They jabbered furiously in languages I couldn't understand, but one thing I knew for sure. If I didn't give them everything I possessed, they'd subject me to the cruelest tortures."

"That's cheap fiction, not Dickens."

I gulped down some brandy. "I emptied my pockets, but that wasn't enough. The strangers snatched my watch and wallet, but still they weren't satisfied. I begged for mercy but they started stripping off my clothes. I didn't dare to resist and they didn't stop until I was naked."

"A psychiatrist would love this," Gray murmured. "All those repressions, bubbling up to the surface."

"I woke in a cold sweat," I said. "Sobbing with gratitude from the moment I realized that the unspeakable horrors were all in my mind."

"I'd no idea," Katie said.

I realized she was watching me closely, something that gave me an obscure sense of pleasure.

Gray seemed amused. "Don't tell me you sleep in separate rooms?"

"I can't sleep through Phil's snoring," she said.

I nodded. "Ever since we came back from our honeymoon, Katie has had the suite across the landing from mine."

She turned to me. "You never mentioned this nightmare."

"In fact, there were two nightmares. Frankly, I was too shaken to want to talk about either of them. The morning after the first bad dream, I persuaded myself that I'd allowed Robbie's anxieties to get the better of me. The best course was to power through any obstacles and crack on with writing the story. I set myself a target. Three thousand words in twenty-four hours."

"Glad to hear it," Gray said drily. "If only . . ."

I raised a hand to silence him. "As it turned out, I was deceiving myself. The harder I tried to get the words down on the page, the tougher I found it to write anything. How desperately Collins must have labored, even to scratch out the feeble lines that filled the two sheets I'd seen! It was hopeless. And when I collapsed into bed, the nightmare resumed. This time, the men struck me with their iron bars, the women slashed at me with their knives. They were determined to put me to death. Slowly and in the most agonizing manner."

"And then you woke up?" Gray didn't try to conceal his sarcasm.

Katie gave him a sharp glance. "Don't spoil the story."

I smiled. For once Gray's snide remarks had got under her skin as well as mine.

"As you see, I wasn't actually murdered in my bed. But it was a near-run thing."

Katie's eyebrows shot up. "I don't understand."

"Don't you remember my heart attack?" I asked.

It had happened two months ago. Katie was away from home that weekend. Visiting an old school friend, she said. On waking, I found I was drenched in sweat and struggling to breathe. I felt a squeezing in my chest, pain spreading to my left arm. Dizzily, I phoned for an ambulance and was rushed into hospital. A mild heart attack, they told me. The specialist urged me to improve my diet and cut down on alcohol. By the time Katie came to see me, I was on the road to recovery.

"You never mentioned it was connected with this old manuscript," she said.

"You'd never have believed me," I said. "But in a writer's life, nothing is ever wasted. I knew my near-death experience would make a good story to tell by the fireside."

Gray shook his head in disbelief. "Are you really saying your heart attack was caused by your attempt to write a new ending to *The Mystery of Edwin Drood*?"

"Scoff if you wish. There was something terrible about what Collins had written."

"Don't tell me it was cursed?" Gray said.

"A haunted manuscript." Katie's eyes widened. "Amazing."

"It's impossible to explain rationally," I said. "That story was never meant to be brought to an end."

"You mean, Dickens's spirit refused to accept even his closest friend finishing *The Mystery of Edwin Drood*?"

"*Especially* not his closest friend," I said. "What other people did was neither here nor there, but remember Collins's disdain for the story? His contempt must have cut Dickens to the quick."

"Dickens was already dead by then," Gray snapped.

I watched the flames dance in the inglenook. "Remember, this is a ghost story."

"Wow," Katie said. "Spooky! So what did your friend do with the cursed manuscript?"

"Nothing. I took matters into my own hands."

"How do you mean?"

"I was convinced that whatever evil force was associated with the manuscript wasn't growing weaker with the passage of time, but stronger and more malevolent. At least Collins had managed to put something down on paper. Sayers failed to write anything. So did Robbie. As for me, that second nightmare was even ghastlier than the first. I could see only one answer. The manuscript must be destroyed."

Gray stared. "You're joking."

At last he was taking me seriously. I conquered the urge to preen. My storytelling powers might have waned, but I hadn't completely lost the plot.

"Absolutely not. Robbie is a friend, but he's also a collector. It wasn't simply a matter of money, or the value of the manuscript, but its place in literary heritage. I was pretty certain he'd reached the same conclusion about those two sheets of paper. But I knew that if I consulted him, he could never bring himself to agree to their destruction."

Katie leaned towards me. I inhaled the subtle fragrance of her perfume.

"So what did you do?"

"I burned Collins's manuscript." I pointed to the fire in the inglenook. "That's where it died."

"No!" She seemed thrilled by my daring.

"Yes, I ripped the two old pages, along with a couple of lines that I'd actually managed to write myself, into tiny pieces. One by one, I fed them to the flames. And do you know something?"

"Go on," she whispered.

"As the scraps of papers curled and burned, I swear I heard something through the loud crackling of the fire. A shriek of pain."

There was a long pause.

Gray's eyelids were drooping. I leaned back in my chair and gave Katie a shy smile.

"So, did you enjoy your Christmas ghost story?"

She smiled. "It's certainly . . . different."

"And what did your pal Robbie have to say about what you'd done?" Gray muttered.

I lowered my voice. "Between the three of us, I didn't tell him the truth. I said the manuscript was burned by accident. I'd foolishly slipped it between the pages of a newspaper, which I then chucked into the fire. I offered to pay him what the manuscript might fetch on the open market."

"But it must have been worth a fortune!" Katie exclaimed.

"A small price to pay, to rid the world of a force for evil. But you needn't worry about us sinking into debt. Robbie refused to take a penny. Money wouldn't bring the manuscript back, he said. Chances are, he saw through my subterfuge. I'm not a good liar. He could never have burned a unique manuscript, but after his own doomed attempt to complete the story, he understood why I'd felt impelled to do so. I'd done his dirty work for him."

"Fantastic, a happy ending." Katie rose. "Awesome. Okay, I'm off to bed. I'm sure you two have business to discuss."

I beamed at her. "Goodnight, darling."

"'Night, Katie," Gray said sleepily. "Sweet dreams."

As the door closed behind her, I refilled our guest's tumbler. For a few minutes we sat sipping our drinks in a companionable silence before Gray uttered a moaning sound and clamped a hand to his forehead.

"Are you all right?"

"Not . . . feeling too good," he mumbled.

"No?"

His breath was coming in short gasps.

"Giddy, are you? Disorientated?"

"Uh . . . uh-huh."

It seemed to take an effort for him to speak. His lips had acquired a blueish tinge.

Excellent. I'd judged the dosage to perfection. Even as I watched, he lapsed into unconsciousness.

I got to my feet, although it proved quite a struggle. I'd drunk more than I intended, but Katie hates drinking spirits. I couldn't risk adding sleeping pills to the mulled wine, and if I hadn't kept Gray company by knocking back the brandy, he might have resisted the urge to indulge in his favorite tipple.

It took some time for him to die, longer than I'd expected. My plan was to dispose of his body in the old well in the grounds, but I felt in desperate need of rest. A short doze would do me good, I thought. As I settled down on the sofa, I heard a noise from upstairs. Footsteps on the creaking floorboards.

Was Katie coming downstairs?

I hauled my aching limbs off the sofa and opened the door of the sitting room. There was no sign of my wife, but I had to make sure she wouldn't interrupt me while I hid Gray's body. My plan wasn't subtle, but it's a mistake for a murderer to over-complicate things. The first step was to tell Katie that Gray had stormed out of the house following a drunken argument.

It took a huge effort, but I made my way up the stairs. Katie's bedroom door was ajar. Interesting. Lately, she'd taken to locking me out.

Was it possible, I wondered, that she was tiring of Gray? This evening, she'd hardly bothered to flirt with him. Perhaps there was hope for us yet. Perhaps I wouldn't need to murder her as I'd murdered Gray and then leave both lovebirds together forever at the bottom of the well.

Exhausted as I was, I felt my heart lift. Did the pair of us have a future together, after all? That would be the best Christmas gift of all. It would be . . . well, *awesome*.

"Phil, is that you?"

Her voice was trembling. *She's excited*, I thought.

I pushed the door open. Katie was sitting on the side of the bed in her blue pyjamas.

"You're wide awake!"

She smiled. "Is Gray dead?"

I froze. "What?"

"He is, isn't he? I can tell by your expression. Wow, you committed a murder! Incredible!"

I gaped at her. "What are you talking about?"

"You wanted to kill him, didn't you?"

"You . . . you guessed?"

317

She beckoned and I slumped down beside her, desperate to take the weight off my feet.

"Of course. You're quite transparent, you know. And Gray was right about one thing. Your powers of invention have faded away."

"I don't . . ."

"You've been rereading one of your old books. *The Mistletoe Murder Mystery*, wasn't it? Where the betrayed wife poisons her husband's mistress? You even marked some of the passages, it was almost as if you wanted me to find out."

I groaned. "You've been snooping in my study."

"Sorry, Phil, I know it's your private fiefdom, but I'm incurably nosy. That look in your eyes whenever Gray and I were talking was a dead giveaway. I could smell your jealousy a mile off. Creepy!"

"It . . . it's because I love you."

Telling the story had taken a physical toll. I was laboring to get out the words.

"And you thought that after disposing of my lover, you and I could find happiness together?"

"Well," I began miserably. "Why can't we . . . ?"

"I don't believe you," she interrupted. "I think you meant to kill us both and dump our bodies somewhere. Probably in that disgusting old well. Just like the henpecked husband hid the body of his rich wife in *The Ding Dong Bell Murder*. One of your most hackneyed plots, I must say."

"Katie, please." I was fighting for breath. *Not another heart attack*, I prayed. "I . . ."

"Not that it matters," she said, "but I finished with Gray ages ago. After we had that spa break together."

I frowned, struggling to take in what she was saying. "You mean . . . ?"

"Let's face it, an agent was never my first choice as a husband. Bartley Innes, on the other hand, he's a hunk." She gave me a teasing smile. "I always dreamed of marrying a brilliant writer. Thanks to you, I've flushed the whole older-man-with-family-money fantasy out of my system. I'm ready to party with someone my own age."

My brain was fuddled. Did she mean to blackmail me over Gray's death?

"Funny, isn't it, just like Dickens's explanation for the death of Edwin Drood?"

I stared at her, bereft of speech.

"Don't look so bewildered, Phil. It's really simple. The stuff I put in your brandy is doing the trick. You murdered Gray, only to discover that the situation which created your motive ceased to exist before you committed your crime." She laughed. "Not that anyone but me will appreciate the delicious irony after your death. Everyone else will need to be content with a crude sensation. *Crime writer kills agent, then takes own life.*"

"You . . . you can't . . ."

"Oh, but I can." She giggled. "You even wrote a suicide note."

I shook my head, but the words wouldn't come.

"Don't you remember? The scrap you wrote about the murder of Edwin Drood? John Jasper's confession?"

I did remember, and I trembled.

She laughed. "'*Jealousy drove me to take another man's life and now I must expiate my sin by taking my own*'? Incredibly convenient, mind-blowingly perfect. Everyone will presume you wrote that about Gray."

Tears of despair pricked my tired eyes.

"You thought you'd destroyed it, but I made a copy to substitute for the original. Careless of you not to notice, Phil. It was like an early Christmas present. I felt sure that little snippet would come in handy one day, even though I'd no idea it was connected with your yarn about a haunted manuscript."

As my eyes closed for the last time, I found myself unable to utter a word.

Unable to tell her that Gray was right. My creative spark was as dead as my agent. The tale I'd told about the manuscript wasn't something I'd made up.

Every word was true.